CANNED GOOD

a novel

CANNED GOOD

a novel

Sabrina Stephens

authorHOUSE®

AuthorHouse™ LLC
1663 Liberty Drive
Bloomington, IN 47403
www.authorhouse.com
Phone: 1-800-839-8640

Published by AuthorHouse   09/03/2013

ISBN: 978-1-4918-0617-3 (sc)
ISBN: 978-1-4918-0616-6 (hc)
ISBN: 978-1-4918-0618-0 (e)

Library of Congress Control Number: 2013914986

This book is dedicated to my own circle of friends --
Joy, Theresa, Harriett and Kate.
You are my anchors.

PART ONE

CHAPTER 1

Tuesday, December 9 had been a completely unremarkable day at the bank. Leah Gibson, the bank's regional retail manager, had approved a real estate loan for one of the line lenders, had counseled one of the office managers about her unacceptable, flashback-to-the-eighties wardrobe, and had surprised the downtown office's vault teller with a cash count. The loan commitment letter was transmitted to the lender, the manager with the fluorescent pink poncho was sent home to change and the vault was in balance. When 5:00 came, Leah almost jumped for joy—she was on vacation until the following Monday, and she was leaving tomorrow morning with her posse of girlfriends for Manhattan for a long weekend. This annual trip was one of the highlights of her year. As excited as she was about tomorrow, though, she was just as completely unprepared, and the evening was going to be hectic. Leah had to pack, print her boarding pass, and take her dog to the kennel. Their flight left tomorrow morning at 9:40 a.m.

And God knows she needed a vacation. The credit crisis was in full swing, and banks were being closed down by the Feds. Customers were worried about the safety of their money, and bankers were terrified about losing their jobs. Huge Wall Street mainstays had closed their doors, and regional financial institutions were struggling to survive. The small community banks like Leah's employer, East Coast Bank, were caught up in the tsunami as well. Deposits were leaving, chasing the highest yield in the market, and loan demand had completely dried up. The drop in activity had already cost three area tellers and two loan assistants their jobs at East Coast. Other banks had given entire lending departments their pink slips. The city was already littered with career bankers, discarded and expendable in the wreckage of the economic crash. Most had turned their sights away from the Virginia coast for employment in the absence of any local jobs, willing to relocate in order to salvage a future in the industry. Others had reinvented themselves entirely or gone back to school to go in a new direction. Many remained unemployed, hoping for an end to the madness and a local position to avoid uprooting their lives. Banking was just not an enjoyable career right now.

Leah sighed out loud, hoping to expel the sudden heaviness in her chest. She was on vacation and needed to think happy thoughts. She wondered if Meg, Toni and Siobhan were ready to go, and she was now buoyed by the thought of her friends scurrying around like she was, double-checking their bags and making preparations with their families for the five-day absence. The close-knit group of women *was* her family after all.

Leah's mom had died on Easter five years ago after a four-year battle with breast cancer. Her dad had never really been in the picture, but he had died from cirrhosis a couple of years before her mom. Both of her parents were only children like she was, and the only living relative she had was a great-aunt who lived in the sticks and was so old she probably went to the school prom with Moses. Aunt Fiona was her Grandmother Belle's older sister. Grandmother Belle, or Gran Belle as she was affectionately called, was her mother's mom. When Gran Belle became a widow in 1981, she asked Aunt Fiona to move in with her. Leah knew her grandfather only from old photographs, but she had spent every summer and Christmas as a child visiting Gran Bell and Aunt Fiona. She and Aunt Fiona spent a lot of time together working in the garden, the orchard and the kitchen. The rural home was truly in the middle of nowhere, and every day was filled with work of some kind from sunrise to sundown. Wistfully, Leah tried to remember ever complaining. She couldn't. Even today, she considered the small mountain farm her childhood home.

Not that she would recognize it now, though. Since Gran Belle's death when Leah was in college, she had only been to visit Aunt Fiona a handful of times. Once Leah's banking career had taken off, there just never seemed to be enough time, or honestly, enough inclination to drive the almost seven hours to the northern foothills of North Carolina to visit her aging aunt. Leah did manage to send her a Christmas card each year and had sent her flowers for her birthday every year since Gran Belle had died. Aunt Fiona reciprocated, sending her a card for both her birthday and Christmas. Each one included an index card with a family recipe written on it in a legible, but shaky, penmanship that matched Aunt Fiona's signature and same one-word closing, "Enjoy!"

Leah chuckled at the thought of her cooking. She had not cooked a single meal since she was in college. She had filed the cards in her metal box of keepsakes, though. Maybe one day she would get married and have a daughter with whom she could share family recipes and domestic activities. More likely, the group of friends she considered her sisters would inherit the box and wonder why their quirky friend Leah kept a box of recipe cards when she didn't even own a decent set of cookware.

Once the suitcase was packed and placed at the door, Leah turned her attention to Pander, her beagle. Pander was pacing around the house, keenly aware that her usual routine was about to be disrupted. She narrowed her beady dog eyes at Leah and plopped down on the floor, whining and moping. Leah sat down on the couch and pulled the dog into her lap. She stroked her soft hair and nuzzled her neck. "I'll miss you too, Pander," Leah said softly. "I'll be back on Monday, and by then you won't even want to come home. You'll hook up with some handsome stud at the kennel and be content to get laid for the next five days. You'll have to remind me what that feels like," Leah said as she stood to take her canine hussy to her crate. Within minutes, she was out the door.

After Leah left the kennel, she stopped at the drug store and picked up a bag full of travel-size toiletries and headed back home to finish packing. When she was through, Leah printed off her boarding pass and put it into her purse. She placed her purse on the table at the door beside her suitcase. She smiled, satisfied that her preparations were complete, and she was ready to jet to the Big Apple. She looked at the clock in the den. It was 7:35 p.m.

She walked into the kitchen, pulled a mug out of the cabinet next to the sink, filled it with tap water and pulled a teabag out of the pantry. She warmed the water in the microwave, dropped the teabag into the water and retired to the den to watch television for a few minutes. As Leah settled into her oversized chair, the phone rang.

She smiled as she put her mug on the coaster, wondering which one of her friends needed something at this eleventh hour. "Hello," Leah answered with a smile in her voice.

"Leah?" said a decidedly male voice in her ear.

"Hi John," Leah replied, confused and concerned that the bank's regional president and her long-time mentor was calling her this late at home. "How are you?" she asked.

"I don't want you to go to New York, Leah," he blurted out.

"John . . .," she said, then went silent, momentarily at a total loss for words.

She heard him sigh, but he didn't seem able to speak either. Fear rose in her throat, and she felt nauseous. After what felt like hours, Leah finally asked, "Why don't you want me to go to New York, John?"

He breathed deeply, obviously to steady himself then replied, "Because I don't want you to go spend a lot of money."

The words reverberated in her head, making her ears ring. She leaned back against the chair and asked woodenly, "Am I losing my job, John?"

"Leah, I'm so sorry . . ." he mumbled, "The bank needs to cut costs and with your salary and your managerial role, your position has been eliminated."

"John, the reason I have this managerial role is because you promoted me because I was the number one retail lender in the *entire* bank for the last four years," she stated.

"I know . . ." he said. "I'm sorry, Leah, so, so sorry."

Baloney, she thought. *You were afraid to go to bat for me.* "What happens now?" she asked.

"This change was not supposed to be announced until next Friday, but I just couldn't let you get on that plane," he said.

"I'm getting on that plane," Leah replied sharply. "Five days is not going to change this decision, is it?"

"No . . ." he stammered. "But do you really want to spend money when you're going to be unemployed?"

"Yes, I do," Leah stated. "I'll deal with it when I get back since I may NEVER have the chance to go again."

"Oh, Leah, you'll find another job," he said almost patronizingly.

"Where, John?" she asked, stung by his cavalier response. "Do you know of a single bank hiring?"

His silence was the only answer she needed. "I've got to go, John. I need to get some sleep."

"I wish you wouldn't go, but I understand," he said. "I'm as devastated by this as you are."

"Uh, not quite or did you get your pink slip too?" Leah asked, almost angry at his comment. "As a matter-of-fact, did anybody else lose their job or was it just me?"

"Just you, this time," he said. "I don't know what's going to happen next."

"Oh, you'll be just fine," she said. "I'm glad you called me, though. I would have hated to get the news by e-mail or the grapevine, you know. Good night, John," she finished.

"Good night, Leah," he replied, and he hung up the phone.

Leah sat immobilized for what must have been a half of an hour. Her tea had gone cold, and the television spouted "blah, blah, blah" incoherently in her ears. She simply couldn't process that she had just lost her job, her career, and her income. She wasn't the type to cry hysterically, but she was afraid. She was unemployed in a shrinking business in a declining local market in a horrible economy. *Holy shit . . .*, she thought.

She picked up the phone to call Siobhan but then changed her mind. She would tell them together tomorrow morning on the airplane on the way to New York; otherwise, the trip could be in jeopardy altogether. Siobhan's practical side would try to talk her out of going, Toni would want her to share her feelings, and Meg would just want to beat the crap out of John and every other male executive at East Coast Bank. Siobhan was a lawyer, Toni was a clinical psychiatrist and Meg was a pharmaceutical sales manager. They were her best friends, and they were as different from each other as three people could be.

Siobhan Mauldin-Haas was an attorney, and she was married to an architect. She had three kids—all boys. She had worked her way through school at Georgetown, both undergrad and law, and graduated near the top of her class. She had numerous, lucrative job offers in the District, but decided instead to move back to the Virginia coast to practice law with her brother. Mauldin & Mauldin handled criminal and family cases. Her brother, Gil, handled the criminals and Siobhan represented the families, or what was left of them by the time they paid her a visit. The firm was very successful and therefore, so was Siobhan. She was level-headed, incredibly bright and well-rounded. She had a great marriage to Robert, and they had a common love of history, architecture and pottery—all the things that would have put most people in a coma. Their boys—13, 11, and 8—were interested too, and they managed to take the coolest trips as a big, happy family to go visit ancient ruins, dig for artifacts or tour landmark buildings. The rest of the crew dubbed Siobhan their "phone-a-friend" go-to, especially for useless trivia. She stored more crap in her gray matter than anyone could use in several lifetimes.

Toni Dalton was a single mother with a lovely, sweet 8-year-old daughter, Lucy. She lived with her mother who, for the most part, was unassuming and easy-going. Toni worked crazy hours at the local hospital on the seventh floor—the cancer ward. She dealt with death and dying on a daily basis and the devastation the awful disease often left for the survivors. Somehow, though, she managed to have a healthier, happier outlook than anybody Leah knew. Toni was a beauty too. She was the hunk magnet everywhere they went together, but she rarely dated. She, instead, devoted her precious free time to her daughter except every other weekend when her daughter was with her father, Toni's ex-husband. He was dubbed "The Bastard" by her friends because he just couldn't keep his little penis in his pants when he was married. Toni was civil to him, though, for their daughter's sake. She also had the satisfaction of knowing she had cleaned his clock royally in the equitable distribution phase of their divorce, thanks to Siobhan's keen mind and a plethora of incriminating photos.

Meg McConnell was a hoot. She was a regional sales manager for one of the biggest pharmaceutical companies in the world. She was aggressive, confident and persuasive—all the personality traits that made her so good at what she did. Meg was a "zero bullshit" kind of woman and if a thought entered her fiery Irish brain, it exited her mouth when she was in her tight circle of friends. She was brutally honest and fiercely protective of "her clan." Meg was rarely critical, but almost always on target and insightful with her casual observations. She was an outstanding golfer and had graduated from UVA after a free ride on scholarship. Ten years later, she still played from the championship tees and routinely crushed the men she played. Meg never boasted, though. She was surprisingly professional and diplomatic, and by the time she and the other golfers, almost exclusively male clients, retired to the clubhouse, she had them eating out of her hand. Not that she was interested in any of them. Meg's long-time "roommate," Courtney, was her only love. They had been together for over 10 years, but they had completely different friends. They were perfectly secure in their relationship and were never jealous of each other or the other's friends. Courtney preferred the bookstore geeks and coffee; Meg preferred her working girlfriends and Miller Lite. The lifestyle was definitely unconventional, but it certainly worked well for them.

Leah wondered how to break the news to her friends. She didn't want them to feel sorry for her, but this situation was too big not to ask for some kind of help. *God*, she thought, *what am I going to do?* The market simply had no banking jobs and the future looked bleak as the economy appeared to be continuing to deteriorate.

She had always defined herself as a banker after all, having been in the industry for the decade since she graduated from college. Leah had been a superstar at East Coast Bank, but her reputation was solid throughout the entire banking community in the region. She had been courted often by institutions of every size in the market, but had stayed at East Coast because she was loyal to the bank. Until tonight, she thought the bank was loyal to her too. Now, for the first time in her adult existence, she was NOT a banker. *And what do you do about that, Leah?* She couldn't just move down the street, rent an office and hang out a sign that said Bank of Leah, "Get Your Loan Here!" *Who are you now?*

Leah looked at the clock—8:32. She needed sleep. Instead, she stood up, went to the door, picked up her keys and walked out the door to her car. She drove east on Laskin Road, straight toward the Atlantic Ocean. She grabbed a cup of coffee at the Starbucks and turned left onto Atlantic Avenue, parked at the King Neptune Statue and got out into the crisp December air.

The boardwalk at Virginia Beach was deserted and thankfully, Leah was alone with her dark thoughts and churning guts to try to clear her head. As calm as the night looked above, the sea sounded angry, waves crashing violently but rhythmically on the shore in front of her. Emotion bubbled slowly into her chest, and she breathed heavily. She felt . . . what? Anger simmered low inside her, and fear and desperation bounced around in her head. The feeling that engulfed her, though, the one that overwhelmed her suddenly and completely was sadness, and she felt herself crumbling. As she collapsed in a heap on the boardwalk, she sobbed audibly as her tears flowed, hot and salty against her face. Leah cried uncontrollably, not only for the loss of the professional career she had built and loved, but more for the sudden end of the only way of life she had ever known as an adult.

CHAPTER 2

Why is she not answering? Siobhan hung up the phone, vowing not to call Leah again after her fourth attempt to reach her. Something was wrong here. Leah was never out of pocket for long. It was 6:00 a.m.—correction, now it was 6:35 a.m., and Leah knew Siobhan was going to call her at six sharp. They still had driving arrangements to finalize and waiting until the last minute was driving her crazy. Perhaps Leah was just in the shower, Siobhan considered.

She dialed Toni. Immediately, her good-natured friend answered, "Good morning!" Siobhan took a deep breath.

"Good morning, sunshine," she said to Toni, "Are you ready to blow this town?"

"You bet, counselor," Toni answered. "Am I driving us to the airport or what?"

"I don't know. I've been trying to reach Leah all morning. Have you spoken to the Queen this morning?" Siobhan asked.

"No, but I did speak to Meg. Courtney's bringing her to my house since it is on the way. Besides, since only Meg and maybe her luggage will fit in that little sports car of hers, we knew she wasn't driving us," Toni said playfully.

"Hmm," Siobhan muttered. "If that woman has not called me by seven, I'm going over there."

"Why, Siobhan?" Toni asked. "Is something wrong?"

"I don't know because she won't answer the phone," she replied, evenly but firmly.

"She's probably just in the shower," Toni remarked.

"I know," Siobhan said. "All right, here's the plan—I'll go get Leah and drive over to your house. I'll pick you and Meg up there with your luggage and drive us all to the airport in the Suburban, okay?"

"That sounds like a good plan. What time will you be here?" Toni asked.

"I'll be there at 8 a.m. so we can get to the airport in plenty of time to check in. I'll see you in about an hour. Finally! Leah is beeping in on my phone. Bye Toni," Siobhan finished, relief washing over her.

She flashed over to Leah. "Please tell me you had some really hot, young guy you had to politely kick out of your bed," Siobhan said to Leah lightly, trying to expel her concern.

"Nah," Leah remarked, "Just me and my hand." Siobhan burst out laughing.

"You are crazy, Leah," she said, still giggling. "I'm coming to get you in 45 minutes. Are you ready?"

"I'm ready for the Big Apple, baby! The question is, is the Big Apple ready for us?" Leah asked.

They disconnected. Leah took a deep breath and walked to the bathroom. She looked into the mirror and was shocked to see what appeared to be her Gran Belle staring back at her. She felt like she had aged forty years in one night. *Pull yourself together,* she told herself sternly.

Leah had arrived back home from the boardwalk after 1 a.m. She had cried to the point of exhaustion and actually fell asleep along the shore propped up like some pathetic drunk against the railing of the boardwalk. The cold finally woke her and she stumbled back to her car and drove home. She set her alarm for 5:30 a.m. but never really fell asleep, tossing and turning in her bed as thoughts of her new-found unemployment wracked her with fear and doubt. When the alarm went off, she got up and dragged herself to the shower. She fell fast asleep sitting on the shower ledge until the water turned cold and jolted her back awake. By the time she pulled on her clothes and combed her short, curly blond hair, it was 6:45 and Siobhan had called her four times.

After the specter she just saw in her mirror, Leah knew she had to get a move on to pass muster with the super-observant Siobhan. Once they were airborne, she would tell her best friends she was available for hire. She silently prayed the four would support her decision to throw caution to the wind and keep their plans and not be judgmental and ruin the vacation with regret or even worse, pity.

Leah squeezed Visine in abundance into each eye, made a cup of Earl Grey tea and managed to put on her makeup and fix her hair in record time. At 7:45, Siobhan rang her doorbell. She swung the door open, plastered a smile on her face and broke into a horrible rendition of "New York, New York." Siobhan hugged her neck and they hurried with Leah's bags out to the still-running SUV. As soon as the doors closed, Siobhan asked, "Coffee, right?"

"Is the earth spinning on its axis? You know it, sister—Dunkin' Donuts, extra large hazelnut coffee with a touch of cream," Leah answered.

With coffee in hand, the pair pulled into the cobblestone driveway where Toni lived. Standing outside in the chill with their bags beside them were the obviously-anxious Toni and Meg, waving like lunatics to greet them. To whip the group into even more of a frenzy, Siobhan blew the horn and Leah rolled down her window and whooped, "Woohoo!" The neighbors probably thought Toni was mixed up with a bunch of hoodlums.

After the bags were loaded into the back of the vehicle, the four piled in and drove the short drive to the Norfolk International Airport, all the while discussing their fluid and fun-filled trip to The City. Siobhan dropped them off curbside then went to park her Sherman Tank in the long-term parking lot. Once she joined them, they went through security without any delays and waited for the plane to begin boarding. In all of the activity, Leah had almost forgotten that her world had been turned upside down yesterday. She suddenly felt like she was going to be sick and walked as casually as she could to the nearest snack counter and promptly ordered herself a Coke Zero to settle her stomach.

"You okay?" Meg asked behind her. "You looked like you were about to hurl."

Leah smiled at Meg's frankness and answered, "I just didn't get much sleep last night because I was so anxious." *Well, anxious is honest, right?* Leah thought to herself as she took an ice-cold gulp. She linked her arm through Meg's, and they walked back over to the seats near the gate door where Siobhan and Toni were perched with their bags.

Leah fiddled in her bag for her IPod; she reorganized her cosmetic case and pulled out her Blackberry to check her messages. She was restless, and when she stood up, her friends were all three staring at her curiously. Leah felt her face go red, but she tried to recover. "What?" she asked with a smile she forced.

"Leah, sit down and relax," Toni said. "I know you hate flying but you're acting like a maniac."

"Okay," she sighed. She let her well-known fear of flying cover the fear of her impending announcement. She hated being untoward.

Finally, the flight attendant called the passengers to board the plane, and they all rose, giddy with excitement, presented their boarding passes and climbed aboard. The small jet had two seats on each side. Siobhan took the window seat next to Leah, and Meg took the opposite window with Toni on the aisle next to Leah. Siobhan squeezed Leah's hand and asked, "Did you take your Dramamine?" As she spoke, the plane taxied down the runway.

"Nah, I popped a Valium instead," Leah answered as the landing gear left the runway. As her friends laughed, she knew it was time to get her news off her chest. She looked at each of them smiling with a happiness she didn't feel and just spit it out the best way she knew. "Hopefully, there won't be much turbulence after I tell you my news . . .," she stated flatly.

Siobhan's head whipped around to look at her, Toni furrowed her brow, and Meg simply asked, "What news?"

Tension among the four was suddenly high, and Leah took a deep breath to steady her nerves. The plane pushed up into the clouds and banked left once they were over the Atlantic Ocean, taking them northward toward New York. Siobhan reached over again for Leah's hand, sensing somehow this was not going to be good news.

"I got laid off from the bank last night—whacked because I made too much money and because my promotion to a management position left me no longer useful . . .," she trailed off, trying to keep her composure.

"O-My-God . . ." Siobhan stated, pointedly emphasizing each word.

Toni added, "Oh, Leah . . ."

Meg chimed in, "Those stupid peckers!"

Leah waited for a few seconds before she continued, hoping to provide some time for her friends to let the news sink in before they really responded. Those responses were the ones she was dreading more than the knee-jerk surprise comments she just got.

And she was spot on to dread them because the next fifteen minutes was torture. Siobhan cross-examined Leah about every word exchanged last night between her and John. She asked Leah about her performance over the last several months, trying, but failing, to subtly question whether Leah's dismissal was for cause or not. Toni asked Leah if she was angry or upset. She strongly recommended that Leah work through all of her negative emotions before she made a real plan on what to do next. Meg was steamed. She wanted to know if any of the sorry lot of loser boys that worked with Leah got axed or not. When Leah told her no, she muttered a string of profanities and swore that a strong woman always got shafted first in the good old boy networks because she threatened the security of the men in the organizations. Men simply hired young pretty assistants to do the hard work for them at a fraction of the cost of a woman executive who could do the job herself.

Leah felt the Valium artificially relax her while her friends continued to get more wound up and emotional. She was tired, and she really didn't have much to say about the situation this morning. She had answered their questions and responded to their concerns, but she was too numb emotionally right now to worry about the future. While her friends talked around her, Leah closed her eyes for a second and promptly fell fast asleep for the rest of the flight.

CHAPTER 3

Siobhan looked over at her sleeping best friend. Leah looked cherubic with her short blond curls, pink cheeks and lips and her stress-free expression in slumber. No wonder she had been such a case at the airport. Siobhan was certain Leah had had very little, if any, sleep.

She wondered why Leah didn't call her last night. Was she too stunned, too upset, too angry or too embarrassed? Or was it a combination of all of those feelings? If Siobhan was honest with herself right now, she was a little angry and a lot sad—angry because Leah had not needed her shoulder for support or even to cry on and sad because Leah had been all alone in her darkest hour, isolated in her home as her professional life disintegrated before her eyes. Siobhan sighed.

Leah was a complicated woman. She was proud, but also humble. She was independent, but almost always surrounded herself with people she loved. She was the consummate professional, but the most down-to-earth human being Siobhan had ever known. They could talk for hours on the phone, over a beer or after a movie, but Leah never really bared her soul. She was much more curious and genuinely concerned about everybody else.

Now, though, Siobhan knew Leah really needed to worry about herself. Leah was afraid, and her fear was justified. Banking was undergoing a metamorphosis, shedding employees at a frightening clip. Where was Leah going to find a job? What would she do if she couldn't stay in banking? Siobhan was driving herself crazy. These were questions she should be asking Sleeping Beauty—and she would, but not right now.

Right now, they were nearing JFK and the four Commonwealth Crazies were going to enjoy themselves full tilt for the next five days. They were going to do a lot of eating, drinking, shopping, and site-seeing—and very little sleeping. Siobhan and the rest of the crew would sleep when they got back to Virginia Beach.

Siobhan looked across the aisle. Toni was flipping through a magazine, while Meg was rocking out to something upbeat on her I-pod. Neither of them seemed too out-of-sorts over Leah's predicament. Why was she? Siobhan had a really bad feeling about Leah's job prospects. To take her mind off of the situation, she pulled out her book and began reading.

As the pilot announced their approach to New York, Siobhan looked out the window. The Hudson River snaked below her, and the city gleamed as the sun danced off the iconic skyscrapers. She felt a rush of excitement as the landing gear was lowered. Siobhan was glad Leah was still asleep since she hated the landing of the airplane almost as much as she hated take-off.

When the wheels hit the runway and the red "Welcome to New York" sign rolled by her window, she smiled over at Toni as she took Leah's hand.

"Wake up, sunshine," Siobhan said quietly as Leah stirred. "We've arrived in the Big Apple and we're ready to go take a bite."

"Good God! Did I sleep the whole flight?" Leah asked groggily. She was shocked and looked across Siobhan out the window to verify her whereabouts.

"You did," Siobhan said, "but that's okay. Sleeping beats freaking out about the landing any day. Besides, you obviously needed it."

"I must have," Leah added. "But there will be no more of that sleeping stuff, sisters. Save that for the old folks' home!"

As they exited the plane, Toni said, "Let's go find Hassid," referring to the limo driver they met five years earlier on their first trip to the city. He was reliable, knowledgeable and personable. He also knew that the four Virginia women were a bunch of suckers. After negotiating a reduced fare from SoHo back to their hotel five years ago when Toni flagged him down in the rain, Hassid had actually doubled his fare after each of the riders tipped him stupidly well. He gave the women his card and told them to call him anytime they needed a ride. They called him three more times during the trip as well as numerous times each subsequent trip. Hassid always made enough money off the crazy crew that he could take the following week off every year and still have money in his pocket.

As expected, a grinning Hassid was waiting at the curb with his sign "Welcome VA Beach (es)!" They all laughed and gave him a quick hug before they piled into his SUV limo for the ride to the Hilton just off Broadway.

As usual, New York City was magical during the holidays with its lights, animated windows and storefronts, and street decorations. Even the people were friendly, helpful and patient—well, more than usual anyway.

As Hassid pulled them to the curb at the hotel, everybody pulled out their wallets to lavish him with cash. When Leah pulled out a $20, Siobhan pushed her money aside, and said quietly, "I got this, Leah."

Leah looked at her like she had lost her mind. "No, Siobhan, I've got it," she answered.

Siobhan shook her head and insisted, "I've got it this time."

At this point, everybody was watching and waiting. Accepting graciously, but embarrassed completely, Leah quickly said, "Thank you," and exited the vehicle. The look exchanged between Meg and Toni was not lost on her, though.

Trying to control her anger and regain her composure, she hurried ahead to the lobby to check in. Leah was determined she was not going to let her current unemployed status ruin this trip, and she vowed to herself that she was not going to let the others feel obligated to pay her way. She would talk with Siobhan about her "pity payment" when they were alone.

After they finished at the check-in counter, they chattered comfortably as they rode up the high-rise elevator to their room. They were excited and had decided that they would take a stroll this evening to Rockefeller Center and grab a slice at John's on the way back. Tomorrow was Ellis Island and the Statue of Liberty during the day followed by dinner at Angelo's and nose-bleed seats to see *Wicked*. Everybody but Leah had read the book. She just couldn't muster much enthusiasm for that kind of fantasy fiction. The other three gushed about the book's literary genius, the darkness of the story and the decidedly adult nature of the relationships in the book. Leah hoped the play was much less intense.

When they had settled into the room, Meg announced that any walk around the city had to be preceded by a round of drinks at the hotel sky bar. She tooted the melody to "Charge" and tried to hurry them along by clapping her hands like a drink coach. They were all laughing so hard they were crying.

Leah, still groggy from her super nap, told them to go ahead and she would catch up. "I need to wash my face and freshen up," she said.

Meg put her hands on her hips and pretended to scrutinize her up and down. "Well, alright, missy, but you better not wait too long! I'd hate for you to have to chug cosmos to catch up," she said, "That could be one ugly sick."

"I'll be down before you finish your first one, crazy," Leah said.

"I'll wait with you, Leah," Siobhan said. "God knows since I have to sleep with you, I'm going to make sure you don't get behind after that mental picture."

"Aw, Siobhan, are you sure?" Leah asked.

"Sure as shit," Siobhan answered, causing the whole room to dissolve again into laughter. Meg and Toni let themselves out, still giggling as the door closed behind them.

"Fools," Leah said as she walked toward the bathroom.

"We all," Siobhan echoed. As Leah was grabbing her cosmetic bag, Siobhan grew serious and followed her to the bathroom.

"Leah, are you going to be alright on this trip?" she questioned.

Leah looked at her in the mirror, put her bag on the sink and turned to face her best friend. "I'm going to be fine on this trip, Siobhan. It's *after* this trip I'm not so sure about," she said quietly.

"Do you think it was wise to come up here and spend money when you are out of work?" Siobhan continued.

Leah sighed audibly and answered, "Yes, damn it, I do, and I sure don't need you to throw me a pity party like the one back at the curb when we got here, Siobhan. I'm a big girl and you're my best friend, not my mother."

Siobhan felt like she had been admonished enough. "Excuse me for giving a rat's ass, Leah. You spring this on us, and I'm just trying to help you get through it."

Leah walked over to her and calmly put her hand on Siobhan's arm and said, "But I'm not your project, and I just stepped into this world. I'm a long way from getting through it, girlfriend, so I just need you to hold my hand when I hold it out, not fill it with your charity, okay?"

Siobhan felt like crying, but she understood. Leah had pride after all. "Okay," she answered, "But next time shit hits the fan promise me you won't go through a night like last night alone. I am your best friend. You should have called me. The thought of you by yourself all night with that burden makes me incredibly sad, Leah."

"There are a whole lot of things worse than sad, Siobhan," Leah stated, then she lightly added, "Like getting drunk off of cosmos. Now let me get my face washed!"

In just a few minutes, the two were out of the room riding the hotel elevator up to meet Toni and Meg. When they arrived, their drinks were waiting on them cold, potent and fruity. Their laughter filled the bar and Leah looked lovingly at each of them, savoring this moment of happiness, frivolity and camaraderie. She sighed contentedly and hoped that this moment filled with their abnormal antics would sustain her until she found another job and her life could get back to normal.

CHAPTER 4

By June of the following year, though, normal was still nowhere in sight. With her severance package exhausted, over 500 resumes in circulation with only two call-backs for an interview and living on unemployment, Leah was feeling everything between mania and depression on a constant basis.

Her bank account had dwindled to three figures and she was behind on her mortgage payments. Leah was in serious jeopardy of losing her home. She advertised for a roommate, but realized the rent she needed to make her first and second mortgage was so much higher than the standard apartment rental rates in Virginia Beach that she would likely not find one. She had called the bank, her former employer, and asked for a loan modification to reduce her payments, but with no income she didn't qualify—like that was some kind of newsflash to her.

Leah enrolled in online and college classes and got her real estate license. She attended free motivational, sales, and career seminars through the chamber of commerce. She networked in two civic groups and volunteered with fundraisers with two non-profits in the area. Still, after six months of unemployment she had nothing in the way of a job offer to show for it.

She was broke, and Leah knew her financial situation was far more serious than even her best friends knew. She rarely went out with the girls anymore because the conversation always seemed to be about her. Besides, Leah could barely afford food for her house, let alone drinks out at a bar. Plus, she was sure she was a mental albatross around their necks. Leah saw it in their eyes. They wanted their old Leah back, carefree and happy—and of course, employed—but they, like Leah herself, were helpless. Nobody seemed to have answers as to how to fix the situation.

Unemployment provided her with enough income to eat, put gas in her vehicle and pay her utility bills. She had disconnected the cable, turned the thermostat up to 78 degrees in June, and started shopping at the huge discount grocery instead of the chic specialty store in her neighborhood. Leah also rarely left the house. When she did, she made certain to combine a week's worth of errands to conserve on gas.

Tonight, though, she had promised Siobhan, Toni and Meg that she would join them at their favorite Mexican restaurant for dinner. Leah planned to spend a maximum of $15. She would drink water with a lime and limit her entrée to under $12 so that she could leave a 20 percent tip. If the restaurant had a beer special, she would keep the entrée under $10, and drink one beer alongside her water. Sadly, these planning sessions were now a daily part of Leah's routine for survival.

Preparing for her evening out was a chore, though. She hadn't bought anything new to wear since she lost her job, and everything in her wardrobe looked as old and tired as she felt. Leah finally decided on a pair of jeans and a black shrug over a red camisole. Instead of giving herself a quick final review, she simply stared at herself in the mirror.

Leah looked like the recluse she had become—pale, lifeless and sunken. She looked withered and sat momentarily trying to remember the last time she went to the beach or got any real exercise. Shaking away the tears that threatened to spill over her freshly-mascaraed lashes, Leah knew it had been over six months—pre-unemployment—since either.

Taking in a deep breath and retreating to her bathroom to load up on bronzer, she forced her mind to a static emptiness. To think was to invite fear and desperation back into her house, and Leah just couldn't visit with them right now. Instead, she shut off the lights as she grabbed her purse and keys, locked the door behind her and got in her car and drove away. Leah knew they would be there waiting for her when she returned.

CHAPTER 5

Anybody else would have probably lied to Leah and said she looked great, but Meg was not going to lie. Meg had arrived first and was stunned when Leah walked in the door. Her long-time friend looked like hell, and when Leah hugged her, Meg took Leah by the shoulders and told her sternly that she needed to get out of the house and get some color. Holed up in a townhouse all day was not only unhealthy physically, it was mentally grueling as well, and if you needed proof Leah Gibson was Exhibit A.

"Come walk with me for an hour tomorrow evening, Leah," Meg insisted. "It will be great exercise and the sunshine will get rid of that ghost-like skin in no time."

Leah smiled and answered, "I might. What time are you going?"

"Anytime you want to go, woman," Meg answered. "How about 6:00? I'll pick you up."

"I might," Leah hedged, but Meg was not going to take no for an answer.

"Say yes, and I'll leave you alone," Meg teased.

Leah sighed and felt hemmed in, but she answered good-naturedly, "Yes, and I'll leave you alone."

Meg laughed, "That's my girl!"

With her afternoon tomorrow set, Meg hailed the waitress and ordered another beer. Leah asked for the draft beer special and a glass of water. As their drinks arrived, Toni and Siobhan walked through the door together arm-in-arm, smiling and waving to Meg and Leah.

Leah felt like they had orchestrated their arrival outside, and given each other pointers on how to react to her appearance, how to encourage her, and how to delicately ask about her job prospects. Their smiles were just a little too broad and their gestures just a little too animated. Maybe she was just being paranoid and sensitive, but Leah suddenly wished she had stayed home.

After all of them had their drinks and a bushel basket of chips and salsa had been brought to the table, the conversation seemed to come easier and was more fluid. Toni was taking her mom and her daughter to Hershey, Pennsylvania for a week over July 4th, and she was so excited. They were staying at a hotel with a spa, and she had planned a chocolate bath soak for them.

Siobhan was up to her eyeballs in baseball right now. While Robert coached the team on which their two oldest played, Siobhan was coined the team mom for her youngest son's team. They had had five nights of baseball every week through the spring, and while the regular season was now finished, the playoffs had just started. Secretly, Siobhan prayed for an end to the madness soon—very soon.

Meg was working like a maniac. She had been out of town much more than she had been in Virginia Beach, traveling to conferences for what felt like weeks on end. She had planned absolutely nothing for the upcoming holiday week and couldn't be happier. Meg and Courtney hoped to take in the local fireworks over a homemade picnic and a bottle of wine.

As if on cue, they now turned to Leah for an update, and she was suddenly at a total loss for words. The silence rang in her ears, and she felt close to an emotional breakdown. She looked down at her trembling hands and began to softly speak. "I am still unemployed. I've sent out 500 resumes and have gotten two call backs, one for part-time, minimum-wage retail work and the other for a commission-only mortgage lending position—so, no and no. I'm two months behind on my mortgages, I have $184 in the bank, and I don't have the money to do a damn thing for July 4th except watch the fireworks from my car, which is where I will probably be living, while eating two-for-a-dollar hotdogs and a 79 cents Big Thirsty from the corner store." Leah took a deep breath as she finished and looked up at her friends, her eyes glistening with angry tears precariously suspended on her lower lashes.

Her friends were now the ones at a loss for words, and Leah could tell that she not only had proven to be a real killjoy tonight, she had also made them very uncomfortable. Siobhan was the first to break the silence that had descended on the table. "Are you still collecting unemployment," she asked.

"Yep," Leah answered, "All $494 per week which is less than 25 percent of what I was making in December."

Toni inquired, "Have you thought about a roommate?"

"Yep," Leah replied a little too sharply, "I only advertised for three months online and in every local publication in the market. I got nothing, zero."

"Have you applied with the federal government? They're hiring for the census and for some positions with the FDIC," Meg commented.

"Twice," Leah countered, "And they never contacted me. What else?"

"Hey, Leah," Siobhan said as she reached over for her best friend's hand, "Don't get upset tonight. We care about you, and we just want to help you!"

"I'm beyond help, sister, so let's drop the 'me' talk and concentrate on dinner. My life is as dull as a first-grader's crayon," Leah said. "Let's just move on."

But the conversation just lagged. Mercifully, their waitress came to the table, recited the nightly specials, took their dinner order, refreshed their drinks, including Leah's water, and retreated to the kitchen. When she was gone, the silence threatened to return, but Meg saved the night by talking about her last business trip to California.

She recounted how she landed in San Francisco, got in her rental car and drove alone to the Sonoma Valley. Meg described the acres and acres of vineyards, orchards, and fields of crops for as far as the eye could see and how the vastness of the land made her feel incredibly small in the world.

Leah summoned the image in her mind, and it stirred some deep part of her memory that momentarily transported her from Virginia Beach to her Gran Belle's and Aunt Fiona's small farm house in the foothills of Western North Carolina. She saw the apple orchard, the greens garden, the rows of staked heirloom tomatoes, the massive fig and persimmon trees and the berry patch clearly in her mind's eye. She saw her Gran Belle at her quilting loom, and Aunt Fiona in the kitchen canning green beans from the garden. Leah suddenly wanted to be there. She sure didn't want to be here, but she was jolted back to the table by Toni calling her name.

"Where are you, Leah," Toni questioned.

"Oh . . . I was just picturing the place that Meg just described," Leah said wistfully, "It sounds lovely and a lot like my grandmother's farm."

"I didn't know you had a grandmother," Siobhan said suspiciously. "Where does she live?"

"Oh, she's been dead for more than a decade, but she lived on a small farm in the foothills of North Carolina with her sister, my Aunt Fiona," Leah said.

"Is your aunt still alive," Toni asked.

"Yes, but she is ancient—ninety-one," Leah said with a smile on her face, "I haven't seen her since college I'm ashamed to say. I used to spend each summer with them on the farm."

"*You* on a farm? Now I've heard it all," Meg said with a loud laugh. "Your idea of cooking is Raman noodles in the microwave, and I don't think I've ever seen you eat a piece of fresh fruit or cook a vegetable that wasn't flash frozen in a factory in the Midwest somewhere."

"I grew up cooking, canning, freezing, quilting, crocheting and sewing," Leah answered defiantly.

The table of friends broke up with laughter. Leah looked at them, anger rising as she asked herself, '*Who are these people?*'

"Oh, Leah, tell us more about your dynamic domestic prowess," Siobhan snorted playfully.

"Just never mind . . ." Leah answered, silently boiling.

"My invitation to Sunday dinner must have gotten lost in the mail," Toni teased.

"Drop it, okay," Leah pleaded, "I shouldn't have said a damn thing."

"Hey, c'mon now," Meg said as she dropped her arm around her, "We're just joking around, Leah. We love learning things about you we never knew!"

Leah felt her face go red, ashamed of herself among her best friends. *What the hell is wrong with me,* she asked silently. One word, she reminded herself—unemployment. "I'm sorry," she said emotionally, "I'm just all out of sorts, I guess."

The girls reassured her, and the tension was broken. Conversation flowed easily as dinner arrived, and Leah felt herself relax for the first time in months. They discussed mutual friends, the local theater production, books they were reading—all those safe topics that stayed away from negative connections to what was happening in Leah's life—joblessness, the recession, and the banking crisis.

As the night was winding down, Leah reached across the table to take Siobhan's and Toni's hands into her own. She rested her head on Meg's shoulder and almost whispered, "Thank you so much for tonight. I really didn't want to come because I know I bring you down with the sorry state of my life right now, but I'm glad I did."

She could see they were moved by her words, and they squeezed her hands and pulled her closer.

"We love you, Leah," Toni whispered, concern tingeing her voice.

"I know, and I love you too," Leah answered hoarsely.

"Don't shut us out, though," Meg warned, "Else, I am going to bug the crap out of you," she finished, and they all laughed.

"Besides," Siobhan added, "You'll find a job soon and all will be right with the world."

CHAPTER 6

By the week before Christmas, though, all was still not right with the world. After 53 weeks of unemployment, all savings exhausted, credit cards maxed out and her home in foreclosure, Leah's world continued to implode.

She rented a small, $400-per-month garage apartment in a less-than-desirable part of town, sold much of her furniture, and took about half of her clothes and other belongings to the goodwill store. Leah carefully managed to budget every dollar, but in the end, there just were not enough of them to keep the status quo that her former six-figure salary afforded her.

On the day the bank sold her house on the courthouse steps, Leah sat alone on the couch in her new apartment holding her dog Pander and cried until she was exhausted and broken, her eyes swollen virtually shut and her throat raw. She finally succumbed to sleep sometime in the early afternoon and didn't wake up until nearly 8:00 p.m. when Pander whimpered and moaned to go out to relieve herself.

Leah put Pander on a leash, grabbed her thick winter coat, and walked out into the brisk December night. With her uncombed hair, baggy sweatpants and unwashed face, she was certain that others would be more afraid of her than she would be of them, but she didn't care. Leah mindlessly walked where her dog led her, and she was numb to the cold, the stares of passersby and the direction she was going.

As a distant church bell chimed 9:00 p.m., Leah snapped out of her trance-like state. She looked around, disoriented by the houses, the street signs and the landmarks. She sighed loudly. She was lost.

The irony of being lost struck her as hilarious and she began laughing, at first a little, then uncontrollably. She sat down on a park bench and leaned over to compose herself. Pander looked up at her like she was insane. Leah thought maybe she was.

As quickly as the laughter started, it gave way to tears, and Leah pulled her knees up, rested her head on her arms and sobbed. She hated this life—broke, lonely and aimless. She was an anonymous, invisible wanderer in a strange place, and she ached for her old life back.

Leah knew that those days were gone, though, and the reality of her new existence left her in despair. She was isolated from her friends, unengaged from the working world, and living in virtual poverty. Her unemployment would be running out soon, and if she didn't find work, she would have to apply for food stamps and welfare. Leah's health insurance alone was over $500 per month, or one-quarter of her monthly income.

And she did enjoy good health, thank God and thanks to those wonderful Parker genes she shared with her Aunt Fiona. Perhaps she should go with a less expensive, high deductible health plan. Leah was only one bad break, one terrible illness away from bankruptcy anyway. She would study the insurance plans tomorrow.

Tonight, though, she needed to pull herself together and find her way back to her apartment. She pulled out her smart phone—the one remaining attachment to her former ultra-connected life—and put in her new home address and the intersection where she currently sat feeling sorry for herself. Leah was stunned as she looked at the directions and distance. She and the amazingly fit Pander had walked almost four miles. It would be after 10 p.m. when she got home.

Not that Leah had anywhere to go tomorrow, though, and she sure wasn't tired considering that she had already slept a full night's sleep this afternoon. She stood and started walking, her mind now fully engaged and alert as she followed the directions on her phone.

In her quest to figure out which way to walk, Leah realized she had cleansed herself of self-pity. Next week was Christmas and she had not bought, nor did she intend to buy, a single present. Leah was going to make a card to send to Aunt Fiona and she planned to find something she could make for her girlfriends. Besides, homemade gifts would at least give *her* the satisfaction of knowing that some vestiges of her self-sufficient upbringing were embedded inside her somewhere.

She had found some direction while finding her way back home. The irony was wonderful this time. Leah's mind raced, and she felt suddenly invigorated. She might survive this nightmare after all.

CHAPTER 7

Christmas fell on Friday this year, but to Leah, it was just another day of the week. Siobhan had invited Meg and Courtney, Toni and her mother and daughter, and Leah to Christmas dinner. Leah really didn't want to go.

Besides having nothing to wear, she really didn't have anything to say. While she was thankful for her friends, Leah wanted to go sit through the stares of pity, the emotional pep talks and the gentle probing like she wanted a sharp stick in the eye.

She knew the wonderful group of women wanted to the best for her, but none of them could describe what the best was anymore, including Leah herself. She more than anybody wanted to be back in the working world, but carrying the label "long-term unemployed" made her virtually untouchable in the banking world for rehire. She wondered what the problem was. Who had she wronged? What was she missing? Leah sighed. Who knew?

In the meantime, she had taken online courses and passed her licensing for insurance, securities, and annuities. She had also gotten proficient in web design, social media and most of the computer-based accounting programs. Leah's skill set was more versatile than ever, but she also felt more disconnected from the business world. She didn't even look like she belonged there anymore.

Her hair hadn't been professionally cut in almost a year, her clothes were unstylish and old, and she rarely used make-up or donned attire that was acceptable outside of a gym or college dorm room. Leah did manage to walk about four miles a day, usually alone with Pander, and she had reverted to cooking her own meals to save money. Her diet was much healthier too.

For the dinner tonight, Leah had made an apple streusel pie, an old family recipe that Aunt Fiona had sent her in 2006. The pie was surprisingly easy to make and after a couple of times, she had even gotten creative and made mini-streusels in ten plain white ramekins she had bought for $3.00 at the thrift store down the street. She smiled to herself. Leah was going to shock the dinner party tonight for sure.

For Christmas presents, she also went homemade. She purchased a small box of half-pint Mason jars, lids and rings from the clearance shelf at the superstore in her neighborhood. Leah pulled out her recipe box from Aunt Fiona and was thrilled to find one for homemade bath salts, sent to her in 2002.

She could picture Aunt Fiona and Gran Belle making and using the concoction since the old farmhouse didn't house a shower for the longest time, only a tub. Leah bought coarse and fine kosher salts, a quarter of a yard of cream-colored, discontinued fabric and two spools of colorful two-for-$1 ribbon at the superstore. Then, she drove to the organic produce store on the swankier side of town to buy vanilla bean, lemon balm and lavender. The total of her purchases was less than $20.

After she mixed the aromatic ingredients together in her blender that she had formerly only used for margaritas, she filled the mason jars, put on the lids, covered the top with fabric, put on the ring and covered the ring with ribbon. Leah then carefully labeled the jars with Organic Lavender, Organic Vanilla or Organic Lemon. When she was through, she admitted to herself that she would like to get any one of them as a Christmas gift. Honestly, she was proud of her accomplishment.

Now, though, Leah was almost sick at the thought of the teasing she would receive as she passed around the pies after dinner and the gifts around the tree. She remembered their dinner at the Mexican restaurant vividly. Why couldn't they just say "wow" or "thank you" and leave well enough alone?

She was being a sorehead again, she thought, and she knew she shouldn't be so sensitive and defensive. Leah had nothing left in the pride department anyway.

When she pulled up to the beautiful Tudor-styled Haas home, she realized she was the last to arrive. Leah took a deep breath and realized that she was shaking. She was nervous, almost like she was going into a job interview. She closed her eyes momentarily and whispered,

"God, give me peace, give me joy, and give me strength to enjoy, not endure, the company of the people who love me most."

She got out of the car, grabbed her covered basket of pies and the wrapped box of gifts and walked to the door. Seconds after she rang the doorbell, Leah found herself wrapped in the warm embrace of Siobhan whom she realized she had not seen in almost three months. She felt her tears well up from sadness followed immediately by relief and happiness in the comfort of her best friend's arms, and she uttered, "I've missed you, Sio."

Siobhan pulled her inside and said, "I've missed you too, Leah. Let me take the box from you. C'mon in and take your coat off and put it on a hook in the mudroom. You can put your dish in the dining room on the buffet. Everybody else is in the den."

When Leah got to the den, Robert and the Haas boys sat mesmerized watching NFL football on TV while the women were gathered around the Christmas tree admiring something in the middle of the group. As she walked closer, she realized exactly what they were doing.

The box of homemade gifts sat on the ottoman in the center of the circle and they were taking turns pulling each jar out, reading it and passing it around. As if on cue, they turned to her with joy, amazement and delight in their eyes. Leah felt her face go red.

"Did you make these," Toni asked in a voice filled with wonder.

"Well, yes, I did," Leah stammered.

"Can I smell them," Meg asked.

"Of course," Leah answered, "I brought a jar of each scent for you all."

As Meg removed the lid, Siobhan looked over at Leah, watching her face. *Our reaction is very important to her,* she thought.

"Divine," Courtney said, and Leah exhaled, unaware before now that she had been holding her breath.

"I could just about stick my tongue in the lemon one," Meg said, "but I won't! This stuff is too good to waste!"

"How did you learn to do this, Leah? I guess you weren't kidding when you said you worked on your grandmother's farm," Siobhan commented thoughtfully.

"Actually, the recipe came from my Aunt Fiona in 2002," Leah answered. "The farmhouse didn't have a shower when I was growing up, just a claw-foot tub, so I guess she devised the mixture out of necessity. She is very ingenious."

"Well, I think you must be a chip off of the block, then," Toni added. "These gifts are special, made by your hands from your heart."

Leah felt the tears rising in her eyes, and she walked quickly over to sit beside Siobhan on the hearth of the fireplace. "I'm glad you like them. I can't think of any people more special than you bunch of fools," she said with a smile on her face.

After a few more minutes of catching up, the whole crew moved en masse to the huge dining room where the table was set for 12, even though they only numbered 11. Siobhan believed it was unlucky to set a Christmas table with an odd number—strange, but true.

As they filled their plates with turkey, dressing, ham, potato salad, green beans and the rest of the fixings, Siobhan reminded her boys to save room for dessert. "Lilly at my office made a pumpkin cheesecake," she said. "It goes great with coffee."

"There are mini apple streusel pies over there too," Leah mentioned off-handedly, but the whole room suddenly went silent. *Crap,* she thought, *can't this girl catch a break?*

She felt her face blaze anew as every eye at the table stared in her direction, silently demanding an explanation for her secret skills or at least an introduction to the stranger she had become to them. Leah just sighed and said, "Again, family recipe—2006."

"Wow," Robert almost yelled, "this is fantastic! I am going to go get the vanilla ice cream to pass around," and he quickly rose to go to the freezer.

Siobhan smiled at Leah, and Leah returned the smile almost shyly, hating the fuss, but relieved that the pie was so well-received. Siobhan asked softly, "Who wants coffee?" When seven hands went up—every adult at the table—she asked Leah to help her.

"Of course," Leah answered, and they rose and went to the kitchen. When she rounded the corner, Siobhan hugged her suddenly. "What was *that* all about?" Leah asked her, pleasantly surprised.

"I'm just so proud of you. You amaze me with your hidden culinary talents, your gift ingenuity and your modesty, Leah. Now I know what you've been holed up in that apartment doing for the last three months," Siobhan said, then immediately regretted her choice of words.

Leah slowly put down the two mugs of coffee in her hands and turned to Siobhan, she felt angry tears assault her eyes this time, and her throat felt dry, her breathing suddenly ragged. Fury coiled in her stomach as she struggled to restrain her anger, her hurt and her pain. "I haven't been *holed-up* in my apartment, Siobhan, but then how would you know since you have never come by? Hell, you've called me *twice* in the last three months, so why this sudden interest in my daily routine," Leah almost spat. "I'm sure it is hard to see my crappy little life down here from your pedestal way up there, but don't worry, I won't come skulking around anymore. I would sure hate to mar your picture-perfect life."

By this time, Meg, Courtney and Toni had heard the argument and come to the kitchen door, Robert had shuttled the boys back to the TV, and Toni's mom and daughter had gone to the den to look at the Christmas tree. Courtney scurried to join the others in the den. Meg walked over between Leah and Siobhan and asked, "What's going on in here?"

"Oh, nothing," Leah raged, "I'm just getting a lesson on the evils of my reclusiveness."

"Leah! I didn't mean to hurt your feelings," Siobhan cried, "but I guess you took my innocuous remark as a license to hit below the belt. I will remind you that the telephone is a *two-way* communication device, my friend!"

"Hey, hey," Toni said softly trying to soothe feelings and calm nerves, "Let's talk through this like people who love each other, okay?"

"Well here's the deal everybody—I have gotten five financial licenses, three more computer certifications and attended dozens of seminars, job fairs and networking and charity events. I am not going to work for minimum wage, and if you think that decision is wrong, I don't give a damn. I can barely scrape by on unemployment when my measly hole-in-the-wall rent and health insurance is almost half of my monthly earnings. I have put out probably a thousand resumes, made dozens of applications, and I am just tired of no response. I am sick of all of it, especially people who think they understand one minute of one day of my life," Leah finished, and she crumbled to the floor with her back against the kitchen cabinet and cried.

Siobhan was crying too, and Toni was torn as to who to comfort first. She finally squatted down beside Leah and embraced her as she sobbed when she saw Meg, who initially looked like a deer in headlights, walk over to Siobhan and pull her close in a hug.

After a few minutes of silence, Toni stood and poured two more mugs of coffee and handed each of her best friends a cup. Then, without any coordination, Meg, Toni and Siobhan sat down on the kitchen floor beside Leah as closely as they could without sitting on each other's lap, silently communicating how much they loved each other.

Leah was still sobbing, Siobhan still sniffling. Meg, like usual, broke the silence, "You could have just thumb wrestled, you know."

They laughed and warmth returned to the kitchen. Finally, Leah said, "I'm sorry, Siobhan. I was mean-spirited and out of line. Jealousy is an ugly emotion."

"I'm sorry too, Leah," Siobhan whispered, "I'm just frustrated—albeit not half as much as you are—that you can't find a real job. This town is just sucking the life out of professionals like you who can't find work."

"Well, maybe this new year will be the charm," Toni said on a positive note. "At least the early predictions are that it will be better than this year. I'll be happy to see this one go for you, my dear," she said to Leah.

"Amen, sister," Meg added. "This economy sucks!"

Leah took a deep breath and said the words that had been bouncing around in her head for months, making them real, "I may have to move away."

Siobhan started crying again and put her head on Leah's shoulder and sobbed, "I don't want you to move."

"I know—me either," Leah said, "but I only have so many opportunities in Virginia Beach, and it is expensive here. Believe me—poverty stinks."

"Well, I am going to hope that job with Hospice is going to pan out," Toni said positively, "and maybe this year will be your year."

"C'mon girls, bring your coffee and let's go eat some pie," Siobhan said. "I have never heard Robert exclaim praise like he did over that streusel. I've got to have some."

"I'm going to eat a piece of your cheesecake too," Leah said as they moved back to the dining room table with their coffee and desserts.

As they talked about the weather and the upcoming New Year, Meg stopped them for a coffee toast. "Here's to a better new year—may it be your new beginning, Leah," and they tapped their mugs together festively as joy and happiness once again filled the room.

CHAPTER 8

By March, though, Leah realized that she was not the one getting the job with Hospice for which Toni had so highly recommended her. In the end, an inexperienced, but beautiful, 20-something who probably earned half of what Leah would have cost got the job. She didn't get a phone call from Hospice. Leah just saw the hiring announcement in the newspaper two weeks after her third interview. Even Toni had not called to break the bad news to her.

In the following months, Leah's despair turned to resignation and the phone calls to and from her friends became less and less frequent. She guessed they had run out of things to say. Leah sure had. Besides, they had lives to live with their families, and she was certain the last thing they needed was regularly dealing with her seemingly hopeless situation.

This year, July 4th came and went so suddenly that, for the first time in seven years, the crew didn't get together for their Mexican fiesta in June. Leah felt further apart from them than ever, almost as if the friendships themselves were disappearing off into some distant horizon. Sometimes in the middle of the night, she would wake up, alone and afraid. For the first time in her adult life, Leah had nowhere to turn. Instead of a quick e-mail to "talk through" her deepest, darkest fears to Siobhan, Toni and Meg, she simply turned her head into her pillow and cried herself back to sleep.

As the summer faded away in late September, Leah's concern and fear turned into full-blown panic. Her unemployment was going to run out at the beginning of November, and she still had no job prospects after a summer of sending hundreds of resumes out at a torrid daily pace. Faced with zero income, she knew she wouldn't be able to afford to pay for her apartment, let alone her insurance. Leah virtually quit sleeping at night, and instead took Pander on long, rambling walks or paced around her small apartment wringing her hands and talking to herself or her dog. By noon every day, she was completely exhausted and would doze off in her chair or at her small dining table in front of the computer. Leah was no longer living. She was simply taking up space.

On October 8, as she was making a pot of chili that was big enough to eat now, reheat it for the next couple of days, and freeze some for later in the month, she realized today was Aunt Fiona's ninety-second birthday. Leah gave the pot one more stir, put the lid on to let the chili simmer, grabbed her phone and sat down to call her elderly aunt. She had remembered to mail her a birthday card late last week.

On the third ring, Leah's sudden excitement was instantly crushed when a decidedly male voice answered, "Hello."

Confused, she quickly checked the number and seeing that she dialed correctly, she replied, "Hello? May I speak with Fiona Parker please?"

"Who is this," the now irritated voice boomed into her ear.

Undeterred and now somewhat irritated herself at his irascible tone, she answered, "This is Leah Gibson, her niece. Who are you?"

Immediately, his tone changed and he replied, "Well, Good Lord, my dear, this is Tom Cunningham from next door! It's nice to hear from you, but your Aunt Fi is not doing so well today. How are you?"

Leah conjured up Mr. C's weathered face and smiled. He was crusty and cranky, but he had always looked out for her grandmother, her aunt and when she would stay at the farm, her too. She lied, "I'm doing fine, but I hope Aunt Fiona's going to be okay. What's wrong?"

"Well, besides being ninety-two, Doc thinks she may have pneumonia, and you know that woman is as stubborn as a mule! She won't go to the hospital. Maybe you can talk some sense into her," he said with a sigh.

"Put her on the phone then! She better not make me have to drive up those hills and drag her there," Leah replied.

"That might be just what the doctor ordered," Tom answered, "Hold on."

After about a minute or so, Leah heard her aunt's distinct but very weak voice say, "Hello, sugar. How's my favorite banker?"

Leah's heart sank because she hadn't had the guts to tell her aunt about her unemployment dilemma, so she ignored the question and scolded good-naturedly, "Oh, no, you're not going to make this conversation about me, young lady! Mr. C tells me you've been sparring with Doc Evans again with your impeccable medical credentials. Is this true?"

Without as much as a pause, Aunt Fiona fired back, "Well Tom has a big mouth, and Doc Evans is not as smart as he thinks he is! I am fine. You'd think that they'd listen to somebody who's lived in this body for 92 years. I just have a cold, Leah," she reassured.

Leah wondered if she should make the drive to Ashe County, North Carolina. Turning the thought over, she asked, "Do you need me to come help you?"

"Good Lord, no," Aunt Fiona said exasperated. "I'll be fine. Besides, what are you going to do here? Watch the turnips grow with me?"

Leah laughed at her aunt's fighting spirit and then said, "That doesn't sound half bad right now! Perhaps I can come up after Thanksgiving. Would you like that?"

"Nothing would make me happier than for you to come home, my dear—nothing," she said sincerely.

"Oh, Aunt Fi," Leah said overcome with emotion. Evoking the word "home" flooded her with memories of the farm, the orchards, the garden, the house. She felt like she might cry. Gathering herself, she added, "I'll be home after Thanksgiving, okay?"

"Okay," Aunt Fiona said with a smile in her voice.

"And one more thing," Leah added, "Pull out some more of those wonderful recipes for me! I've been making several of them for about a year now, and I think I'm ready for some new ones."

"How wonderful," Aunt Fiona replied, "I'll show you some of my favorites, and we can make them together when you come home."

"I can't wait," Leah said, "Now you go get some rest, birthday girl. I'll see you in a couple of months." They said goodbye and Leah hung up the phone.

For the rest of the day as she cooked, cleaned and sent out another batch of resumes, she kept a smile on her face. That night, as she laid her head down on her pillow, Leah, though tired, slipped contently off to sleep as she realized that for the first time in almost two years she had something to look forward to.

CHAPTER 9

November blew in with a hellacious winter storm that sent temperatures plummeting and snow falling at record levels. The sky stayed depressing, dishwater gray for weeks. Everyday seemed to bring some kind of precipitation—cold rain, sleet, or snow. Virginia Beach was a soggy, sloppy mess.

Worse, Leah hadn't been able to pay her rent in full this month, and her bitch of a landlord came knocking on her door every day demanding the balance. Her last unemployment check—her ninety-ninth—would arrive on Friday. She knew the entire balance was already spent between rent, insurance, and her power bill. She was eating food that she had frozen over the last several months every time she ate, sometimes only a late lunch or an early supper. She washed down the vegetable soup, the chili, the lasagna or the chicken casserole with iced tea or tap water since she could no longer afford good coffee.

Leah's situation was dire, and she knew she was going to be evicted from her apartment. She needed to figure out what to do rather quickly. What would she do with her furniture? Where would she go? How would she feed herself and Pander?

All the questions overwhelmed her and she felt herself shaking, quaking really, all over. She needed help, and she needed help quickly. Leah pulled out her phone and dialed Siobhan at work.

"Mauldin and Mauldin—how may I direct your call," the pleasant receptionist asked.

"May I speak with Siobhan? This is Leah, and I need her help," Leah said with unusually urgency in her voice.

"Oh, I'm sorry Miss Gibson. Mrs. Haas is in court this afternoon. Would you like to leave her a message or do you want to speak to Mr. Mauldin," she inquired.

"Just let her know that I called and ask her to call me as soon as possible, please," Leah responded. Dejected, she hung up the phone and tried not to panic.

Next, she called Meg's cell phone but only got her voicemail. Leah left her a short message asking her to call when she could.

Last, she called Toni at work. When she answered the phone, Leah breathed a sigh of relief. "Hi Toni, this is Leah," she said quietly, "Have you got a minute to talk?"

"Hey, you—I've missed you," Toni replied sweetly, "I'm getting ready to go into a family conference, but I want to catch up. Can I call you after work?"

"Oh, sure, that would be great," Leah lied, "Call me when you have time to talk."

Toni was silent for a split second then asked, "Are you okay, Leah? You sound like something is wrong."

"I'm fine, Toni. Just call me later," Leah said. As she hung up the phone, she sat immobilized for what felt like an hour. When a chill ran down her arms, she realized she was cold, and Leah got up to go grab her quilt.

She sat back down on the couch and covered up from her neck down to her feet. Pander jumped up beside her to get in on the quilt action. Leah pulled her close and the dog licked her face then lay her head down on Leah's lap. The thought that her only comfort came from her four-legged companion unbraided her, though, and she began crying, softly at first as she stroked Pander, then harder as her desperation became more apparent.

Finally, as Leah accepted the fact that within weeks she would be homeless, the dam holding back her emotions and her fears broke, and she sobbed deep, gut-wrenching tears that wracked her body and left her trembling, weak and scared. Deep moans escaped from her that echoed of hopelessness and desolation, and she could only wrap her arms around herself and rock back and forth trying to find some small measure of comfort. Even Pander seemed to sense the seriousness of the situation for she was shaking and skittish and uncertain what to do.

On wobbly legs, Leah eventually rose from the couch and walked over to the lone window in her small abode and looked outside. A light, wet snow had begun to fall and already the tops of the cars along the street were blanketed in white. The city no longer looked like a wonderland; instead, it looked like a lonely, cold, snowy prison where she had been condemned to solitary confinement.

Leah suddenly wanted out. She looked wildly around the room, located her keys and started toward the door. Just as suddenly, though, she stopped. *Where am I going*, she asked herself.

Out of answers and drained of energy, Leah simply sat back down on the couch and pulled the quilt over herself and her dog again. Then, she turned off her phone, stretched out lengthwise, closed her swollen eyes, and fell fast asleep.

CHAPTER 10

Siobhan sat tapping her pencil on her desk, decidedly distracted and obviously irritated. The snow was falling again outside and as if a 12-hour day spent in the courtroom with emotionally-wrecked clients in a custody battle was not trying enough, now she had to navigate perilously slick roads on the drive home. She sighed and stood to pack her briefcase, grab her purse and finally go home.

It was 7:30 p.m. and Robert had left her a message that he was taking the boys out for pizza. He had promised to save two slices of her favorite topping-laden pizza to bring home. Siobhan was relieved and felt so fortunate to have married a thoughtful, considerate, and kind man. Never mind that he was incredibly handsome, smarter than she was, and as funny as anybody she knew. Most importantly, after all of their years together, she loved him more than ever. Thinking about her family as she sat alone in the office irritated her even more.

If she was truthful, her irritation was not from needy clients or from too little time with her family, however. Right now, the source of her frustration was Leah Gibson, one of her best friends. Siobhan was worn to a frazzle watching Leah's life spiral to rock-bottom. She had made suggestions for Leah to volunteer at various charities, make application at several law firms seeking paralegals, and take relevant courses at the local college. Leah just seemingly tuned her out and made no effort to follow up on any of them.

Two years out of work was a lifetime, Siobhan thought. Maybe Leah had forgotten how to work, forgotten that a morning routine was important to maintain, and forgotten that pride over low pay didn't pay the bills. Or, maybe Siobhan was being harsh. She just didn't know anymore.

It was easy to assume she knew how awful this recession had been on Leah because she had been there for every blow it had delivered to her best friend. Siobhan's view, though, was always tempered by her own seemingly blessed existence as she came home each night to a beautiful home, a wonderful family and every amenity her success as well as Robert's provided.

Leah had nobody. Nobody, that is, except Siobhan, Toni and Meg, and they had all let her down. Siobhan knew it and felt enormous guilt that she didn't proactively do more. Not financially, because Leah sure as hell wouldn't accept charity, but emotionally and physically. All of Leah's friends knew what she needed—an ear, a phone call just to say hi, a visit to her god-forsaken apartment with a pizza in hand just to sit and watch a movie—but what she needed was also the hardest to continually supply. The kind of support Leah needed was emotionally draining and sad, and it left her friends feeling helpless, anxious and unfulfilled.

Siobhan felt tears well up in her eyes. She just wanted Leah to find work, to find meaning in her life again and to find somebody special with whom she could share it. Siobhan knew why she wanted all of those things, too, and the acceptance of the fact that she dreaded having to shoulder Leah's despair and wished for somebody else to do it sent tears in torrents running down her cheeks. She was a crappy friend, she thought.

She dried her eyes and pulled herself together. She needed to get home, wanted to be there already. Siobhan grabbed her bags and picked up the message from Leah and put it in the top of her purse. She would call her best friend tomorrow.

Chapter 11

Toni looked at herself in the mirror one more time. She touched up her purplish-pink lipstick and smoothed her violet dress in the back. She hoped Carter liked the way she looked tonight.

Over the last six months, she had increasingly grown to care what Carter liked and thought. Toni admitted four months ago that she was in love with him after two months of denials and fake detachment. Now, just weeks before Thanksgiving, she wondered how she had ever existed without him.

Carter Monroe was kind, quiet and intensely passionate. He was a pediatric oncologist at the hospital, and Toni had never met a man so committed to helping sick children get well or making dying children stay comfortable. He had seemed almost too good to be true, and unlike the other female nurses, radiologists and doctors, Toni somewhat noted but then promptly ignored what a co-worker deemed Carter's "awesomeness."

Carter couldn't ignore her, though. He would pop into her office late in the afternoons to talk about their patients, their families, their prognoses and their illnesses. Toni proved to be a sounding board for him, and in early July, he asked her to go watch fireworks with him—on the mall in Washington, DC. She was completely stunned, but she politely declined, telling him that she was spending the holiday with her daughter, Lucy.

Without missing a beat, Carter said he was inviting Lucy too so his daughter, Olivia, would have someone her own age to keep her company. Toni was out of excuses. She wanted to go, telling herself that Lucy would love the Capitol's fireworks, but she hardly knew Carter Monroe. How could she say yes?

But as she had slowly grown to know him over the last couple of months, Toni had seen his tenderness, his humor, and his intelligence. Carter had also allowed her to see his vulnerability as he discussed the loss of his wife in a car accident; his uncertainty about the role of faith in his life; and his awkwardness with women. That is, every woman on the hospital staff except Toni. She asked him why.

Carter told her, "You're different, Toni. You're like an anchor—steadfast and sure under a hellish undercurrent."

Toni answered, "An anchor is also heavy, cold and invisible when it's working."

Carter had laughed so hard and so deeply that he had supported himself on the doorjamb of her office to keep from rolling around on the floor. The sight of him had made Toni smile, and she realized she liked Carter Monroe.

When he finally responded, "Toni Dalton, you are perfectly petite, smoking hot and on my mind far too much—so an anchor was a bad description," Toni knew she was hooked.

She accepted his invitation, and the four of them drove to Washington the day before Independence Day. They visited all of the monuments, rode the Metro and went to a performance at the Kennedy Center. They stayed in a townhouse near the Capitol building that belonged to a friend of Carter's. On July 4th, they staked out the perfect spot on the mall early and listened to the music from a wide variety of bands and ensembles. They ate from the well-stocked and delicious picnic basket Toni's mother had prepared for them, and the girls danced around and acted silly like typical eight—and nine-year-olds.

Toni and Carter split a wonderful bottle of white wine and discussed every topic from religion to politics to television shows to movie stars. Toni realized that she could truly be herself around Carter and he told her, "I like myself a whole lot better when I'm with you, Toni. You complete me."

With that honest remark, Toni was lost. That night, as the girls slept upstairs and were completely exhausted from the day in the sun, Toni invited Carter into her bedroom. He took her into his arms and made love to her over and over, taking Toni to heights of passion she had previously only read about in romance novels. He was an incredible lover, and he held her all night long.

The next morning, he got up early and made everybody French toast for breakfast. When he called her to eat, he unabashedly kissed her passionately in front of the girls. Toni smiled, and the girls just giggled. From that day until now, she and Carter had been inseparable.

Toni had kept her relationship with Carter secret from everybody except her mother and Lucy. Their hospital co-workers were clueless that they had been seeing each other. More importantly, though, Toni had kept all of her friends in the dark. She had asked herself why so many times she refused to think about it anymore. She knew why. It would be just one more blow to Leah, so she decided to keep Carter a secret from all of them.

Now with the holidays rapidly approaching and her relationship with Carter seemingly leading to a permanent status, Toni knew she needed to tell Leah, Siobhan and Meg. She wanted them to meet him, get to know her Mr. Wonderful, and show them how much they loved each other. Toni knew they would be ecstatic for her, especially Meg and Siobhan because they knew the kind of love she had with their own soul mates.

Leah would be thrilled too, but Toni was certain that the relationship would also reinforce in Leah a kind of loneliness during the darkest time of her life. Toni sighed to try and rid herself of the heaviness that had settled in her chest.

She could feel Leah's despair and several times this year the feeling threatened to devour Toni. When Leah was passed over for the charitable giving director position with the local Hospice, Toni cried so hard and so long that she missed work the following day. She meant to call Leah, but she just never got around to it. After days turned to weeks, the overwhelming guilt began to fade. As Toni's workload increased, she ploughed herself into her work with gusto. Several months later at the end of March when she spoke to Leah, she didn't even think about the position Leah had lost. She had just been too busy with her own life and career.

Now, Toni realized that she forgot to call Leah back yesterday like she promised. She had again put her almost decade-long friendship on the back burner to focus attention on her relationship with Carter. Not that there was anything wrong with her decision, Toni countered to herself. Leah, though, was all alone and she needed her friends, her only solace from the cruelty the economy had shown her.

Toni sometimes wanted to reach out and hold her close just to comfort her, but Leah was like a drowning child, flailing dangerously and holding on so tightly that she threatened to take Toni down with her. The friendship that had sustained her for so many years was now just . . . difficult. God, with friends like her, Leah didn't stand a chance, Toni thought.

She shook the depressing thoughts away as best as she could and smoothed her dress one more time. Toni would call Siobhan and Meg tomorrow to set the date for their Christmas gathering. For Leah, she would order Chinese and pick up a movie to take over to Leah's apartment where they could spend some time together, and Toni could make sure Leah was doing okay. She would also tell Leah first about Carter.

Perhaps, then, Leah would understand why Toni had been missing in action for the last six months, and maybe she would forgive her absence in the friendship. Toni's true motive for a visit with Leah was like a slap on the cheek, and she scolded herself in the mirror as she admitted what was now painfully obvious. *You suck,* she said silently to her reflection. Toni didn't need to visit Leah tomorrow to obtain her blessing on her relationship with Carter. In truth, all Toni really needed was absolution.

CHAPTER 12

Meg stared out the window as the airplane banked over the Atlantic Ocean on its final approach toward Virginia Beach, toward home. She had so much on her mind, so many things to consider, and so many decisions to make.

She sighed audibly, and the man next to her looked up, seemingly annoyed. "I'm sorry. Does my breathing bother you?" she asked him sternly. Of course, he didn't reply. He was a jerk, but he didn't look stupid, Meg thought.

Taking a cleansing breath, Meg conjured up her beautiful Courtney, and the stress buzzing in her brain began to quiet down. Perhaps this evening they could open that great bottle of red wine they had been saving for the perfect occasion and settle in beside the fire to watch television or a movie. Meg didn't want to go out, even to eat. She was sick of restaurant food, traveling anywhere, and other people. All she wanted was calm, quiet and Courtney.

Over a home-cooked meal and a glass of cabernet, Meg would tell Courtney about the promotion she was offered this morning. "The opportunity of a lifetime," her boss had called it, and it certainly was. Her acceptance of the position would make her the youngest executive vice president in the entire multi-billion dollar company. She would have perks too numerous to list and a new salary that more than doubled what she currently knocked down, including her incredible bonuses.

The role came with a caveat, though, and that one requirement had Meg tied all in knots. If she accepted, she would have to move much closer to Washington, DC. Doubt wracked her brain, fear churned in her gut. What if Courtney didn't want to move? Would she go anyway? Could Courtney let her go? Would Meg survive without her?

Quit assuming she is going to say no, she told herself. Meg took another deep breath. This time, the man beside her didn't so much as glance her way.

Meg also had to consider her friends. Next to Courtney, they were the most important people in her life. She needed them, and they needed her. Not that she had been available to them for the last six months, though. Meg had literally spent more nights in hotel rooms this year than she had in her own bed. She was sure her tireless work ethic won her the prized role which she had now been offered.

But travel was tough on relationships, and Meg remembered that Courtney had expressed her displeasure numerous times in the last several months with her long absences. Worse still, she hadn't seen Leah, Toni or Siobhan in months—months! She hadn't called them lately either, and the thought reminded her that she never returned the missed call from Leah yesterday.

Meg's mind settled on her best friend. She simply could not fathom how someone so vibrant, positive and beautiful could be unemployed for so long. Bankers must be idiots, she decided. Well, more specifically, the dark-suited men in the executive and senior management positions must be idiots. Leah's charm alone threatened male bankers. Meg had seen it first-hand.

Five years ago, Leah's bank hosted a kick-off party before Virginia Beach's American Music Festival. Her boss gave her ten tickets to sell for the exclusive event. Never one to let her friends miss out on a party, Leah had called them and asked them to cough up the $200 per ticket. She sold all ten in three phone calls. Siobhan bought four tickets for her and Robert and her brother and sister-in-law. Toni bought two tickets so she could take her mother, and Meg bought the remaining four tickets for her and Courtney and her boss and his wife.

After her initial success, Leah was given ten more and asked to sell them as well. Pouring over her lists of customers and contacts, Leah sold the second ten in two more days. Now amazed by her sales prowess, she was challenged to sell as many tickets as she could by the end of August or one week before the event. Over the next two weeks, Leah called every contact and contact of her contacts that she could find. All told, Leah sold a total of 50 tickets, and her sales efforts alone netted the bank's charitable foundation $10,000.

At the beginning of the party, the bank's president got up on the stage to thank the event sponsors and welcome the standing-room-only crowd. Then, he specifically called Leah by name and asked her to come to the stage. As she stood beside him, he gushed about her contribution to the foundation's cause, her dedication to the bank and her remarkable sales skills. Leah, though somewhat embarrassed by the attention, smiled graciously the whole time at her entourage.

Leah's friends and customers were so proud of her, and the remainder of her evening was spent accepting hugs, handshakes and thanks for a job well done. To add her part to the celebration, Meg went to the closest bar and grabbed two beers, one for herself, the other for Leah. As she waited for the bartender to bring them to her, she overheard the conversation of two slick guys standing beside her. They were obviously bankers in their standard-issue black tuxedos, and from their green-with-envy comments about Leah, they were obviously bastards too.

As they accused Leah of everything from sleeping with men in the executive suite to stealing ticket sales that belonged to them, Meg knew her best friend would always have a target on her because of her success. After she got her beers from the bartender, she "accidentally" ran into the guy standing closest to her. When he looked her in the face and smiled, Meg smiled back broadly, turning on every ounce of devilish charm she could muster.

As she sashayed away, she was certain the bastards watched her walk directly over to Leah, tap her on the shoulder, then turn around. Yep, they were watching her. All of the color had disappeared from their faces, though. Meg casually asked Leah who the guys at the bar were, pointing to them for effect and never taking her eyes off of them. Leah gave her their names curiously, telling Meg they were colleagues of hers at the bank.

Meg smiled at them, raised her beer to them, then leaned over and whispered in Leah's ear, "Watch your back with those two, Le. They are not only jealous of you, you scare them to death."

Leah looked at her seriously for a moment then nodded. She never even looked back in their direction. Perhaps she knew how they felt. Perhaps she just didn't care.

However she felt, Leah never mentioned it again. But the thought that those losers kept their job and Leah didn't made Meg furious now. She knew why Leah had lost her job, and why she had been unable to find another in this sorry little banking town.

Leah was female and fabulous, and that was in complete opposition to how banking business was done in many small towns and cities across America. The good old boys club was alive and well in banking. Old farts cultivated young bucks by modeling that a hard-working, pretty young assistant was the key to looking good and moving up the ladder. The "secretaries" did all of the work while the "officers" knocked off at lunchtime on Fridays to go play golf and left early most other days to go "develop business" at the country club bar. An independent, hard-working and successful "girl" officer threatened their executive privilege. As a result, for a lazy bunch of idiots, they worked amazingly hard to undermine her at every opportunity.

Sadly, the idiots won, and Leah lost her job. In fact, she had lost everything. Well, not everything, Meg thought. She still had her friends.

Or did she? Meg considered how their tightly woven group of best friends had seemingly begun to fray. She hadn't seen them or talked to them in months; they had foregone their annual Mexican fiesta this year; and nobody had called to orchestrate a Christmas celebration. Their friendship was changing, had changed, just like their lives. Life was never static, Meg thought.

God knows Leah needed a fresh start like Meg was getting. Perhaps Leah could move up near the District too. Meg would call her best friend tomorrow and discuss it. They could catch up, and Meg would make sure Leah knew she would always be there for her whether she was here or there. She would also call Toni and Siobhan and plan their Christmas party. Satisfied that she had a plan to get together, Meg banished thoughts of friends for now and turned her mind back to Courtney.

She smiled as she did. Courtney would be waiting at the airport for her. Meg looked out the window as the plane, now on the ground in Virginia Beach, taxied toward the terminal. She was nervous, but her doubts had ebbed considerably. She and Courtney loved each other enough that they would make Meg's exciting career opportunity work. They could move to Maryland where they would make their relationship permanent—a domestic partnership they called it. Meg wanted it now more than ever, and she planned to propose to her lover tonight. She had waited for this moment for years, having bought a beautiful carved jade band to mark the occasion not long after she and Courtney had moved in together. Meg was suddenly giddy with anticipation, and she stood quickly, grabbed her carry-on bag and waited to exit the plane. She looked through the plane's open door, hoping to catch a glimpse of Courtney. She saw that it was snowing—hard. She sighed contentedly. They had the whole night ahead of them—just the two of them.

Tomorrow, Meg would concentrate on helping Leah start over. Meg was going to force her hand, push her hard, motivate a change—she wasn't going to take "no" for an answer either. Leah Gibson had to re-invent herself and get back to the land of the living. Meg wondered what Leah would do and where she would do it. After two years of unemployment, however, Meg was certain of two things—Leah Gibson was never going to be a banker again and her eventual departure from Virginia Beach was far more certain than Courtney's or even her own.

CHAPTER 13

Leah woke with a start, somewhat disoriented and freezing cold. Pander jumped off her lap and walked to the door. She needed to go outside. Meg walked to the window, wiped the condensation off of it with her sleeve and peered into the white wilderness.

Virginia Beach was blanketed with snow. Leah guessed at least six to eight inches had fallen by the looks of the banisters. Traffic was non-existent, and she didn't see a soul in sight. Leah looked at her watch. It was only 7:00 a.m.

After a few minutes, she realized today was Saturday. Not that her weekend days were any different than Monday through Friday. She was simply marking time, flipping days on a calendar, existing but not really living. Now with the cold, wet, and dreary weather, Leah couldn't even take Pander on their long daily wander. She had to take her outside for a few minutes, though.

Putting on her enormous coat, the one she had used for years in New York City when she and her friends made their annual Christmas trip, Leah called Pander over to see if she would wear the sweater she had crocheted in the last couple days. The dog sweater was red with black around the collar and leg ends. Leah was quite proud of it actually. She had been at the discount store last Friday, wandering past the end-caps where all of the discontinued and seasonal items were marked down to sell.

A crochet book and starter kit with the bright red yarn caught her eye. The whole kit was $5.99. Leah picked it up and read the package. The pillow on the front reminded her of her Gran Belle's mudroom bench cushion and transported Leah back decades when she used to lay on the bench while Aunt Fi and Gran Belle would hang herbs and flowers to dry on the open porch. She loved that pillow so much that she wanted one like it to take home to her room.

Never one to miss a teaching moment, Aunt Fi showed her how to crochet that summer. Leah learned the stitching easily and before she left to go home that summer, she had crocheted a small pillow using the leftover yarn she loved. Years later, when she left for college, her mother packed the pillow to go with her. Leah didn't argue. She wanted a piece of home to take with her.

Unfortunately, her roommate threw a party shortly after Leah's arrival, and the pillow that she had so lovingly made, used and brought with her to college was ruined by a cranberry juice cocktail spilled by an obviously drunk girl from down the hall. In an attempt to make it all better, her roommate then tried to clean the pillow by putting it in a washer. The pillow was unrecognizable afterward. The crochet was unraveled and the stuffing was ripped out. Leah threw the remnants in the trash—albeit reluctantly.

Snapping back to the present, she wondered if she could still crochet. She put the package in her basket and then rifled through the yarns in the sale bin to see if she liked any of them. Leah chose four skeins because they were only $1 each and the yarn was pretty.

When she got back home, she read the first four chapters of the book, and then gave the stitches a try. Surprisingly, Leah picked up right where she had left off so many years ago, and the methodical movements both comforted and appeased her. Before she retired to bed last Friday, she had crocheted a beautiful winter scarf from the yellow skein. Yellow was Toni's favorite color, and Leah decided she would give her creation to Toni as a Christmas gift this year. By the time she went to bed on Tuesday, she had completely exhausted the four skeins of yarn she purchased plus the red and black skein included in the kit from which she crocheted Pander's sweater.

When she considered her color selections of yarn now beautifully transformed into long, fringed scarves, Leah marveled at her subconscious mind. The four skeins were the favorite colors of her best friends and herself—yellow for Toni, sea foam green for Siobhan, purple for Meg and powder blue for herself. The connection left no doubt what she would give to them this year as a gift, and she knew they would love it. Leah also knew she would blow their minds when she told her friends that she crocheted the scarves herself.

As she opened the door to go outside, she was greeted by a stiff, northerly gust of the coldest wind she had ever felt. Even Pander paused at the door as if she was reconsidering how badly she needed to go, but she finally ran to the nearest bush, relieved herself then made a beeline back to the apartment door. *Smart dog*, Leah thought.

Now cooped back up inside the apartment, Leah wondered how she would fill the day. With no yarn, no money, and no call-backs from her friends, her options were quite few. She could watch television or she could get dressed and go to the public library to read or access their internet for free. Leah considered the weather. She could watch television.

She sighed. She was already bored, and it wasn't even 8:00 a.m. She wondered what her friends were doing. Leah sure knew they weren't watching anything on television. They were probably sleeping in since they didn't have to work today. Perhaps they would call later.

As if she had communicated her thoughts telepathically, Leah's phone rang and she had to curb her enthusiasm not to run to get it off the counter. It was Meg!

"Hi Meg!" she exclaimed. "I've sure missed you."

"I've missed you too, sweetie pie. This weather is el-shitay, huh?" Meg said. "No matter, though, I'm on my way over to kidnap you. You're coming over to the house, and we're going to get in the Jacuzzi, drink wine, eat pizza and catch up."

Leah laughed nervously as she looked around her postage-stamp apartment, then answered, "I could probably be talked into going even though I'll have to consult my calendar I'm just so busy. I haven't had a shower yet this morning. Have I got time?"

"Absolutely," Meg answered, "The roads are awful so it will take me about forty minutes to get there. How would you like a large hazelnut coffee with just cream from the DD?"

"My mouth is watering just thinking about it, Meggie," Leah said, and she got choked up at just how lucky she was to have a friend like Meg.

"You've got it then, my queen," she answered. "I'll see you just before 9."

As soon as she disconnected she began straightening the apartment. She folded her blanket, put the scarves on her bed, and hung her coat on the hook in the closet at the front door. Then she ran to the bathroom, turned on the wall heater, shut the door and went to get her clothes. She pulled out her bikini for the Jacuzzi and grabbed a sweater, jeans and her boots to wear. As she was scurrying, the phone rang again. Fear ran through her that Meg couldn't make it, and she hesitated. *Selfish*, she said to herself.

Leah picked up the phone. It was Toni. "Hey girlfriend!" she said excitedly.

"Hey girlfriend, yourself," Toni replied. "What are you doing?"

"Meg is on her way over to whisk me away to her house for the day," Leah answered happily. "What are you doing?" she asked Toni.

"I wanted to come see you and catch up. Hey! Maybe Meg will let me come over," Toni said, then continued, "If that's okay with you, Leah."

"That would be great! Hey, I've got to get in the shower. Will you call Meg and tell her the plan? Better yet, have her call Siobhan and see if we can all get together, okay?" Leah exclaimed.

"You bet! Get in the shower, and I'll see you at Meg's. I'll call Siobhan and arrange the par-tay with her. I can't wait to see you. I've missed you terribly," Toni admitted.

"I've missed you too—all of you," Leah said. "I'll see you later!"

Leah was almost delirious with happiness, a perma-grin plastered on her face as she raced to get ready. What had started out as another day from hell in a long list of boring days from hell now held the promise of excitement, change, comfort and joy. It also promised coffee, pizza, wine, movies and her three best friends.

"Screw the weather!" she said with a smile to Pander. Today was just the buoy she needed to raise her sunken spirit from the deep.

CHAPTER 14

Leah squealed like a 12-year-old as she opened the door to Meg's sports car, startling Pander who was under her arm and causing Meg to let out a wild victory yell. Leah laughed, hoping the commotion woke up her nasty landlord.

As she climbed in the car, tossed her bag behind the seat and strapped Pander and herself into the seatbelt, she reached over and kissed Meg on the cheek when she saw the extra-large coffee waiting for her. She was giddy with excitement.

They drove and chatted casually as Meg navigated the hazardous streets back to her house. Meg told Leah that Siobhan was coming over in about an hour, and Toni planned to join them for lunch—on her. Leah responded, "Today is like an answered prayer, Meg. I was so stir-crazy in my little apartment that I almost scared myself."

"I'm sorry I've been so unavailable, Leah," Meg replied softly. "Work has been hectic, but you have been very much in my thoughts." The sincerity of her words touched Leah deeply, and she reached over and squeezed Meg's arm as they pulled into her garage. They got out quickly and rushed into the warmth of the house.

Leah walked comfortably to Meg's guest room and put her bag on the bed. Pander found a pallet in the corner made just for her, and she walked around it several times to check it out before she finally approved and plopped herself down. Leah smiled at Meg's thoughtfulness, silently considering herself to be both lucky and undeserving of such devotion. She had not been an easy person to be friends with over the last two years.

When she walked in the den, she found Meg sitting on the couch with trays full of muffins, bagels, croissants, fruit and cream cheese waiting for her. Leah was once again overcome with the emotions in her heart, and she sat down beside Meg, put her arms around her neck and cried with happiness. Meg simply stroked her hair. Finally, she broke the silence by saying, "Life has been so unkind to you, Le. What can I do to help you?"

Leah sniffled, trying to pull herself together, and softly replied, "Just *this*—connection, friendship, and fellowship with no judgment. I'm broke, but not broken. I'm cut off from the working world, but I've become incredibly self-sufficient in many ways. You wouldn't believe it, actually," she finished.

"Tell me!" Meg said, genuinely interested.

"I'll tell you what," Leah said as she stuffed a grape into her mouth, "as soon as the whole gang is here, I'm going to tell you things about me that are going to shock the shit out of you." She smiled mysteriously at Meg who let a huge grin spread over her face.

"Ok, then, but I want to hear it as soon as they get here," she said, and Leah promised her she would. Meg then asked, "So what are you going to do to survive now that your unemployment is going away? I'm concerned for you, Leah."

"I know, Meg, and I'm more than concerned, I am scared to death. After this month, my landlord is going to kick me out. I'm not going to have enough money to pay my rent anymore," Leah answered honestly. She sighed and shook her head to keep her tears at bay.

"What are you going to do then? Do you need to move in here for a while?" Meg asked.

"No, I'm not going to do that to you and Courtney. I truthfully have refused to think about where I'm going, Meg. I'm just so scared. I'm going to be homeless, penniless *and* jobless," she said as her tears threatened again.

"Leah," Meg said firmly, "you've got to think through this situation pragmatically, but quickly. Don't make a decision out of panic or desperation. Plan, then get a plan b, and even a plan c, if necessary," she added.

"You're right, Meg," Leah stated, "but I get so paralyzed with fear that I can't think through it alone."

"Well, you're not alone anymore, sister," Meg assured her. "You've got all of us today to help you think it through."

"Thank God for you—all of you," Leah said softly.

The doorbell rang, and Meg sprang to her feet. "That must be counselor Haas. I'll be right back!" Leah smiled, and she realized that she was excited and anxious to see Siobhan. She couldn't believe she had not seen her in months. She was even a little nervous, she thought—weird!

Leah closed her eyes and took a deep breath to help her relax. She heard the door open followed by an ear-busting squeal. As Leah's eyes opened, in the next instant Siobhan flew over the back of the sofa like a wild woman and landed with a thud in Leah's lap. Meg was doubled over with laughter, and Leah was so surprised that she almost choked on the grape she was poised to swallow. As Siobhan planted kiss after kiss on her face, Leah hugged her so hard she was afraid she might crack her ribs.

Overcome with sheer joy, Leah's tears flowed in a solid stream as she held onto her best friend. She put her head on Siobhan's shoulder, powerless to stop her tears, while Meg came and sat beside her. In the next few minutes while Leah let her emotions flow then ebb, Meg quietly updated Siobhan on Leah's current state of existence.

When she finished, Siobhan, obviously stunned at the depth of Leah's desolation, searched for the right words with the right solution to help solve her best friend's crisis. Leah could almost see Siobhan's legal mind working, but she knew the only person that could resolve her life's dilemma was herself. "You can't fix my situation, Sio," Leah finally whispered, "so stop beating yourself up over it. My shabby state of being is nobody's fault."

"But what are you going to do? Where are you going to go? I want to help you anyway I can," Siobhan said, almost desperately.

"I don't know, I don't know and I know you do," Leah answered. "Hopefully, my best girlfriends can help me make a plan since I seem so impotent at thinking my situation through by myself. But— and she paused for emphasis, "I don't want this weekend to be all about me—that would be zero fun—I want us to relax, re-connect and laugh—a lot."

"You've got it," Meg said. "Now, who is up for a pedicure?"

Siobhan squealed again, this time in tandem with Leah, to express their approval and excitement. Leah was suddenly embarrassed as she remembered that she probably hadn't even thought about her feet in at least two years. "My feet are so flaky they could be mistaken for one of these croissants," Leah deadpanned.

Meg and Siobhan disintegrated with laughter, but Meg managed to add, "That is gross, Leah! But just to be safe, let's move to the master bath with just this fruit tray, because I'm still hungry and I'd hate for you to end this weekend a few digits shy of a foot." As they groaned with good-natured disgust, they grabbed their drinks and the fruit and almost skipped to Meg's home spa, eager to pamper themselves and bask in the love that only best friends can give.

CHAPTER 15

Toni arrived at Meg's just before lunchtime, bringing all the necessities for each of them to enjoy a facial after they noshed. Toni treated the gang to a scrumptious lunch of roasted vegetables, huge slices of spinach, mushroom and gruyere quiche and prosciutto bites stuffed with feta cheese, sun-dried tomatoes and fresh basil. To top it off, she brought out four towering pieces of New York-style cheese cake adorned with fresh raspberries and dark chocolate shavings. The whole meal was simply spectacular.

Stuffed to the gills, the quartet retired to the master bath where they applied facials scrubs, masks and moisturizers to their skin. Meg had apricot and vanilla candles burning, and the whole atmosphere was intoxicating and soothing as they chatted casually and enjoyed each other's company.

Finally, as they retreated to the den and gathered close to the fireplace, snuggled up in robes and slippers, they began discussing their lives, comfortably filling in the spaces of the recent hiatus their friendships had taken. Leah, hoping to get all talk of her life crisis out of the way first, asked if she could share and update the circle of friends first. When everybody in unison agreed, she said, "Okay, but hold that thought—better yet, Meg, you and Siobhan update Toni to this point while I run to the bedroom just a sec."

As Meg brought Toni up to speed with Leah's landlord situation, her lack of job prospects and her unemployment income status, Leah ran to the guest room, unzipped her overnight bag, and lovingly removed the scarves she crocheted for her three best friends in the world. As an after-thought, she wrapped her powder-blue scarf around her neck. She pulled out the three pieces of tissue paper she brought and quickly wrapped each, sealing it with a gold sticker out of the pack of six she purchased for 25 cents from the discount bin at the dollar store.

When she walked back into the den, Leah was overcome with emotion as she watched her friends talk about her, their heads shaking out of concern, their expressions showing their worry. She truly was blessed with friendships—deep, real and solid. She cleared her throat and easily garnered their attention as she sashayed back into their midst, swinging her scarf. They were rapt.

"I have something for each of you," Leah said, "that I made especially for you." As she handed each their package, she encouraged, "Go ahead and open it!"

"What do you mean you 'made' this scarf, Leah?" Siobhan asked. "Do you mean you knitted it?"

"Oh, yellow . . .," Toni cooed.

"I love it, Leah," Meg added.

"Good! No, Siobhan, the scarves are crocheted, not knitted, and yes, I crocheted each one of them—and this one," Leah said, holding up the ends of her blue scarf. "I bought the yarn, I thought somewhat mindlessly, to see if I still remembered how to crochet. When I realized I did and started crocheting, I was amazed that my subconscious mind had chosen four skeins of yarn that happened to be our favorite colors—weird, huh?!"

"Wow . . . wow . . .," Siobhan said.

Leah turned to Meg and said playfully, "I told you I was going to shock the shit out you!"

"Well, you damn sure did, woman," Meg said as she wrapped the scarf around her neck, got up and planted a kiss on Leah's neck. Leah giggled and plopped down between Toni and Siobhan.

"Okay, so while I am jobless, penniless and soon-to-be homeless, I have discovered that I am, quite amazingly, a self-sufficient, thrifty, domestic diva—uh, Siobhan, you're mouth is open," Leah joked. "I can crochet, quilt and sew; make homemade candles, soaps and bath salts; and can fruits, vegetables and soups. Honestly, I do all of them quite well, too," she finished.

Clearly her friends were amazed. Toni said, "You've learned to do all those things since you've been out of work?"

"No," Leah said, "I actually learned how to do all of these things when I was a child. I just forgot that I knew how—and how much I loved it. Unfortunately, none of these hidden traits will pay the bills in Virginia Beach, my dears."

"But they might," Meg said seriously. "Have you checked in with the Agricultural Extension Agency? What about the Department of Agriculture?"

"No, but I am fairly certain that having a business degree instead of a master's degree in agriculture, horticulture, botany or earth science wouldn't get my resume a second glance, let alone an interview," Leah replied candidly.

Siobhan sighed. "So what are you going to do for employment here, Leah?"

"I'm not going to be able to stay here, Sio," Leah almost whispered. "I'm going to see my great-aunt Fiona in a few weeks—i.e. when I get kicked out of my apartment. I am going to spend some time with her on the farm, take an inventory of my life, my skills, and then decide what to do."

"Where does your aunt live again?" Toni asked.

"She lives in the mountains of North Carolina, about an hour northeast of Boone. Girls, it gives 'the middle of nowhere' a whole new meaning," Leah added. "The closest town is West Jefferson."

"God, it sounds . . . cold, I mean, quaint," Meg teased.

"The winters there can be brutally cold," Leah stated, the thought causing her to shiver, "but the summers I spent there were idyllic."

"Are you going to stay until the summer?" Siobhan asked fearfully.

"I don't know, Sio. I am going to stay as long as Aunt Fi needs me. I'm all she has left," Leah said then asked, "If I do stay until the summer, will you come see me?"

"I'd love to come see you," Siobhan said sincerely.

"I'll come too," Toni added.

"I won't," Meg said curtly. When her friends' heads snapped in her direction, she snorted loudly, "I'm kidding! I am actually going to invade your farm, sister! I can hit golf balls for miles!" The whole crew laughed then pelted Meg with popcorn.

"So, I have a plan then," Leah said then repeated, "I have a plan." As her three best friends in the world smiled and nodded in unison, she felt at peace for the first time in two years. Leah was leaving Virginia Beach. Leah was going home.

CHAPTER 16

In the coming weeks, Leah would hearken back to her weekend in paradise at Meg's time and time again. She marveled at the drastic changes in Toni's life with her engagement and impending marriage; she was thrilled for the magnificent career opportunity ahead for Meg and Courtney in the nation's capital; and she and Siobhan had grown even closer by simply growing apart long enough to spread their wings and flourish as individuals.

Leah realized, probably for the first time in her life, that she was a better friend to everybody when she was a good friend to herself. She was learning to admit her weaknesses while acknowledging that she had strengths that were real, sustainable and important to her development as an individual hell-bent on remaining relevant, connected and independent.

Not that she wasn't scared to death about leaving Virginia Beach and everything that she had known for more than a decade. She was. But laced into that underlying fear, Leah also recognized excitement and opportunity—not necessarily regarding employment, either. The changes in her life—the imminent move, the separation from her friends, the return to her childhood utopia—felt somehow like an upcoming adventure for which she needed to prepare but not over-think.

And she had a long list of preparations. She had sold most of her furnishings by listing them online and had made arrangements for the buyers to pick up the couch on Saturday morning, and her tables and bedroom suite on Wednesday night. Leah was spending her last night at Siobhan's house. She had just yesterday notified her landlord that she was leaving by December 1. Both were thrilled to be ending their rental arrangement. Last, but certainly not least, she had to alert her Aunt Fiona that she was on her way to the hills of North Carolina, maybe for a long time. Leah looked at the time on her phone. It was 8:03 a.m., and Aunt Fiona had probably been up over two hours.

She dialed the number she knew by heart and waited anxiously to hear her aunt's familiar, soothing voice. On the fourth ring, though, it was Tom Cunningham that answered. Leah was immediately concerned. "Mr. C?" she inquired warily.

"Leah!" he said lovingly, "it is sure good to hear from you, girl. Your aunt fell outside on the ice last night—she's fine, but she needs to stay in bed today."

Leah sighed then asked, "Is she up to speaking with me? I want to tell her I'm coming home."

"Well, good Lord, yes," he all but exclaimed. "I can't think of anything that will heal her quicker—or make her listen to me. That woman is as stubborn as a mule and mean as a moccasin when she is told to stay in bed."

Leah laughed, "Put her on the phone, then, and I'll see if I can help you out!"

"You bet, missy! Hold on while I walk the telephone back to her. I don't want to spoil the surprise, though, so I'll tell you right here—I'm glad you're coming home, Leah. Ms. Fiona needs you—not that she'd admit it to you or anybody else," he finished.

"I'm glad I'm coming home too, Mr. C," Leah said emotionally. "Honestly, I need her as much as she needs me right now, so I can hardly wait."

"Don't wait long," he said ominously, "She is going to drive me into an early grave if you do. Alright, my dear, here is the queen of Buffalo." Leah laughed at his mock exasperation as he handed the receiver to her aunt.

"Hello?" Aunt Fiona said innocently into her ear.

"You know Santa Claus is not going to come to your house if you're naughty, right?" Leah teased.

"The last thing I need is another man in my home anyway," she answered spiritedly.

"Well, would an unemployed, penniless, homeless niece be welcome?" Leah inquired candidly.

"Oh, my dear—you are always welcome here. This is your home, and I am your family. I am sorry about your situation, though. How long are you going to stay?" she asked.

Leah sighed. She said softly, "I don't know, Aunt Fi—maybe a long time if that's okay. I have so much to tell you."

"Wonderful!" she exclaimed, "You are coming home. I always knew you would. When will you be here?"

"I'm leaving Virginia Beach on Sunday morning so I should be there by dinnertime," she replied, her excitement level rising as she continued. "I have a few things to wrap up here or I would have been home for Thanksgiving."

"Well that would have been nice," Aunt Fiona said, "but at least I'll have you here for Christmas. That way we can cook and sweeten up Tom's disposition. He's such a sourpuss."

"He's standing there listening to you, isn't he?" Leah giggled.

"Like a hawk watching a chick," she said.

"Aunt Fi!" she warned good-naturedly, "You better listen to him. I need you to be as good as new when I get there."

"I will be, Leah, I will be. I didn't break a bone. I'm just bruised. You don't need to worry about me, you need to worry about Tom—he may have bruises *and* broken bones by the time you get here," she added.

"I'll be home shortly to referee!" Leah finished, "I'll see you then, Aunt Fi. I love you."

"I love you too, Leah. Goodbye," she said as they disconnected the call.

Leah wrapped her arms around her waist and hugged herself, temporarily satisfied that she was making the right decision to leave Virginia Beach. She wouldn't think about what she was leaving behind. Instead, today she would focus on the adventures ahead of her when she got to where she was going.

A smile spread across her face. She would pack up her kitchen today and her bedroom tomorrow, leaving only the bare necessities to pack up before she left. Wednesday, she would spend the day baking and preparing goodies for her friends while the buyer of her bedroom suite and tables arrived to whisk them away. Thursday was Thanksgiving, and she was planning to join Meg and Courtney for dinner. Friday, she would pack up the rest of her belongings, load her vehicle, and clean her then-empty apartment before sleeping on the couch one last night. Then, on Saturday morning, the buyer of her couch would arrive and take it away, leaving only an empty apartment. Then, Leah would make the drive across town where she and her friends would gather at Siobhan's for their Thanksgiving dinner and celebrate the dawning of a new chapter in her life. Leah hoped to make the gathering fun, memorable and satisfying for everybody since this would possibly be her last holiday in Virginia Beach with her friends, and she had plenty of surprises in store for them for which she had been planning since the summer. Finally, early on Sunday morning, she would leave this life behind. *Surreal*, she thought.

Leah sighed out loud. She had basked in this moment long enough. Now it was time to go to work.

CHAPTER 17

The Thanksgiving celebration on Saturday proved to be the greatest of blessings that Leah had ever known in her life in Virginia Beach. She and her local family of best friends and their respective families gathered at the Haas home at noon to celebrate all of the amazing joys, changes, and opportunities that had touched their lives over the last year as well as the promise of them in the year to come. It was a day full of cheers, jeers and tears as Meg so observantly pointed out.

Leah instantly loved Carter, and was so happy that Toni had met a man who was worthy of her love, intelligence and passion. The couple was planning a small July 4th wedding at sunrise on the beach followed by a two-week honeymoon all over Europe that included Toni's mom and the two girls. They were already searching for a new home, one of their very own with room for everybody, but no old memories present. The girls got along so well that they wanted to share a room, but Carter and Toni knew that as they grew from girls into young women, each may want a room of their very own someday too. Toni's mother protested moving in with them at first, fearing she may be a distraction or not needed as much by the combined family. Carter called her and invited her to lunch where he alone spent over an hour imploring her to reconsider because they all needed her too much. His gesture not only convinced her mother to make the move, it touched Toni very deeply that he wanted all of them in this marriage, not just her. Very obviously, Carter adored Toni and Toni was head over heels in love with Carter.

Meg and Courtney were moving to Severn, Maryland in early January when Meg would begin her new executive role. In a sign that the move was meant to be, Courtney received word on Tuesday that she had gotten the coveted position for which she applied at Georgetown University in their library archives. She was positively giddy. Meg was excited too, but she was also somewhat nervous since her new role moved her squarely into the executive suite of her company as well as into direct contact with powerful politicians, lobbyists and Washington insiders on a daily basis. They had months of work to do in the next five weeks, including preparing, listing and selling their home plus moving to the new bungalow they found to lease last week.

Changes were afoot for Siobhan as well. Last week, the Chief District Court Judge, Wallace Pettigrew, announced his retirement. Before his announcement, though, he and several other judges paid Siobhan a visit and implored her to seek his seat on the bench. She was honored, humbled and stunned. Refusing to commit on the spot, she went home that night and discussed the opportunities and the risks with Robert and the boys. Then, Siobhan called her brother and asked him to have coffee with her the next morning. Of course, as hard as it was to lose half of the Mauldin & Mauldin team, Gil echoed Judge Pettigrew and Robert—Siobhan was exactly what the court needed, and the challenges of the bench were exactly what she needed. After receiving such rousing and universal support, Siobhan decided to go for it. The election was in the spring, and she would likely run unopposed. That, of course, meant that she would be on the bench and out of private practice very shortly thereafter. Between now and the election, though, she had a ton of work to do.

Leah had very casually brought three huge boxes with her to the den right after they finished their Thanksgiving feast. They sat around her like massive boulders, silent and still, but nonetheless, demanding attention. As they talked, Leah alone seemed to overlook their presence. Siobhan, Toni and Meg, though, were about to die of curiosity. Leah continued the discussion in no hurry. She started by telling her friends that she had spoken to her Aunt Fi, and while she was excited to be going to help her and stay with her, she still had not been able to wrap her head around the fact that the Buffalo community in northwestern North Carolina was going to be her new home. Leah also told them she was scared—of losing touch, of disappearing, of being irrelevant with her best friends.

When she saw tears trailing down their cheeks, Leah smiled and said, "But you have to know I'm not going to let that happen, right?"

They answered, "Right" emphatically and in unison, and Leah took a deep breath.

She continued then, "You aren't interested in what I have in these boxes are you? I could just put these at the door for you to take with you when you leave or open later if you'd prefer."

"Like hell!" Meg exclaimed, "Give me that box!"

As she bubbled over with laughter, Leah told them her rules for opening the gift box to each of them. First, they had to open one layer at a time at the same time. Second, they had to promise to send her silly photographs using each gift in the next twelve months. After they agreed to Leah's rules, she slid each a box marked with her name on it.

The first gift to each of her girlfriends was wrapped in tissue paper. On top, Leah had penned, "A reminder of the warmth of my love."

"Aw!" they cried together. Then, they tore into the package. The discovery of the contents prompted squeals of delight all around. Leah had crocheted each of them a pair of fuzzy booties that matched the scarf she gave them at Meg's girls gathering. She knew the pictures her friends would make with the booties would be priceless, and Leah smiled wider at the thought.

The next parcel was heavy and in a wrapped box. On the lid, Leah had taped a card that read, "A true friend is the essence of life." Inside, they found small jars of homemade bath salts, bath oils and a facial scrub. Of course, they opened each and breathed in the wonderful aroma. Rose, lemon, cucumber, vanilla and mint filled the room.

The largest of the gifts was next, and the package was the reason such large boxes were warranted. The message on top was, "Picnics, the beach, the stars and fireworks are meant to be shared with friends." When they opened their boxes this time, they were stunned into silence. This past summer, Leah began sewing fabric squares together, hoping to make a quilt. She found the sewing so therapeutic and soothing that she just kept sewing, picking up remnants of material off the discount racks in the craft section of the superstore. She also found old shirts, shorts and tablecloths for next-to-nothing prices at the local goodwill that she cut up into fabric squares. By the end of September, she had pieced together three large, blanket-sized squares. Excited by her patchwork, she went to the fabric store and bought batting, spray adhesive, and a large roll of water-resistant black nylon. Within days, she had finished three outdoor picnic blankets, each unique in its color scheme and textures, all lovingly made for her best friends.

Siobhan got up and went across the room, sat on Leah's lap, wrapped her in her arms and cried. Meg and Toni would have done the same if Leah had any more lap to share. Instead, they sat sniffling and crying, overcome by emotion at the love and care embodied in Leah's gifts to them.

Finally, Leah whispered, "Come on, Siobhan, you've got one more." Siobhan stood and wiped her eyes then sat back down among her treasures. When they reached into the bottom of their boxes they found a simple box wrapped in brown paper. Written across the paper in Leah's handwriting were the words, "Good friends are kisses blown to us by the angels. Write the words on your heart anytime you think of me."

Inside each box was a journal with a cream-colored muslin cover with a ribbon-tied closure—Toni's in yellow, Meg's in purple, Siobhan's in sea foam green. Embroidered on each were hearts in matching colors. Leah smiled as she met Meg's eyes then she said, "I want you to write in here every time you think of me this year, anything you want."

"I will," Meg said to her.

"I will too," Toni promised.

"I won't," Siobhan said with fresh tears streaming down her cheeks. The comment prompted all of them to stare at her, shocked. Then she laughed, "I'm kidding! Did you give me a back-up journal?"

They took turns hugging Leah, thanking her for the gifts, and discussing plans to stay connected through visits, photos, and phone calls. It was late, and they all realized that this was goodbye. In an attempt to keep from falling completely apart, Leah told them that each of them had another gift box waiting on Siobhan's screen porch. "Hey," she said before they got all choked up again, "I had to clean out my freezer, okay? I have a lasagna, chili and chicken casserole wrapped up for each of you—dinner for those busy nights ahead."

After everybody else had gone home and the Haas boys had gone to bed, Leah offered to help clean the kitchen with Robert and Siobhan. Siobhan would have none of her help, though. She told Leah, "You have a long drive ahead of you tomorrow, Le. Go get a good night's sleep. We'll get this."

"Okay, then. Thank you for everything today, Siobhan. I'll never forget this day as long as I live," Leah told her sincerely.

"Me either, Leah," Siobhan answered, "Me either. Good night."

Leah kissed Siobhan and Robert on the cheek and called, "Good night" as she walked out of the kitchen to the guest room. Within minutes, she was in bed and fast asleep, satisfaction and emotional exhaustion combining to send her dreamlessly toward tomorrow, the first day of the next chapter of her life.

Twenty minutes later, Robert and Siobhan finished cleaning the kitchen, turned out the lights and headed for bed. Halfway down the hall, Siobhan told Robert she would be there in a few minutes. She returned to the den where she had lovingly repacked the box of gifts Leah had made for her and reached inside to retrieve the journal. She turned on the lamp beside the easy chair and sat down. Siobhan clutched the journal to her chest and let the sadness of the moment work its way out of her system. Her best friend was moving almost seven hours away, and she felt bereft, lonely and even a little frightened. Sure, her life in Virginia Beach would still be great, but Siobhan also knew it would never be the same without Leah, her rock for the last decade.

Siobhan sighed and wiped her cheeks with the heel of her hand. She was tired. Before she got up to go to bed, though, she reached over and took a pen from the drawer in the side table. Then, she opened the book to the first page of the journal, dated her entry as November 27 and very simply wrote, "Oh Leah, I miss you already."

PART TWO

Chapter 18

On her way out of Virginia Beach just before daybreak, Leah left Siobhan's Bay Colony neighborhood and drove the short distance east to the beach to walk the shoreline, smell the salt air and feel the magnitude of the ocean one more time. Pander slept peacefully on her bed on the passenger seat beside her. Notwithstanding that it was still a cold late-November morning, Leah parked her car, bundled up in her huge winter coat and walked over the crosswalk to the beach alone. The wind was out of the east, brisk but not brutal, and the waves were dark gray, almost black, against the dawning sky. Icy pink shards of light shot heavenward from the horizon, promising a spectacular sunrise for the winter observer brave enough to wait for it. This morning, Leah had the beach to herself to witness the moment the sun's crown first sprang up on the distant eastern horizon over the Atlantic, and she caught herself holding her breath as she waited.

When the sun finally broke though, she exhaled and broke into a huge smile. The ocean was seemingly on fire in a path from the horizon all the way to the waves crashing several yards from her feet, secretly promising Leah an illuminated way forward on a journey just beyond, out of sight. The thought gave her cold chills, and she rubbed her arms through her heavy coat to try to warm them. Leah reached into her purse and pulled out a snack-sized plastic bag. Then, as she slowly made her way back to her vehicle, she squatted down when she reached the deep, white sand farther from the sea and scooped up several handfuls of the cool granules, letting each slowly slip through her fingers. Finally, Leah took two more handfuls and dropped them into the bag. She was crying now, and her chest hurt with emotion. Gasping sobs escaped her throat, and her shoulders shuddered with each one, forcing her to steady herself in the sand to keep from teetering over. She was truly going to miss Virginia Beach and all of the places here, like this one, where she had created so many wonderful memories and made so many close friends. She inhaled deeply, finally regained her composure, and blew the air out audibly.

"Time to go," Leah said out loud to the sea. Then, she stood up, dropped the bag of Virginia Beach sand into her purse, clapped the sand away from her hands, and without turning around again, she climbed the steps of the crosswalk, got into her SUV and began her long journey west.

The streets of the city were virtually empty as she passed through downtown, and she felt like a stranger quietly tip-toeing out of a house. Leah was fairly certain her absence would go unnoticed by all of Virginia Beach except her handful of true friends, and she realized her more than ten-year tenure at the bank had seemingly never even existed to the other bankers still in the bank's employ. She pondered all those early-morning meetings, late-night seminars, and weekend training sessions, and Leah realized that all of the team building and relationship nurturing among the employees was just crap. They weren't friends. They were simply co-workers, even job competitors, whose only allegiance to her ended the moment the bank vault closed and they locked the doors behind them. Not one of her former co-workers had telephoned, e-mailed or come by to see her since she lost her job, and Leah knew that that sad fact said much more about the people she worked with what now felt like a lifetime ago than it did her.

During her mental musing, she had left the city streets of Virginia Beach and was now flying at warp speed down the interstate, barreling toward her new home in northwestern North Carolina. The trip was virtually due west from Virginia Beach, and she had calculated that she would arrive around 2:00 p.m. at Aunt Fiona's. A fresh blanket of snow had fallen last night in the high country, and Mr. C had warned her on the phone this morning to be very careful coming up the mountain roads once she left US 221 in West Jefferson. The country roads in the outlying communities, including Buffalo, were often left covered by snow and ice for days at a time, and were only passable for drivers with snow chains or four-wheel drive. Fortunately, Leah drove a four-wheel drive SUV, and she was not in a hurry even though she was excited about seeing Aunt Fiona, the old home-place, and the lovably grouchy Mr. C.

Pander stirred beside her, and Leah reached over and stroked her furry companion's neck. As soon as they got on Interstate 85 then crossed over into North Carolina, she would stop at the first rest stop so they could both stretch their legs for a while. It was a Sunday morning, so the interstate and even the highways further west would be uncluttered with workday traffic. Leah stopped just west of Durham, North Carolina at a remarkably clean and convenient rest stop that even sported a dog park for Pander. She let the dog explore each tree, sniff the grass for "foreigners," and run around like some phantom animal was chasing her. Leah lingered with a cup of coffee out of the vending machine and turned her face toward the sun to eke out any warmth through the chill of the late-autumn day. She sighed with contentment, and her smile prompted the older man to her right to smile back at her.

After the emotional goodbye with her friends last night as well as her tearful parting this morning with Siobhan, Leah would have sworn she would be completely drained of life. On the contrary, though, she felt alive, upbeat and excited, like she knew deep down that leaving Virginia Beach was the right thing to do. Siobhan knew it too, and she shared with Leah this morning that she believed something big, meaningful and good was waiting for her in the mountains of North Carolina. Leah didn't aim quite that high, but her best friend's confidence in her was humbling. Her plans included reducing Mr. C's schedule of care for her aunt significantly as well as finding some kind of employment that was both interesting and afforded her the opportunity to eat and clothe herself.

As she drove, Leah noticed the subtle changes in the landscape of the Tarheel state as she drove west. The sandy soil of the Triangle gave way to the red clay of the Triad, and the terrain now looked much less like a pancake and more like boiling water, rolling up and down. As she approached Winston-Salem, she decided to stop again and eat lunch, stretch her legs and let Pander do the same. Leah had been on the road for over four hours. When she exited the car, she realized that the air here was much colder than the breeze on the eastern Virginia shore this morning or even the Durham rest stop, and she literally ran Pander around the vehicle several times to let her do her business and get some exercise at the same time—quickly. Leah fed Pander once they were back in the SUV and poured some water into her bowl. Then, she went into the fast food restaurant where she had stopped, used the facilities and ordered a salad and an iced tea off the Dollar Menu. Thirty minutes after she pulled off Interstate 40, she was again heading west around the historic tobacco town, marveling at the beauty of the skyline, the tastefully repurposed industrial buildings, and the towering smokestacks that evidenced the city's proud heritage.

She knew she was nearing her destination when she left the high-speed interstate at Highway 421 and looked ahead at the hazy blue-gray mountains on the northwestern horizon. The terrain grew hillier, the road increasingly curvy as Leah traveled, prompting a strange exhilaration to creep into her chest, and she breathed deeply to keep her excitement at bay. As she drove, she pondered how Aunt Fiona would look, if the old farm house would be a disappointment without the benefit of the eyes of youth, and whether she would fit in, find employment, or make friends. She knew she would be attending church every Sundays as long as Aunt Fi had breath left in her body. The thought was comforting, though, and Leah wondered if she could still remember any of the hymns, the creeds, or even the Lord's Prayer. "Lord, I'm probably going to hell," she said out loud. Pander just looked at her with curiosity.

Arriving in the bucolic town of North Wilkesboro, Leah noticed frost on the shaded patches of grass, on branches of loblolly pines unexposed to the sun. She put the back of her hand on the driver's window to verify that the temperature outside was continuing to fall the farther west she traveled. It was indeed colder.

The Blue Ridge Mountains loomed just ahead, close enough now to see the snow that capped the higher peaks above their tree lines, and Leah's excitement once again bubbled to the surface. Bundled up now in her coat, scarf and cap, she stopped at a gas station to fill her SUV before she began the steep, winding climb up Highway 421 to Deep Gap where she would then take the last of the federal highways, US 221, into West Jefferson. Then she would travel a couple of miles north of town on state highway 194 before she would likely leave dry, cleared pavement.

The Buffalo community in northwestern Ashe County is set deep in the higher elevations of the North Carolina high country. Many of the residents are multi-generational family farmers who raise burley tobacco or beef cattle or keep dairy cows or chickens. The livestock grazing in the fertile valleys between the peaks often were the only visible evidence of the families and farmhouses tucked into the recesses of the mountains. The people here were private by choice and self-sufficient by necessity.

Not that the folks were unwelcoming or unkind, though—they weren't. They helped each other, bartered with each other, and worshipped with each other. They were also diligent workers. The growing seasons were short and the winters were long, so idle time was almost non-existent and social gatherings, while infrequent, were well-planned, usually in conjunction with the local churches.

In the first five years of the new century when real estate became the hottest commodity, some of the poorer family farmers sold out to developers who promptly broke the land up into postage-stamp sized lots and built mini-mansions on as many as they could, as quickly as they could. For a while, city dwellers seeking a country estate, a summer retreat or a skiing getaway descended on the area like apocalyptic locusts. Some fell in love with their new homes and immersed themselves in the community, attending church, bake sales, bazaars and tractor pulls. Most of the transient property owners, though, deemed themselves too sophisticated, too refined to associate with the locals. They framed the hillbillies in terms of "Hee-Haw" or "Deliverance" and felt it was prudent to keep their distance.

After the real estate bubble burst, half-finished new subdivisions failed, property values sank and the empty lots grew increasingly unkempt and wild as the promise of new home construction evaporated. Finally nature took over, until the only reminders of the existence of many of the subdivisions were the painted signs with renderings of the non-existent amenities and never-built homes, now rotting and weathered in the elements.

In addition, many of the out-of-towners abandoned their vacation homes, walked away from their lots, and left the area without a second thought, hoping to write off their real estate investments mentally in addition to financially.

The new families that came and stayed, though, were now part of the community fold. They exchanged goods with their neighbors, participated in church and area festivities, and kept a watchful eye out for trouble that might threaten the fabric of their mountain homesteads.

As the slowly sinking sun just began to touch the top of the highest mountain, Leah made the left turn onto Buffalo Road. Snow remained under the trees, in the pasture ravines and on the boulders out of full sun. The narrow road had at least been scraped today, but it still had patches of ice and snow along the outer edges and in the middle. Carefully, Leah navigated the hairpin turns that mimicked Buffalo Creek flowing alongside. To her left, Three Top Mountain towered against the gray sky, its triple peaks currently shrouded in fog. Ahead of her to the right, White Top stood tall and wide, its name apropos today with its thick cap of snow. Leah passed the horse farm, the brick church in the bend and finally the little white wooden chapel opposite the entrance to her family's farm. She had arrived.

Breathing deeply, hands shaking on the steering wheel, Leah turned slowly onto the steep gravel driveway that always reminded her of the climb of a roller coaster before the hair-raising drop just over the crest. The farm boasted no gravity-defying drop, though. Just above the tree line, the land flattened out and the drive spilled over into a rolling valley, filled with an apple orchard, a small pasture and an enormous garden. Behind the white clapboard farmhouse, a picket fence corralled a chicken coup, a smokehouse, a raised-bed patch of herbs and a stunning rose garden, currently winter fallow. Leah sighed, tears filling her eyes, emotion welling up in her chest. She smiled then wiped away her tears. Relief washed over her, and she parked her car out of the driveway near a stand of maples. The farm was still utopia. Leah shivered, perhaps from the cold, perhaps from the exhilaration, and reached over to stroke a now wide-awake Pander. "Come on, girl," she said as she hastily pulled her dog near, opened the car door, and made her way toward the house, "We're finally home."

CHAPTER 19

Tom Cunningham saw Leah coming up the driveway, and he stirred Ms. Fi's pot of vegetable beef soup once more then casually walked to the den where she was resting on her couch. "Leah's on her way up the drive," he said calmly, but very loudly since Ms. Fi's hearing was only slightly better than totally deaf, and she refused to wear her hearing aid.

"Wonderful!" she exclaimed, "But you don't have to yell."

Tom snorted out a small laugh, but he didn't say anything else as he walked over to the couch and gave her his arm to help her to the door. They sure were a sorry welcoming committee, he mused—a 92-year-old stubborn mule of a woman and a lonely 70-year old widower with nothing better to do than keep his neighbor company, but they were going to welcome little Leah nonetheless. He had tried to get his son, Cal, to come with him today, but he was more ornery than Ms. Fi, and he said he was going to the hardware store to catch up on his bookkeeping this afternoon after church instead.

Cal was a certified woman-hater, and Tom had long ago quit trying to encourage him to go out or introduce him, or in this case, re-introduce him to anybody. Cal needed friends whether they were women, men, old or young. He ran a small, but successful hardware and garden store in the community, but rarely socialized outside of work. Tom knew Cal was lonely since his wife of 10 years, Marissa, packed up and moved to Nashville, Tennessee to pursue a career in country music five years ago. As Tom expected, her career was as well received as a fart in church, but she had stayed in the city hoping for a more prosperous, exciting marriage than the stable, dull life she had in Ashe County with Cal.

Not that Tom missed her, though. She was a petulant, lazy, arrogant person who made sport out of belittling others. Marissa was also superficial, and her out-of-control spending almost put Cal in the poor house. Cal had tried so hard to make her happy to no avail, and after she left, he continued to believe she would ultimately come back to him. When the divorce papers arrived in the mail, though, he gave up then simply retreated from society. To this day, he continued to beat himself up because he just didn't measure up somehow or provide well enough for Marissa. As a result, Cal was withdrawn, sad and bitter. Tom knew Cal's sulking was a waste of his life. His son was 38 years of age, tall, with strawberry blond hair, just beginning to go gray at the temples. He was a rugged outdoorsman and built like an athlete with broad shoulders and a small waist. Cal was a catch.

Tom had been the same way 35 years ago, but he had married well right out of school at N. C. State University to the woman of his dreams, Claire. They had made a great pair, and they loved each other and were crazy in love for the next 40 years until she died eight years ago from cancer. The horrible disease threatened to kill him too as he watched his beautiful Claire waste away from its effects, and sometimes he would sneak away to the church late at night just to yell at God or cry or plead for a change in circumstances.

Claire never wavered in her faith, though, and she constantly talked to him about the second half of his life without her, what she dreamed and what she expected. She expected him to serve others by helping his neighbors and community, and by serving the church through giving of his time and talents. She also made him promise to never give up on their son, Cal. It was Claire's dream for Cal to have children so he could teach them all of the wonderful things that life offered, all of the magical ways love, happiness and faith provided. Tom didn't forget his promises to Claire, and his life since her death had been lived pursuing the fulfillment of them.

Besides helping Cal move on and heal, he had taken responsibility for the care and watch over Fiona Parker, his neighbor just up the hollow. Ms. Fi was old as the hills and tough as nails. She had barely slowed down since she turned 90, and she churned out more work than women half her age. In this brutal part of the country, she had been a mainstay through summer droughts, brutal winters, spring flash floods and meager fall harvests. Ms. Fi was an amazing farmer, botanist and mechanical engineer. She was also exceedingly smart, wickedly funny, and remarkable insightful for someone who had never really left the high country.

When he and Ms. Fi rounded the corner at the kitchen, he grabbed their winter coats so they could walk out on the porch to welcome little Leah. She protested, of course, and told him to hurry. When Tom opened the door, the cold air blew briskly from right to left down the porch, and he shepherded Ms. Fi to his left arm to shield her from the blast while they waited. Leah's car door opened, and he heard Ms. Fi inhale and hold her breath. She was excited. Admittedly, he was too. When the compact package that was Leah Gibson emerged from the car with a beagle in her arms, Tom was struck at just how pretty and grown she was. Leah was not little anymore.

Ms. Fi squeezed Tom's arm. "Oh my, she's as beautiful as I thought she'd be," she almost whispered.

"Yep, she is," he answered. "She looks so much like her mother."

"She looks like Belle, too," Ms. Fi answered, and they fell anxiously silent until Leah saw them, and she smiled broadly and sweetly at them, her pace quickening.

"Oh, Aunt Fi, Aunt Fi!" she exclaimed as she ran up the two steps to the porch to embrace her lovingly. "You haven't changed a bit!"

"Oh my dear, what a liar you are!" Aunt Fi said good-naturedly and obviously flattered. "I have missed you so much."

Leah stood back and held her at arm's length, then unabashedly pulled her close again and kissed her on the cheek and replied, "I have missed you too." Then, she turned to Mr. C and gave him an equally loving hug. "Thank you so much for taking such good care of her. I am sure she is an easy charge," she said with a squeeze of his arm and a quick wink.

"As easy as taming a tiger and almost as dangerous," he answered with a smile in his voice.

"He's as demanding as a circus ringmaster, too," Aunt Fi retorted. Leah just giggled at their teasing. "Well, don't just stand there! Let's get her inside before we have to bring an ice pick out to move her."

"Yes, ma'am," Tom relented, and he escorted them inside and closed the door behind them.

Leah stopped and breathed in the smell of the kitchen. The porch, the mudroom, the polished rock countertops were all the same, and the sight choked her up and made her smile at the same time. "I love this house," she said softly. "I can't believe I've been away so long."

"But you are here now, my dear, and that's what's important," Aunt Fi said. "This old house has just been sitting here all these years waiting, and the pieces of it you took with you helped sustain you until you could return. This is your *home* now, Leah. Welcome back."

Leah felt both serenity and satisfaction wash over her, and she quite honestly had never before experienced such an overwhelming feeling of belonging. She shivered as she stood between Aunt Fi and Mr. C and took everything in. Then, Mr. C smiled at her and echoing Aunt Fi's sentiments, he summed up all of the emotion Leah felt with two simple words, "Welcome home."

CHAPTER 20

The first time he saw her, Cal knew without asking anybody, "Is that her?" Leah Gibson had "city girl" written all over her. Her designer clothes, her five-day-a-week gym body, and that prissy house pet she called a dog were dead giveaways. Cal figured she fancied herself smarter than everybody since she was a "professional." He was also certain she would last just a matter of weeks taking care of her 92-year-old great aunt before she grew bored, disgusted or tired of the farm's manual labor.

As he watched her walk down Main Street toward the hardware store, Cal searched for any signs of the little girl with crazy white-blonde curls with whom he used to fly homemade paper kites in the pasture, exchange rotten apple grenades, and pick and eat berries until their stomachs hurt. Nope, he thought, I don't see a trace. Cal got up off the stool behind the register, picked up the stack invoices he had just approved for payment, and walked to his office in the back off the store. Unlike some people, he had work to do besides strolling downtown and window shopping.

The Christmas season began in earnest last Friday after Thanksgiving, and Cal knew that he had to capitalize on the holiday frenzy since January through March were his slowest months. He had ordered a plethora of poinsettias, Christmas roses and Christmas cacti. In conjunction with several of the local Christmas tree farms, he carried numerous varieties of freshly-made wreaths, garlands and swags that were unavailable at the superstore in Jefferson. To maximize the benefit of the weekend crowds of shoppers in town, Cal was planning a holiday sidewalk sale next Saturday too.

He had been collecting homemade goods from local crafters since October. So far, he had collected two hand-carved nativity sets, several birdhouses, a handful of beautiful vine baskets and ten beautiful wooden stocking holders carved in the shapes of Santa and elves. Cal knew he needed more, but he was running out of time.

Lost in thought about next Saturday, he didn't hear the bells on the door jingle when Leah Gibson walked in the store. Walking up and down the aisles, she neared the back of the store where the business office was located. Leah spotted Cal Cunningham immediately and smiled at how much he still looked like the sandy blonde boy she played with every summer when she visited her Gran Belle. Cal was so busy entering invoices into the computer that Leah had to clear her voice to get his attention.

Cal looked up into Leah's smiling face. He started to smile back, but he sure didn't want Ms. Gibson to think she could worm her way back into this community or their lives just by her presence so he took on a more guarded tone. "May I help you?" he asked her formally.

"I hope so, Cal," she said quietly. "I'm looking for sea salt, coarse and fine. Also, do you have any pretty pint or half-pint canning jars for sale this time of year? I want to make some of my homemade organic bath salts for Christmas presents."

Taken aback by her kind tone and her industriously folksy request, Cal was rendered almost speechless at first, and the silence made him blush a little. Leah smiled at him again as she waited patiently. "Um, I don't know about the jars, I'll have to look. I don't have the salt in stock, but I can order you some and have it here in a couple of days if you'd like," Cal answered. "How much do you need? I'd have to order it in bulk for it to be reasonable."

"Well, I can make some for the other neighbors and the women at the church, I guess, but I'm as poor as a church mouse, Cal," Leah replied honestly. "I guess the smallest bag of each would make about three dozen pints or six dozen half pints. That's a lot of bath salts," she finished, now a little embarrassed herself.

Cal's mental wheels were turning, though. He stood, crossed his arms and leaned against the doorjamb facing Leah. He said cautiously, "Tell me about these bath salts. Could I sell them at my craft fair next weekend? Who buys them and what exactly are they?"

Leah shook her head, and laughed good-naturedly, "Mr. Cunningham, you are such a male. Bath salts are used to scrub and smooth women's skin. They are organic, they smell good and they work. Any women who bathe would buy them, especially when they smell them."

Cal dismissed her poke at him then continued, "How long will it take you to make four dozen half pints to sell?"

Leah smiled, "Two minutes to mix each scent, ten to fill the jars, and an hour to decorate that many. I could sell a half pint for $5 to the public easily. These salts make great small gifts and stocking stuffers," she answered. Her mind was already racing ahead down the road Cal had steered her. "That would be $240 less the cost of the supplies," she summed up quickly, then Leah looked straight into his eyes and asked directly, "How much are you going to charge me to display them?"

"Charge you?" Cal asked incredulously. "I'm not going to charge you to display them. Here's a newsflash, Ms. Gibson, the people in West Jefferson aren't on the take all the time like where you come from. We don't treat strangers any differently than we do our neighbors," he finished, hoping the last dig at her inexcusably long absence didn't escape her.

Cal definitely hit a nerve, and Leah's smile disappeared almost immediately. She took a deep breath. Cal wasn't sure if he hurt her feelings or made her angry because Leah Gibson was silent for what seemed like ages. It made him uncomfortable, and he shifted his weight from his right foot to his left.

When Leah opened her mouth to speak, though, Cal very quickly wished he could take back his mean-spirited words, but he couldn't, and he knew he deserved the barrage she unleashed. She almost whispered her retort.

"Well, Cal, then you must be a shitty businessman. Your customer service skills are completely vacant too or maybe you just don't need business, or at the very least, my business. If you've got a personal bone to pick with me then I can think of a whole lot better places and times for that conversation. I came into your store to transact business and to see the grown up version of the young boy with whom I had so much fun and made so many fond memories in my childhood. I truly apologize for bothering you because all I have found today is a bitter man incapable of treating a customer decently and an old acquaintance even cordially. I'll go see if the Wal-Mart in Jefferson can help me," Leah finished, turned without further adieu, and left as quietly as she came.

When he heard the bells chime at her exit, Cal leaned up against the wall and sighed. "What the hell is wrong with me?" he said out loud. He had no excuse for his behavior. Cal knew he needed to apologize right now. Besides, they could help each other, he thought. He took off at fast jog through the store, out the door and in the general direction from which he had seen her come.

Finally, he rounded the corner and spotted her approaching her SUV. "Leah," he yelled, and she turned around. He kept running until he was right in front of her. She had defiant tears in her eyes. Out of breath, he stopped and breathed deeply then met her eyes. "I'm sorry," he said quietly, but sincerely. "I'm an asshole *and* a shitty businessman. Come back to the store, and let's talk turkey. I'll even buy you a cup of the best coffee in the high country," he added.

Leah smiled slightly and nodded, "Okay Cal," she said. "Let's talk, but be fair with me because I'm a sucker for a great cup of coffee."

Her comment made Cal smile, and as they walked back down Main Street, he realized that Leah Gibson was the same ball of fire she had been almost twenty years ago, and he wasn't sure if that fact excited him or scared him to death.

Chapter 21

By Wednesday, Leah had all of her supplies arranged in the mudroom off the kitchen. She had purchased four festive scraps of cotton cloth and some Christmas sticker tags to label each jar. Then, she had Aunt Fi decide which scents she should make with her nose. She had dried lavender from the garden, lemon peel, orange peel and a big vanilla bean. In the end, Aunt Fi liked them all so much that she encouraged Leah to make a dozen half pints of each.

Leah put Aunt Fi to work cutting the jar toppers out of the fabrics with the pinking shears while she used her blender to mix each scent then carefully fill twelve jars. Then she put a lid on each, covered the lid with the beautiful fabric and finally covered the fabric with a jar ring. When they had finished all 48, Leah and Aunt Fi stood admiring their handiwork. The bath salts looked beautiful. Leah loaded them back into the boxes in which the jars had arrived and sat the boxes on the front porch.

On the stove, Leah had a big pot of chicken chili simmering for supper, and Mr. C promised to come by and eat with them this evening. Yesterday, she stopped by the Cal's hardware store to inquire about the delivery of the bath salts. Cal told her he could come by and pick them up at the farm on Thursday. Leah spontaneously invited him to dinner too. He muttered and stuttered looking for an excuse, but Leah wouldn't hear it. She insisted, and Cal relented.

While she was in town, she made a trip to the goodwill store to see if she could find some old N. C. State tee shirts or at the very least some red, gray, white and black ones that she could cut up and turn into a quilt for Mr. C for Christmas. Mr. C had taken such good care of Aunt Fi over the years Leah wanted to show him just how much she appreciated him. She found thirteen cotton tee shirts, five of which remarkably had an NCSU logo on them. Leah was elated. Mr. C was a huge Wolfpack fan, and she knew he would love it. Before she left town, she also purchased a big roll of batting and three yards of black cotton jersey for the backing of the quilt at the fabric store then hurried back home to check on Aunt Fi.

While she had almost fully healed from her fall on the ice, Aunt Fi was still frail, and Leah didn't like to leave her for more than a couple of hours. Aunt Fi fussed at her that she was fine, that she had looked after herself for 92 years, and that Leah certainly didn't need to hover over her, but Leah could tell Aunt Fi enjoyed having her around to help cook, clean and tend to the chores that needed to be done.

Surprisingly, Leah thoroughly loved farm life. While there was not as much to do outside in the during the harsh winter months, she and Aunt Fi were already planning what vegetables and herbs to plant in the gardens in the spring, preparing the terracotta pots for planting bulbs right after Christmas, and choosing the perfect place for a new compost bin they wanted to start with the last of the fall leaves. The prospects for the spring excited Leah, and her mental wheels were diligently turning on how she could earn income through her efforts. The preparation and sale of her bath salts was a good start.

Aunt Fi had made some yeast rolls, and they were ready to go into the oven as soon as the Cunningham men arrived. Leah gave the chili another stir then retired to the den with Aunt Fi. They were both working on Christmas projects. Aunt Fi was knitting a sweater for Mr. C while Leah was crocheting some trivets and potholders with some neutral yarn for Cal's sale on Saturday. She had already crocheted two Christmas stockings in red and green this week when she should have been sleeping. Leah was planning to add them to her goods for sale. She agreed to give Cal 10 percent of her gross sales. He was thrilled with their agreement, and Leah would still make a handsome profit if she sold most or all of her items.

As she crocheted, Leah's mind wandered to Cal. She was not surprised that he was so handsome. She always knew he would be. What really shocked her, though, was just how ruggedly sexy he was—and how strong. The sleeves on his fleece pullover had been pushed up on his forearms while he worked in his office, and the sun-bleached hair was such a stark contrast to his tanned skin. Cal always was an outdoor type like she was. When they were teenagers, they would hike up to the top of the steep mountain behind them then race down as fast as they could. They would also fish together in the creeks and streams for trout. For eight glorious summers until she was 14, they had been inseparable.

Cal was almost four years older than Leah, and when she was thirteen, he was the first guy she ever kissed. The thought of his lips on hers and his arms around her sent her stomach flipping. She had to get a grip because she was so attracted to him even now. They had shared a special bond as they grew up together. They could sit in the front porch swing for hours in a comfortable silence and listen to the cicadas sing and the crickets chirp or just watch the lightning bugs dot the yard and the pastures of the farm. In contrast, they could argue passionately over which school had the best basketball team, his NC State or her UNC Chapel Hill, knowing that they would never agree, but they would argue anyway, always good-naturedly.

Then, the summer she was 14 and getting ready to go off to high school, everything changed. Cal turned 18 late that summer and was heading off to NC State in the fall. After spending the whole school year anticipating the eight glorious weeks of summer with him, Leah instead saw him only a handful of times. When she did, he would brush her off, never making eye contact, and always make an excuse to leave her presence as soon as he could. Leah had been confused by his behavior. Even worse, she had been hurt deeply. She had become completely invisible to Cal Cunningham.

Still, Leah continued to hope that their friendship would somehow be rekindled as she visited the next three years, but it never happened. Instead, the summer after Cal graduated with his degree in Agriculture, he married Marissa Doherty from Boone and set up house with a woman who was Leah's polar opposite.

Leah had met her two times—once when she attended their wedding, then again when her Gran Belle died when she was in college. Both meetings left Leah perplexed, angry even, that a woman who was so obviously shallow, materialistic and aloof could have won the heart of her friend, Cal. Marissa was stunningly beautiful, though, and her long, straight brown-black hair, dark brown eyes and perfectly-proportioned body were impossible for anybody, especially any man, to ignore. In the end, Marissa's desire to make it big, or at the very least, strike it rich, left her constantly dissatisfied, unfulfilled and wanting with the life Cal had provided in Ashe County, North Carolina.

What a fool, Leah thought. Marissa left a handsome man who adored her, a lovely home surrounded by a family who cared for her and a kind community that provided security for her. What it didn't provide, though, was precisely what Marissa wanted and felt like she deserved—fame and fortune. Leah wondered when Marissa's search came up empty whether she would come skulking back to Cal. *Probably,* she mused.

Pander's sudden outburst of barks, growls and whines startled Leah out of her daze, and she looked at the clock. It was dinnertime. She got up and went to the kitchen, turned the oven on to 400 degrees, and pulled the bread basket out of the cabinet. Pander was still making a fuss so Leah shushed her—to no avail. Finally, she went to the door, opened it and held the screen door so her barking maniac could be unleashed. As the cold evening air rushed inside, Pander simply quit barking. "Go get 'em, killer!" she teased her spineless weasel of a dog, now retreating to her bed beside Aunt Fi's feet.

A rap on the door prompted her to call, "Come in!" just as she popped the rolls into the oven. When she turned around, Mr. C and Cal were looking at her curiously. Leah felt herself blush. She must look like a wreck. She wasn't even sure if she had pulled a comb through her hair this afternoon. Her sweatshirt was tattered, but thankfully, it was clean and paired with an old pair of jeans.

"That's an ugly shirt you have on," Mr. C teased, "or don't you have anything decent to wear for company."

Leah blushed again as she looked at her attire, then she smiled. She had on her UNC sweatshirt. "I wore it just for you. I thought you'd like it," she replied.

"She never did have any taste that way, Dad," Cal added. "She's a hopeless case."

"I'm going to ignore that remark since it is not kind to kick people when they're down—and everybody knows State is way down," Leah added.

The Cunningham men just shook their heads and closed the door. They knew this fight was not one the Wolfpack fans wanted to pick with a Tarheel fan today. While Mr. C shed his coat and went to the den to see Ms. Fi, Cal went to retrieve some logs for the fireplace from the wood pile. He had cut up an old hickory tree that was knocked down after the freak October snow storm when the leaves were still on the trees. The stack of wood it yielded would probably last Ms. Fi the entire winter, he figured.

As he pushed the wheelbarrow behind the house, Cal noticed the old garden shed had been cleaned up and all of the old brush around it cut away and hauled off past the tree line. The front windows had been cleaned, too, and he stopped and went to peer inside. Cal couldn't believe his eyes, and he felt a little angry that his dad had done all this work without asking him to help. Inside flower pots were lined up to be scrubbed, freshly-sharpened shrub and hedge clippers were hanging on the peg board, and two big heavy-duty plastic garbage cans with lids were nearby. Cal was impressed with the work, but he wondered what his father was thinking since Ms. Fi sure wouldn't be able to prune, plant or garden this spring.

Cal stood staring inside, and he wondered if perhaps Leah might hang around through the spring, if she survived this brutal winter. While there was a lot more work to do on the farm, the spring was a beautiful time in the high country. The dogwoods would bud and bloom along with the daffodils first. Then, the purple wisteria would blossom while hanging from the hardwoods followed by the native rhododendrons which made the hillsides and vales look ablaze with the bright reds and oranges of their flowers.

"Are you frozen or thinking of moving in?" Leah asked, startling Cal out of his trance.

"I always did like this old shed," Cal said. "I could have helped with the clean-up, but dad didn't tell me he was working on it."

"He wasn't," Leah answered. "I was."

"You cleaned out all the brush and debris by yourself?" he asked incredulously.

"Well, no," she admitted. "Aunt Fi has helped too."

"Mmm-hmmm," Cal countered. "Yeah, she's a real bundle of energy lately."

"You'd be surprised at how energetic she is—and strong," Leah said. "She cleaned all of those flower pots and washed the two windows. I sharpened the clippers, cleaned up the weeds and brush then simply hosed down the inside to cut down the dust," she finished proudly.

"What are you doing with the two trash containers? Are they full of junk and need to be hauled off?" he asked curiously.

"Heavens no," Leah stated, "Those are my new compost bins."

"You're going to compost?" he questioned.

"Of course, that's why I drilled holes in the top and sides," she said, smiling the whole time. "Besides, I'm not going to let all those leaves go to waste. My future flowers would never forgive me."

Cal turned away from the window and stared at Leah intensely. Leah returned his unflinching gaze, her hands in the pockets of her long quilted coat. Without any further comment, Cal walked to the wheelbarrow and went out of sight to the wood pile.

What is his problem, she wondered. Leah had no idea, but she knew Cal's moodiness and icy attitude toward her had to stop, and there was no time like the present. She followed him to the wood pile to confront him.

"Exactly why do you want to be an ass around me?" Leah asked directly. "What did I do to you or are you just an asshole in general?" Cal didn't stop loading the wood into the wheelbarrow, and he didn't answer either. Leah walked right over to the woodpile and began loading wood alongside him. The gesture obviously irritated him even more.

"You can stop showing off Wonder Woman," Cal responded snidely. "I wouldn't want you to get your nails broken or your muscles strained. Besides, Dad and Ms. Fi aren't around to coo over you."

"Excuse me, but that was *your* Wonder Woman, not me," Leah replied coldly. "Unlike your ex-wife, I haven't had a manicure in over three years, and I run 15 miles a week so I earned these muscles, and I don't need your bitter, forlorn bullshit just because you think every woman is a gold digger, an opportunist or a prima donna. I'm not any of them, so save your crap for somebody else, mister."

Leah very obviously hit a nerve. Cal's face was so red, his breathing so ragged that she could hear it pumping in and out of his lungs. Before she knew what was happening, Cal stepped right over to her and grabbed her around the waist and pulled her roughly up against him. Now, Leah's breath came in a gasp and stayed locked in her chest.

"You don't know me at all," Cal seethed, "but you sure think you do."

Now, Leah was livid. "Touché, Mr. Cunningham," she retorted, and she tried to push him away from her with all her might. His rock-hard body didn't budge. "Get the hell away from me," she finished in a whisper.

As a response, Cal pulled her to him and roughly kissed her, his mouth hot and wet. Leah was no longer sure if her feet were on the ground because her head was spinning like a top. As hard as she fought him, she desired him even more, and that fact made her angrier than she could remember. Finally, she mustered the strength to push him away just as he let her go, and Leah fell to the ground. Cal reached for her to catch her to no avail then promptly tripped over the leg of the wheelbarrow and fell onto the frozen ground beside her.

A loud silence set in momentarily until the hilarity and stupidity of the moment undid Leah. Instead of the tears, yelling and cursing Cal expected, though, Leah began to laugh. At first, the noise was a bubbling giggle from her chest, and the silliness of the sound made him smile. In a matter of seconds, though, Leah was laughing so hard she was holding her sides, and the sight of her made Cal laugh too.

"Well, we're a freaking pair of idiots," she managed. "I can't get angry worth a hoot, and you sure make a crappy Casanova, my friend."

"That's what you call angry?" he asked. "I thought anger would prompt you to slap me or cuss me out, not howl with laughter. I got to tell you, though, I haven't laughed like this in ages, but I'm sorry, Leah."

The comment touched her, and Leah smiled over at him and said, "Maybe that's why you've been so cranky. Maybe you just need somebody to teach you how to laugh at yourself again. God knows, if I couldn't laugh at my situation, I'd have already cried myself to an early grave." Leah pushed herself up and extended her hand to Cal who was still sitting on the ground. He simply looked at her, amused.

"What exactly is your situation, Leah?" he inquired gently, as he took her hand and got up off the ground.

"Get that wood and come on," she said good-naturedly, squeezing his hand slightly as she let it go. "Aunt Fi and your dad will be waiting on us to eat. If you want, we can go for a nighttime walk after dinner, and I will tell you all about it, okay?"

Cal looked at her for a moment in the fading light, and Leah wondered if he was trying to make up an excuse or silently asking pondering whether or not he wanted to go. Finally, he picked up the handles of the wheelbarrow and with the subtlest hint of a smile answered, "Okay, but only if I get to sit on the old chair stump."

Leah chuckled at the memory as they walked back to the farmhouse, and replied softly, "You've got yourself a deal, Cal Cunningham."

Chapter 22

When Leah was thirteen, one of the last huge old chestnut trees on Gran Belle's farm succumbed to the blight that destroyed the entire population of American chestnut trees in the Appalachian Mountains. After it died, Mr. C tried to cut it down, but he found the old tree to be so stubborn and so knotty, his chainsaw blew its motor a little more than three quarters of the way through the trunk. To finish the job, he cut into the trunk with a cross-saw along with Mr. Dancy who lived around the bend in the hollow. When the old chestnut fell, though, instead of breaking off flush the tree split over a huge knot in the wood at its base, leaving a stump that resembled a regal high-back chair.

Leah found the "chair" the very first day she visited that summer, and immediately claimed it as her own secret hideaway for reading, writing and eating pie. Cal had already found the spot, though, and when he beat her to the seat, he showed her his initials cut into in the side of the stump. Not to be deterred, Leah promptly marched back to the house, grabbed the pocketknife out of the utility drawer, ran back to the stump, and carved her own name on top of Cal's initials.

For the rest of the summer, they spent hours there talking about school, faraway places, and their hopes and dreams. They watched the Leonid meteor shower, several spectacular summer thunderstorms and even the July 4th fireworks the town shot off over at Mount Jefferson that summer. As a sign of joint ownership of the chair, Leah and Cal would take turns sitting against the back, the other sitting on the front of the stump leaned up against the other's knees for support. The chair was the site of Leah's first kiss, her first love, and the following summer, her first heartbreak. It was a place brimming with bittersweet memories.

After they finished eating dinner, Mr. C volunteered to wash the dishes, and Leah and Aunt Fi happily agreed. Cal offered to help his dad, but Mr. C shook his head no—the kitchen wasn't big enough for the two of them. While Mr. C was occupied, Leah took Cal to the den to show him the NC State blanket she was making for his dad. Cal was speechless and held it in his hands long enough for Leah to realize he was impressed and even a little envious.

Leah also showed him the crocheted stockings, trivets and potholders she wanted to sell on Saturday, and Cal readily agreed and shook his head in amazement at her handiwork. He asked her in front of her aunt, "When do you have time to do all of this work? My goodness, you've only been here four days!"

Leah was a little embarrassed as she looked at everything, but simply shrugged her shoulders. Finally, she answered, "What else am I going to do? I don't have a job, I don't have internet to communicate with my girlfriends on the coast, and I need the money. Besides, when Aunt Fi and I get to talking, I can churn out more work than I ever imagined."

Cal looked at her but didn't say anything more. Leah, though, looked at him and said, "Do you have time for a brisk, nighttime walk, Cal?"

Cal slowly rose from the couch, grabbed his coat and hers and answered, "I do, but I'm going to have to go home in a minute. I've got to go to Boone in the morning to fetch some tables and tablecloths for the sale on Saturday."

"Okay," Leah answered, and they bundled up, walked out of the house and into the darkness.

The moonless night was still, but cold. Millions of stars twinkled overhead as their eyes slowly adjusted to the darkness, and the frozen ground crunched below their feet. They walked silently, heading toward the tree chair, instinctively knowing the way. When they arrived, Leah smiled. God, she loved it here. Cal sat down astride the trunk, leaving room for Leah to sit in front of him. He didn't invite her to sit down, but he didn't have to—Leah knew what to do, and she sat down and leaned back against him.

She sighed and closed her eyes. She thought about their first kiss as well as their kiss earlier in the evening, and Leah shivered with excitement. Cal, thinking she was cold, pulled her inside his coat. Leah felt sure she would burst into flames she was so overcome by desire, attraction or maybe just those memories. She was content to stay silent.

Cal sighed too, and he put his chin on top of her head. Breaking the silence, he asked her quietly, "Why are you here, Leah? Why did you come back?"

Without turning around, Leah answered in a whisper, "I came back because this is the only home I ever really had, Cal, and quite frankly, I had nowhere else to go—nowhere else I wanted to go. I lost my career two years ago, and I have spent countless hours and days sending out resumes, taking courses, getting licenses and following up on every lead, contact in the market to no avail. I ran out of unemployment benefits three weeks ago, I lost my townhouse to foreclosure, and I am virtually penniless." Leah sighed then continued, "Don't feel bad for me, though, and here's why—in these hellish last two years, I have discovered that I can sew, crochet, quilt, cook and can and that I am quite good at all of them. I have become amazingly self-sufficient because the only person I have been able to count on for day-to-day living is me. My friends don't recognize me or what I have become, but they never knew what I used to be, where I was truly at home and what I was capable of doing. Aunt Fi knew, though. She's been sending me recipes since I was in college." Leah took a deep breath, and leaned back against Cal. She was tired of talking. Besides, what else was left to say?

Cal stayed quiet as he pondered what Leah had said, and he considered what her life must have been like for the last two years. All of his assumptions about her fancy, sophisticated lifestyle were wrong, and he was ashamed of himself for treating her so abysmally this week. Leah had enough on her plate without having to deal with a mean-spirited, cranky ass like him.

Hardly recognizing his own voice, Cal heard himself ask Leah, "Would you consider working at the hardware store a couple days a week, Leah? I really need the help with the computers and the bookkeeping, and you could use the internet."

Leah slowly turned around and looked at him, searching his face for sincerity, honesty. "If you need me, I will help you," she replied, "but I'm not a charity case, Cal."

"I wouldn't have asked for your help if I didn't need it, Leah," he said to her, his eyes never leaving hers. "Besides, it's not like you're going to strike it rich working there."

Leah smiled and answered, "Good thing for you then that I don't care about being rich."

"It's a damn good thing," he laughed.

"I'll accept the job under one condition," she said good-naturedly.

Cal cautiously responded, "What condition?"

"I'll help you at the store if you'll help me plant the garden this spring," Leah said.

Cal breathed a sigh of relief, glad her request was so easily granted then said, "Deal."

Leah grinned in the dark and stuck out her hand to seal the agreement, "Deal."

When Cal grabbed her hand, though, Leah felt the electricity of his touch surge through her body, and she wondered if she was going to teeter off the chair and roll down the hill like a boulder. Cal obviously felt it too because he steadied her by slipping his arm around her back. They were suspended in time for a few seconds, Leah searching his face, Cal stroking her hand with his thumb.

Desire raged inside her as she leaned up against him. He was breathing heavy, and Leah was so close to him now that she could feel the heat of his body on her face and neck. She wanted Cal to kiss her; in fact, she wanted him more than she ever had in those seconds, but Cal reached up and pushed a short blond curl off her forehead then moved her back to arms length. "Can you come in tomorrow afternoon to help me set up for the sale?" he asked her, breaking the sexual tension crackling in the air around them.

Leah, somewhat dazed, simply nodded yes. Cal smiled tenderly, and answered, "Good. I'll see you around 2 if that's okay."

Leah's voice had disappeared so she nodded again. Cal replied, "Thank you for dinner, too. I've got to go. Please tell Ms. Fi I said thank you," and without another word, Cal stood and disappeared into the darkness.

In the cold, black mountain air, Leah leaned against the back of the chair tree, and was overcome by emotion. For the first time since she arrived here at the farm, she felt lonely. She was also completely disconnected from the life she had made in the last decade in Virginia Beach. Leah felt like she was floating around aimlessly, tethered nowhere. She suddenly ached to belong somewhere, to matter to someone. When her tears came, they streamed in hot tracks down her cheeks and onto her neck, and she felt powerless to stop them, immobilized by heartache just like she felt in this very same place twenty years ago when Cal Cunningham broke her heart.

Chapter 23

The Haas house was always crazy around the holidays, but this year proved to be a three-ring circus since Siobhan added a campaign for a seat on the judicial bench to the family mix. She simply could not find the hours in the day she needed to wrap up her pending legal cases, attend all the holiday parties or simply do the dishes and the laundry. Siobhan was exhausted, and she never felt rested in the mornings, even after a full night of sleep or her favorite extra-large cup of coffee.

She needed to finish her Christmas shopping too, but the time and effort required to find the perfect gift for her boys and Robert had proven elusive. She needed to get away. Sensing her need to relax, shop, and simply disappear for a couple of days, Robert planned a weekend getaway for the family on the Outer Banks of North Carolina. Siobhan could hardly wait.

Siobhan snapped out of her anticipatory daydream with a jerk. Today was only Thursday which meant she had a ton of work to do before they left tomorrow morning. She had to finish packing. She finished putting the dishes into the dishwasher, hit start then wiped down the countertops and took the dishcloth to the laundry room before she finally went upstairs. As she opened her dresser drawer, she saw the scarf and booties Leah had given her. Siobhan reached in the drawer and lovingly picked them up.

As she held them to her breast, she thought about her best friend, now some seven hours away in the Appalachian high country. Leah had been gone for only four days and yet, her absence felt like a permanent void in Siobhan's chest. As she stroked Leah's hand-made and thoughtful gifts, she was suddenly overcome with grief—of loss, of loneliness, and of sadness, and great gasping sobs escaped from her throat. She crumbled onto the bed. Siobhan put her hand over her mouth to squelch the sounds, but she was unable to stop her tears, and her chest felt heavy and hollow at the same time.

Thoroughly drained, Siobhan stood, wiped her face dry with the palms of her hands and took the scarf and booties over to her suitcase along with the blanket Leah crafted. She intended to make her pictures with all of her gifts this weekend, and the thought provoked a smile from her that she otherwise didn't feel. In a rhythm now, Siobhan finished packing, saving the journal for last. Before she put it inside, she sat back down on the edge of the bed, picked up the pen from the bedside table, and opened the journal to the second page.

Pouring out her heart, Siobhan wrote:

> *"Only four days gone and I already feel the loss of you, Leah. You're missing in the ordinariness of my daily life, and reminders of your absence are everywhere. Coffee, pajamas, dogs, chili—just about everything recalls some kind of memory of you, with you. Are you making new memories yet? Are you lonely? Do you miss Virginia Beach? Do you miss me? I sure miss you.*
>
> *I know we promised to call each other on Saturday evening, but I am dying here. Watching you leave last Sunday was emotional torture, and I selfishly wonder what I will do without you. I love you, and I am so proud of you and the resilient, independent survivor you've become. Through the hell of the last two years, I've never seen you more determined, positive or self-sufficient. I've never known anybody like you, nor am I ever likely to. I long for the spring to see you again, but I long even more for Saturday when I can hear your voice reassure me that you are going to be alright."*

Siobhan closed the journal and laid it upon her chest, holding it close. She was so tired. She leaned back against her pillow, shut her eyes for just a moment, and pictured Leah making a snow angel in a huge meadow blanketed in a foot or more of snow. Siobhan smiled, maybe in her dream, maybe for real or both, then she drifted off to sleep, frolicking carefree in the winter wonderland and wrapped up in the warmth of her memories.

When Robert came in later that evening and found her fast asleep, he didn't want to disturb her, and he warned the boys that if they woke her he was going to throttle them. Siobhan needed her rest. He was worried about her going full speed, fulltime and burning herself out. This election was taking a toll on her, and Robert was keen enough to notice the bluish circles under her eyes every morning, her weight loss and her fatigue. He was glad they were going away from this madness. The campaign was less than two weeks old, and another three months of it could be Siobhan's demise. He questioned her just yesterday if the judgeship was worth the hassle. Robert wasn't sure from her response that she thought it was.

The laid back, quiet existence of the Outer Banks in the offseason should help her unwind, ponder and recharge—at least, he hoped so. They were going to go to all of the lovely local lighthouses—Ocracoke, Hatteras, Bodie Island and Currituck, the last of which they could climb to the top and see for miles into the Atlantic, across the charming Whalehead Club, the quaint towns of Corolla and Carova, and north into their home Commonwealth. Besides, the arctic winter was supposed to temporarily abate to a more normal pattern, the first days over 60 degrees since late October. Robert saw that break as reinforcement of their decision to take a vacation.

He looked at his beautiful Siobhan in sleep. Even after almost fifteen years together, she took his breath away. She challenged him with her intelligence, nourished his spirit with her peace, cracked him up with her humor, and brought him to his knees with her sexiness. Siobhan Mauldin-Haas was the full package. She was also a damn good lawyer, a fantastic mother, and an incredible lover. Just the thought of her body against him turned him on, and it was maddening to let her sleep.

Robert went over and gently took the journal from her hands. He saw her short entry from last Saturday, and his heart almost broke for Siobhan. Leah was her rock—even when the fabric of Leah Gibson's world unraveled completely—and Siobhan had always needed that support. Her Yin to Leah's Yang, their passion ran as deep in opposite directions as it did for each other. Leah was free-spirited, impulsive, unstructured, but driven by a deep goodness and authenticity that Robert had rarely observed in anybody else. Siobhan was meticulous, disciplined and quietly ambitious, but she was always keenly aware of achievement for the greater good, the benefit of others, and the betterment of their community.

He knew the first time he met Leah Gibson exactly how important she was to Siobhan, and that security and complete lack of jealousy or emotional competition with Leah was what Siobhan said sealed the deal on wanting to spend the rest of her life with him. Whatever her reason, Robert was thankful. He put the journal into Siobhan's suitcase, spread the cotton throw over her, quietly turned off the lamp, and closed the door, leaving his angel to slumber peacefully.

CHAPTER 24

Less than one week into their move, Meg believed that the hand of fate had steered their decision to relocate to Maryland. Courtney was happy working in the District and living in suburbia, and their schedules aligned so well that on most days they could get ready, eat breakfast and ride the Metro Red Line inside the beltway together. Meg hopped off at Union Station within one block of her new corporate office while Courtney continued on to DuPont Circle where she would then hop the bus to Georgetown University.

Even the fishbowl of the headquarters of her pharmaceutical company had proven less daunting than Meg imagined. She had an executive-sized office, an assistant named Charles who was incredibly efficient, smart and talented, and an amazing view down Pennsylvania Avenue that was simply breathtaking as the sun set. Her fellow employees were cordial, driven, and professional and so far, Meg had been impressed with the "zero drama" atmosphere. She found herself re-energized by the culture, and strangely ambitious in her desire to influence the movers and shakers, not just in the District but in the nation, armed with results, facts and products that improved the health and lives of people everywhere.

Meg would have been lying, though, if she said she didn't miss the familiarity and friendships of Virginia Beach. She did—and how. She missed the ocean, the year-round green golf courses, and the coastal vibe that pulsed in every shop, restaurant and business. She also missed Siobhan, Toni and especially Leah, even though Leah was even farther removed from the shore of home than Meg was.

Her mind wandered to Leah, and she tried to imagine what she was doing at this very moment in the mountains of North Carolina late on a Thursday evening. Meg heard bluegrass music and saw lots of plaid shirts and suspenders in her mind, and she laughed at her ridiculously stereotypical mental image. Trying to think more rationally, she saw Leah sitting beside a stone fireplace in a pair of old jeans, a tee shirt and her blue booties, crocheting away. In her mind's eye, Leah was smiling, comfortable, and at peace.

Meg sighed out loud, and wondered why she never saw the methodical and mundane routine of Leah's former life. She was a great actress, Meg realized. When she thought about the last two years, she could scarcely fathom how industrious, inventive and thrifty poor Leah had become. And she really was poor. Leah had been living in a shithole, in a neighborhood that frightened even Meg, rationing the last of her paltry unemployment to the penny. Incredibly, though, she was happier, and Meg was convinced that the Leah Gibson she had known in the sexy, navy suit and heels carrying a briefcase had been the imposter, acting the part of a career banker very adeptly for over a decade. Meg sighed, somehow relieved, and surprisingly certain that Leah, like she and Courtney, had settled immediately into her new home in the mountains.

Snapping back to the present, Meg looked at the time at the bottom of her computer screen. It was late, and she needed to pack up to go home. She had finished a brief which was anything but, and she had a meeting with a congressional aide tomorrow to discuss her concerns over the latest proposed legislation that further threatened the profitability of pharmaceutical companies with more capricious regulations and restrictions. Meg turned her computer off, and as she thought about going home, she picked up her pace. Clearing off her desk, Meg opened her top desk drawer to put away her pen and binder. The journal from Leah caught her eye, and she took it out and ran her finger lovingly over the cloth cover. She opened it up, turned to front page and wrote:

> *The first Thursday in our new homes*
> *"I am finally 'home.' Are you? I hope you are. I miss you something awful, but I promised along with everybody not to call you until Saturday evening. So! I'm telling you first, Leah—I'm popping the question to Courtney on Saturday. Sssh! Don't tell a soul. I'm thrilled, but I'm also terrified! What will I do if she doesn't say 'yes?'*

As she closed the book, a smile spread across her face. This weekend was going to be special. Meg was treating Courtney to a weekend inside the District. Friday night, Meg was going to take her out to the Kennedy Center to see a wickedly funny play called "Shear Madness." Saturday, she and Courtney were going to visit several art galleries and the Library of Congress in the morning then tour all of the presidential and war monuments Saturday night, an idea from none other than her best friend, Leah. In accordance with the pact they made together after Thanksgiving, Meg was going to bring her picnic blanket, scarf and booties, and send the perfect picture to Leah before she phoned her Saturday. The mental image made Meg snicker with delight as she turned off her light and headed for home. She hoped it had the very same effect on her little blonde dynamo in the high country.

CHAPTER 25

Toni leaned back in the over-sized chair in her den, propped her feet up on the ottoman, and breathed in the deafening silence of her home. Carter had taken the girls and her mother to the movies and then the local pizzeria. Toni had worked late to complete work on the file of a cancer patient who was being transported tomorrow morning to Hospice. The "final entry," the last update of the patient's medical chart, was her part of ensuring a smooth transition from the hospital to the Family Life Center where the patient would spend his last weeks, days or even hours, hopefully surrounded by friends or family. It was often heartbreaking work, but the care into which Toni entrusted the patients was so dignified, professional, and peaceful that staying late to complete a chart never seemed to be an inconvenience for her. Instead, Toni insisted this critical component of care should always create a sense of urgency on her part.

She tightened the muscles in her legs momentarily then relaxed them. Perhaps she should go run on the treadmill or go workout to a DVD. *I should*, she said to herself. She already had on her sweatpants and a tee shirt, but Toni just had not been able to muster the strength to put on her tennis shoes so she sat barefooted. Now, her feet were cold. She pushed the ottoman away to go put on a pair of socks then she remembered her booties. The thought made Toni hurry to her bedroom where she opened her dresser drawer.

The fuzzy yellow slippers were right on top, and she picked them up and rubbed the soft yarn against her cheek. She loved her booties, mainly because they were made by Leah, but also because the yellow color brightened her spirit. Toni was suddenly overcome by emotion, and she sat back on the edge of the bed and slipped the booties on her feet. Oh, how she missed Leah.

Leah was the friend who always remembered birthdays, favorite colors, the silliest stories, and when you just needed a hug, a hand or a kick in the butt. Now she was hundreds of miles away, and Toni found herself coping with Leah's move like a person dealing with the loss of a loved one. Her heart hurt, everything provoked a memory, and Toni found herself constantly expecting Leah to call to go eat lunch.

She stood up, and the corner of her journal caught her eye in the still-open drawer. Toni pulled it out, took the yellow feather pen Leah gave her on her birthday last year from her purse, and returned to the comfort of the easy chair in the den. Once she was settled, Toni opened the booklet to the first page and penned:

Coping—December 3

I've cloaked myself in yellow tonight, Le, trying to create some sunshine in the gloominess around me. I miss you so much, and while I miss the big things like the Christmas parties and the trips to New York, it's the little things that tear me up the most. Like this yellow pen, the booties, this journal—all more than things because they are the essence of the kind of friend you are and have always been to me. You are thoughtful, warm, caring and good, but you are also peaceful in spirit and genuine in character. I miss your peace and your authenticity.

I feel like a selfish, self-centered clod who has so freely taken the friendship you offered and yet given so little in return. You have been living a nightmare for several years, and I haven't been there for you. I'm sorry, Leah.

I am sure Carter thinks I am a lunatic because I cried myself into a stupor last Saturday night after we left Siobhan's house. I wanted to go back, hold you close, and tell you I love you, tell you not to leave me. There's that old selfish streak again, huh?

You're the bravest woman I have ever known, Leah Gibson. You belong in those hills because you are a pioneer—an independent, self-sufficient go-getter. I feel deep within me your life is there, and that something really wonderful is afoot. More than anything, I pray for your happiness because you deserve it more and have had it less than any of us. Keep your old friends here in Virginia Beach close to your heart, Leah, and when you have to dig deep to carry on, just think of us to remind yourself just how much you are loved.

Toni closed the journal and smiled. She was warm now, and somehow the room felt brighter and lighter. She took the journal back to her bedroom and put it back into the drawer. Inspired now, she grabbed her scarf and her cell phone and went into the bathroom. Toni took the lemon-scented bath salt from Leah off the shelf and opened it. She then measured out one scoop, dumped it into the tub, and ran the water as hot as she could stand. The aroma filled the room, and Toni breathed in the lemony delight until she felt almost giddy. When the tub was nearly full, she took off her clothes but left on her booties, arranged the scarf around the bath salt on the teak table beside the tub, and got into the hot water. With her bootied feet propped up out of the water beside the table, she grabbed her phone and snapped a picture, and sent it to Leah's e-mail with the caption, "Why I had to wait until Saturday to call you . . ." Almost immediately, the weight of the world lifted from Toni's shoulders, and she relaxed as her stress was dissolved completely by the echoes of her laughter.

CHAPTER 26

Leah nervously paced back and forth across the kitchen floor as she waited for Aunt Fi to finish getting ready so they could go into town for the annual holiday sidewalk sale. She stopped momentarily and looked out the window. Leah smiled and said a small prayer. Luckily, the hard-working shop owners and crafters of Ashe County had a beautiful day on tap for the event. With highs in the mid-50's expected along with abundant sunshine, Leah felt certain the stir-crazy visitors and resident shoppers would turn out in droves.

The winter this year, just like the last one, was shaping up to be cold, wet and dreary. The temperatures had been below average since early October when the High Country received its first measurable snowfall. Now only early December and still only late autumn, Ashe County had already tallied several feet of snow, and November had registered only two days above 50 degrees.

Aunt Fi strolled around the corner, dwarfed by her enormous coat and hat to protect her from the cold. Leah smiled at her, and said, "You look like a Christmas elf, Aunt Fi."

"If I keep shrinking, I'm going to be able to ride Pander like a pony," she countered. "Let's go so the invaders don't get all of the good parking spaces."

"Well, I hope we are covered up by tourists," Leah said, "because they like to spend money. I hope they buy every jar, stocking, and trivet on Cal's table. Heaven knows I could use some walking-around-money."

"Money's overrated," Aunt Fi deadpanned.

"Yes, but it makes paying the power bill a whole lot easier," Leah added then held out her arm for Aunt Fi to hold as they walked out to Leah's SUV.

The ride into town was filled with discussions about Christmas, but before they even had gotten to the holiday menu, they had already turned right onto the highway toward town. As they crested the hill that led into downtown West Jefferson, the sheer number of people down on the sidewalks and in the closed section of Main Street stunned both Leah and Aunt Fi.

"Where do you reckon they all came from?" Aunt Fi asked in amazement.

"I don't know, but I am so happy they are here," Leah all but exclaimed. Pulling out her handicap parking placard for Aunt Fi, they nestled into a small parking space just a few steps from the masses and around the corner from the hardware store.

As they strolled down the sidewalk slowly, Leah looked at the wares for sale by the various vendors. While they had all kinds of jewelry, homemade toys, and even bluegrass music CDs, Leah didn't see anything that competed with her items head-to-head. Leah was cautiously optimistic, but didn't want to appear too anxious about her prospects for income as the neared the hardware store's display tables.

Aunt Fi went inside to sit with Mr. C while Leah walked to the edge of the table to see how her products were selling. Cal was behind the table with a hardware apron on collecting cash from sales. When he saw her, he smiled broadly and briskly began making his way down the table toward her. Leah smiled back, but she was clearly distracted as she looked up and down the table and didn't see hardly any of her items out on the table. *What the hell?*, she asked herself.

A little irritated that he was holding back and rationing her inventory to sell later in the day, Leah tried not to tally how much income she was missing with a crowd this huge and virtually nothing of hers out to sell. As Cal approached, she put her hands on her hips and questioned him sternly, "Why haven't you got all of my products out, Cal?"

His smile disappeared, and he crossed his arms defensively as he stopped just short of her. Then, he leaned down to her glaring face and sassily answered, "What you see is all that's left, you knucklehead!"

Completely shocked, Leah looked at her watch. It was only 11:30 in the morning. Only four jars of her bath salts remained and one set of trivets. Cal just shook his head, and added quietly, "You're mouth is gaping open, Ms. Gibson."

"Oh, shut up," Leah whispered, "and let me savor the moment at least!"

Cal laughed as he looked down the nearly depleted table and remarked, "I could have sold four dozen more by lunchtime, I bet. And those stockings! These two women, obviously not from around here, almost came to blows over them. These people are crazy for your junk, Leah."

"Excuse me, Mr. Cunningham, but my handiwork is not junk. It is art and craft, my friend," Leah replied.

Cal laughed again and said, "Call it what you want, but I call it a very good day!"

"Amen, brother," Leah chuckled.

"I'm going to go check on Ms. Fi, get her a grape soda and a jack pie. Do you want anything," he asked.

"No, thanks, Cal," she said, "I'm just going to go look at the earrings and smell the Christmas trees."

"I bet Lula Caldwell has some really pretty Wolfpack red, white and black ones," Cal said to Leah, knowing she loved Tarheel blue intensely.

"I'm sure she can't even give those away in this tasteful crowd," Leah answered without missing a beat. "I'll be back shortly," she added then spontaneously reached up, hugged his neck and kissed him on the cheek.

Cal smiled and asked her, "What did I do to deserve that?"

"You gave me an opportunity, and I appreciate it, Cal," she said softly.

"With this kind of success I should be thanking you," he said sincerely. "When you get back, let's talk shop some more, okay? We've got three more weeks before Christmas!" Leah grinned and nodded her head. Then she swung around to go shopping, forcibly restraining herself to keep from skipping along the way.

CHAPTER 27

After Leah had browsed through all of the merchants' tables and returned Aunt Fi safely home via Mr. C, she went into the hardware store to see Cal. He had already broken down the outside display because it was virtually bare and was behind the counter on the computer with the most genuine smile Leah had seen on him since her arrival in the area.

"It has been a very good day, Cal," she said jubilantly.

"A very good day, indeed, Leah—mostly thanks to those bath salts. Then those women saw the stockings and madness and mayhem took over. So, today was successful *and* entertaining," he said, chuckling at the thought.

"Plus, the weather cooperated. I don't think we have had such a beautiful day since September," Leah added.

"Well, now that everybody knows we're here and what we have, maybe they will come back into the store," Cal stated.

"Let's hope! What are you doing back there?" she asked.

Cal looked up then answered, "Just putting the sales figures into my sales log."

"Do you mind if I go to your office and check my e-mail? I haven't even looked at it since I left Virginia Beach," Leah said. "I know you'd be shocked to find out that Aunt Fi hasn't got an internet connection at the farm."

"Yea, that's shocking. Help yourself to the computer," he said then added, "Just don't download any of that male porn you're so fond of."

Leah grinned then answered as she started toward the office, "Well, damn! You're already on to my intentions, Cal."

Once settled at the enormous wooden desk, Leah opened up the internet browser and logged into her account. When messages from Toni, Siobhan and Meg popped in, she wanted to cry out with delight. Controlling her emotions, she first deleted the plethora of spam and advertisements then opened the message Toni sent last night. The only words in the e-mail were in the subject line which read "Why I had to wait until Saturday to call you . . ."

Leah double-clicked on the attachment anxiously, certain that Toni had received an engagement ring from Carter. When the picture of Toni's booties propped up on the side of her tub appeared along with the scarf and her bath salts instead, Leah laughed out loud. Toni was deceptively silly underneath her calm demeanor and soft-spoken manner. Leah called her first.

"Leah! How are you, woman?" Toni answered before the end of the first ring.

"I'm great! Hey—I'm not keeping you from the bath or anything am I?" Leah teased.

Toni laughed, and for the next twenty minutes they talked easily and openly about the last week. Leah told Toni about the sale, Aunt Fi, the cold, the snow and the farm. Oddly, she didn't mention Cal Cunningham, though. Toni told Leah about the patient that she moved to hospice care on Friday, their tireless search for the perfect house, and their unfolding plans for an Independence Day wedding.

Leah promised to call again next week, and thanked Toni again for sending the picture. Toni laughed then added, "It won't be the last one!"

After she finished talking to Toni, Leah opened the e-mail from Meg. The message had been sent late last night. When she opened it, Leah sighed, "Oh my" out loud. Meg wrote, "Hey fool! I miss you. Good news, though—SHE SAID YES!" Attached was a picture of Meg and Courtney with the Washington Monument in the background late in the afternoon. They were huddled close together, Courtney in front of Meg, on the blanket Leah made with the scarf Leah made Meg wrapped around both of them. Meg's feet were in the matching booties. Courtney had her left hand turned to the camera, showing off her ring. Both of them wore smiles a mile wide. They were obviously happy.

Leah called Meg who answered amid noise and commotion, "I'm walking down Pennsylvania Avenue—no, I'm too busy to see the President, thank you very much!" Leah laughed and breathed a sigh of relief that their move north had worked out so well.

"Meg, you sound so happy. I hope you both are. Tell me everything," Leah said. About a half hour later, Leah had learned about their house, Meg's new office and staff, Courtney's dream job, and how much they loved being able to spend so much time together. Leah shared that her week of work had been productive, that she and Aunt Fi were very compatible despite over a fifty-five year age difference and that she truly felt at home in the mountains, despite missing her friends and the ocean terribly. Meg promised to come see her in the summer. Leah promised to come to the Capitol for their civil union ceremony. When they disconnected, Leah sighed with contentment.

Saving the e-mail from Siobhan for last, Leah quickly opened it to read. Siobhan simply wrote, "Guess where I am? I miss you so much. Call me!" Leah opened the picture and was surprised by not only the view, but by Siobhan as well.

She was on top of a lighthouse, brick, with miles of water behind and below her interspersed intermittently with only rooftops and ribbons of sand and grass. The view had to be breath-taking, Leah thought. Siobhan smiled out from under a toboggan, her long blond hair blown behind her head by the wind, her scarf wound around her neck and the booties on her hands like mittens, holding onto a black wrought-iron railing. Siobhan had dark circles under her eyes and her face looked thin. *I've only been gone about a week,* Leah thought, and she wondered if her best friend had the flu.

She quickly dialed her number. Siobhan answered immediately, "I swear I didn't think that Saturday was ever going to get here! How is my Mountain Mama?"

Leah breathed a sigh of relief. Siobhan was fine. "I am doing great now that I've got you on the phone. I miss you too. By the way, where the hell are you?" Leah asked.

Siobhan giggled and replied, "We're in Carova on the Outer Banks—hey! We're both in North Carolina! The picture was made from the top of the lighthouse in Corolla. I needed some rest so Robert brought us out here for the weekend. You forget just how beautiful and wild it is here," she finished.

"Windy too, I see. You aren't letting that election get the best of you, are you? You look tired, Siobhan. Nothing is worth your health," Leah gently admonished.

"I know, I know," Siobhan responded. "Only three more months . . ."

"That sounds like an eternity to me! You need to eat and sleep somewhere in your busy schedule too," Leah said.

They discussed what the boys were doing, her boutique Christmas shopping and walking on the beach this morning in the wind. "I won't need a glycolic peel for a year. It felt like I got sand-blasted," Siobhan said.

Leah told Siobhan about her week, describing the fear she felt coming up the driveway when she first arrived that she and Aunt Fi might not get along, but then discovering that they were so much alike and very compatible after all. She mentioned the sale today, the work she did to make and prepare her wares, and her "shopping spree" on the streets of West Jefferson. Leah recounted how she and Aunt Fi spent all day cleaning up the old potting shed and how sore her muscles were the next morning. Finally, she told Siobhan that she had seen and been reintroduced to the first guy she kissed and how his erratic behavior was driving her crazy. "Cal Cunningham needs some Prozac or something," Leah said.

"Whoa, whoa, whoa—tell me about this Cal Cunningham!" Siobhan exclaimed, stopping Leah from just moving on to the next topic. "Is he handsome? How old is he? Is he married? Spill it, sister!"

Leah sighed out loud, already tired of this conversation. She shouldn't have said a word, and she wished she could hit a 'rewind' button. "Let's see—yes, 38, no," Leah said, answering Siobhan's questions but not elaborating.

"Well, that doesn't tell me anything! What does he look like? You've never told me about your first kiss before, Leah! You've been holding out on me," Siobhan accused good-naturedly.

"Oh, come on, Siobhan—I'm not holding out on you! Why would you care about a kiss almost 30 years ago? And besides, there's nothing to tell. Cal's dad is the Mr. C who has looked after my Aunt Fi for years. Cal owns the hardware store in West Jefferson where I am right now and where I earned almost $350 today. He is an old friend. He looks like he always did—athletic, tall, blue eyes and strawberry blond hair. God, you are so transparent, Sio," Leah said.

"You're first love! How sweet," Siobhan opined.

"Jeez! I said my first kiss, not my first love, you knit-wit!" Leah teased. "Oh, Sio—I miss you so much. Have you talked to Toni and Meg?" she asked.

"I told Meg I would call her today. I'm going to call Toni too and see if she wants to go get lunch this week," Siobhan answered. "She's all I've got left of our posse here in town."

Honestly, Leah was a little jealous, but she knew she was being silly, and she tempered her envy by asking Siobhan when they could all get together. "We will all meet in Washington for a weekend this spring!"

Siobhan answered wistfully, "Spring—if I survive until then with this damn election."

"Well, now you have another reason to look forward to all of that madness being behind you, Judge Haas," Leah finished. "I've got to go. Will you call me this week after you and Toni go to lunch? That way, you can tell me about it, and I can live vicariously through you."

"You've got a deal, sister. I miss you too, Leah, and I look forward to seeing you in a couple of months. Hey, send me a picture of that potting shed and the farmhouse. The place sounds like Utopia," Siobhan said.

"As close as it gets, I believe—I promise I will. I love you, Sio," Leah managed.

"Back at you, Le—goodbye," Siobhan said.

When Leah ended the call, she felt her emotions roiling inside her gut. She felt sad, but also far removed from her former life in Virginia Beach, and the opposing feelings confused her. She wondered how, after over a decade in a city, she could move hundreds of miles away and immediately feel at home. She had left friends, acquaintances and everything familiar behind. Leah missed her friends immensely, the ocean more than a little, but she not only didn't the miss the rest of the people and places in Virginia Beach, she hadn't given them a second thought. Her total lack of attachment was strange.

Deep in thought, Leah didn't hear Cal walk in the door. "Planning what to do with your fortune?" he asked.

Leah snapped back to reality quickly and swiveled his chair around, leaned back and propped her black boots up on his desk. As he raised his eyebrow, she replied, "I'm flush with cash, and planning how to own this town."

"With $350, you might get the stray cat across the street and one of those booths at the flea market on the outskirts of town, but I'm watching you, Leah Gibson," Cal teased and made her laugh. "You still have that goofy laugh, but it's good to hear it again," he said quietly.

"It's good for me to be able to laugh again," Leah said sincerely. "There were days, maybe weeks, in the last couple of years when all I did was cry—if I even got out of bed. But for Pander, I might have just evaporated and disappeared into thin air. What's truly the hardest is realizing that sometimes the only person in the whole wide world who needs you is you. Life is hard when you are irrelevant."

"You sure aren't irrelevant here," he said with conviction. "You never have been. Your Aunt Fi has burned the home fires for you since you left the last time. She never stopped believing that you would come back."

"I never thought I would, but now I'm having a hard time believing I didn't come back before," Leah answered.

"For all those bank jobs here?" he teased.

She laughed again then replied, "No, for family—Aunt Fi is all I've got."

"Well, that's something," Cal said. "Now, are you ready to talk business?"

"Damn straight, Papa," she replied, making him just shake his head and chuckle.

"How quickly can you make 96 more half-pints of bath salts, four stockings and a bunch of those trivet things?" Cal asked.

Leah sat up and grabbed a pen and the legal pad off of the desk. "By all means, make yourself at home," he said smartly, but she was already absorbed in her calculations and figure.

When she finished, Leah looked up and answered, "Well, I need about another three hours to finish your dad's blanket. I bought Aunt Fi's present today, so I'm going to say I can have all 96 of the salts by Wednesday, the four stockings by Friday, and I'll have Aunt Fi make the trivets. She loves that sort of work."

"When do you sleep?" Cal asked.

"Hey, $700 is real money. I can sleep in January," she said. "I'd also like to set up a table near the entrance and sell some coffee and crumb cake next week. Would you let me do that?"

"I'll let you do anything that makes us money—within reason. I won't condone wet tee shirt contests or pole dancing," he joked. "Do you need me to get you anything in Boone on Monday?"

"I might. Could I just ride with you?" Leah asked.

Obviously taken aback a little, Cal paused before he answered, "Uh, sure."

"Well, you don't sound sure. What—is this trip your quiet time?" she inquired.

"No, I just thought you could be knitting or sewing or whatever it is you do while I pick up supplies. The weather is going to be terrible," he responded.

Leah snorted then posed her reply, "It is December so snow is expected. As far as managing my time, have I let you down yet? N-O! Besides, I haven't been to Boone in almost 15 years—indulge me, Cal."

"Alright, but I'm leaving early—8 a.m. sharp," he said, relenting.

Leah logged off the computer, stood and walked to the door beside him. Then she smiled her huge, white grin and replied, "I'll have one of those stockings done by then. Come by and pick me up, okay?"

"Okay, just make sure you wear something warm. We're going to get horizontal snow," he added.

"10-4, Papa," she giggled then squeezed his arm fondly and walked out of the store to head home.

CHAPTER 28

Cal stood at the storm door off his den, and looked at the distant western horizon. The wind had picked up, and the storm clouds rose high above the mountain tops like a tidal wave just offshore, threatening and dark. He sighed. Snow was imminent and would likely be abundant by the tone of the forecast. Snow was wonderful for the ski resorts, but not so great for the merchants in town. When a storm this size blew in, most of the citizens simply hunkered down and stayed home. As the owner of the local hardware store, staying home was not an option. Cal had to be open. Instead of selling items for Christmas, though, he would be selling snow shovels and blowers, rock salt and even the occasional generator. He would also need to stock up on his firewood and kindling. The trip to Boone on Monday was now critical.

The weather threatened to cancel all sorts of Christmas events this week. Church services, though, weren't among them. Tomorrow was the second Sunday of the Advent Season, and very little could keep the members of the Buffalo Creek United Methodist Church away this time of year. Only five weeks a year could they sing Christmas carols, light advent candles and watch the Passion play about the birth of the Christ child. Advent was more than a holy season. It was a festive and social season as well.

Cal's thoughts settled on Leah, and he smiled as he stared off into the darkening night sky. When she was a young girl, Leah would go to church with her grandmother in the summers every Sunday. She was baptized at the church when she was six, and grew to love they old hymns so much and so well that she didn't even need to look at the words by the time she was probably ten.

Leah had a good voice, and she sang with enthusiasm. Everybody in the church could hear her singing above everybody else. Her vibrant grasp of the faith was uplifting, and somehow, the church body was buoyed by her presence every summer. On the other hand, though, each summer's end was marked by her departure and the inevitable void without her spunk and joy. Leah Gibson just seemed to bring life and excitement to everybody around her.

When they were really young, Cal had been able to share anything and everything with Leah—his hopes, his dreams and his fears, and she would listen—really listen—then quietly ask him questions, testing his convictions or quelling his concerns. She had both a peaceful spirit and a full-tilt passion for life. More than anything, though, Leah was happy, and her happiness was shared abundantly and freely with the people in this community. As a result, they loved her deeply and genuinely and accepted her as family. His father and mother were no exceptions.

So why did you give up on her, Cal? He had asked himself that question too many times to count over the years. He thought about their first kiss and how he literally felt the electricity of her body move through him. Their attraction had scared Cal then, and honestly, it scared him now. Leah was about four years younger than he was, and he knew that corralling her at fourteen would have been unfair to her. She had never been out into the world, and Cal, even only on the cusp of eighteen, recognized that she needed to have the opportunity to experience more. But, man, he handled his decision to sever Leah's ties to him badly.

That summer when she arrived, Cal simply chose to keep his distance from his oldest friend. He never told her what he was doing or why, Cal just snubbed her. He spent the summer with his friends, working on the farm with his dad, and playing in his spare time on the Blue Ridge Parkway with the Appalachian State University students at Julian Price Park—anything to keep himself physically separated from Leah. Cal remembered seeing all of the pretty girls from the college in their skimpy bikinis playing Frisbee and Hacky-Sack, working hard to get noticed by the guys, but working harder to act like they weren't. He could see through them, though, and their coy and inauthentic actions, and they made him want Leah more than ever.

The evening before his eighteenth birthday that summer, his dad brought home a pineapple cake—his absolute favorite dessert—from Ms. Belle, Ms. Fi and Leah to mark his special day. Cal was humbled by their thoughtfulness and generosity, but he didn't know how to thank them. His dad, never one to mince or waste words, told him, "Just walk over and say, 'Thank you!'" Cal obliged.

As he walked the short distance to the Gibson farm, he thought about making amends with Leah, and he rehearsed over and over what he would say to her. Satisfied that he could repair their friendship, Cal came up the driveway with a bounce in his step. In the waning light of the day, the lights shone in the windows of the Gibson farmhouse, and out of habit, he looked up at the second floor on the west side of the house.

There, standing stark naked in full view, was Leah Gibson, and she was a vision. Cal stopped dead in his tracks and just watched her. She had obviously just gotten out of the shower, and she was smoothing something on her sun-kissed skin. Leah was no longer a child, Cal observed, and she stirred arousal in him instantly. He wanted her, and he saw them in his mind's eye passionately making love, their naked bodies intertwined and slick with sweat. Cal's breathing was ragged, his heartbeat rapid, and he felt wild. He recognized with certainty that if he and Leah were alone, they would not be able to restrain their desire. He was one day from 18, but Leah was only 14 years of age, and Cal knew she was far too young to lose her virginity, even if her body was full woman. He suddenly felt like crying and a little like he was going to be sick, perhaps because he couldn't have her now or perhaps because he never would. Whatever the reason, Cal Cunningham, on the eve of manhood, took his heart full of regret and despair into the shadows of the tree line and slowly made his way back down the mountain.

Now here he was, almost two decades later, reliving those emotions. *Stop!* Cal sighed. His sorry existence, divorced and unhappy, was 100 percent his own making while Leah's predicament, unemployed and uncertain, was the result of a horrific economy and the fact that she had tried to build a life virtually alone. When their two paths crossed again, instead of trying to rekindle a wonderful, old friendship or welcome Leah back into a community that was really the only family she had ever known, Cal had responded by being aloof, distant and cold to her. He was exactly what she said he was—an asshole. *What is wrong with me?*

Oh, he knew. He knew exactly why he was behaving so badly. Cal was afraid—afraid of being spurned after Marissa, afraid of dismantling the wall around his heart, and afraid that Leah would no longer see in him the person to whom she had so steadfastly bonded and belonged years ago. *So I'm an asshole and a wimp*, Cal thought.

Now, he and Leah were going to be alone for hours as they drove to Boone and back on Monday. Thinking about the trip both exhilarated and disturbed him. Cal wasn't worried about struggling for conversation; quite the contrary, he was much more worried about the responses a conversation with Leah Gibson would elicit from him. Just the thought of being so exposed, so open and so honest made Cal want to call the entire journey off. On the other hand, the idea of finding out about Leah's long-term plans, the details of her life over the last fifteen years, and her thoughts about Ashe County after having been gone for so long interested him immensely. He decided the key to a successful trip was to keep Leah talking.

Cal's mental musings were interrupted by his father's voice. "Have you got it all figured out?"

"No, but I'm still working on it," he answered. "I'm just looking at the storm roll in from the west," he continued with a smile in his voice. "I think it is going to be a big one."

His father walked across the room and stood beside him. "I don't think the cloud formations are what has you preoccupied, son. You've got the spunky Ms. Gibson on your mind this evening," he commented. "I'd know that look anywhere."

Cal sighed. He didn't want to argue or debate Leah Gibson with his father, so he just changed the subject. "Do you want to stay here tonight? We can go get Ms. Fi and Leah tomorrow morning for church," he offered.

Tom put his hand on Cal's shoulder then said, "Thanks son, but I'm going home and going to bed. Will you pick me up on the way to get the girls for church?"

"You bet, Dad," Cal replied warmly. "I'll see you tomorrow morning."

While his dad lived only a short distance down the mountain from his home and the Gibson farm, Cal knew he would worry in this weather until he saw the lights from his dad's porch go on. Winters in the high country could be brutal—cold, snowy, and damp, but the reward was the beauty of the springs, the pleasant summers and the idyllic autumns that followed. No doubt, his dad loved these mountains as much as he did. Neither had ever really considered living anywhere else except temporarily like when his dad was in the service or he was in school. The air, the earth, the water—it was in their blood.

The Cunninghams had a good way of life, and Cal had hoped to pass this gift on to a son or daughter of his own. Marissa never wanted children for fear that it would ruin her figure. God, she was so selfish. He supposed that was just as well anyway since any child of theirs would have carried half of her genes.

Admittedly, he thought he loved her when he married her. She was beautiful and savvy, and Marissa Doherty had chosen him among the throngs of young men hanging on her every word the summer before he graduated from N C State. She made him feel special, and she showed her appreciation physically by making love to him insatiably the entire year before they were married. As if she could read a young man's mind, Marissa knew just where and when to put out.

Cal became so preoccupied with having sex with her his last year in Raleigh that he would drive a couple of times a week two hours each way from Raleigh to Winston-Salem to meet her just to satisfy his longing. They would park in his Jeep, take a blanket to an old barn off of some country road, or even pay for a night for a couple of hours in a cheap motel. Her only desire for sex was hard and fast, and Cal did everything in his limited repertoire to satisfy her. As he lay spent and panting from exhaustion, Marissa would calmly get up, put her clothes back on, kiss him on the cheek and head back to Boone. She was maddening.

Cal thought about having her every night, slipping in and out of her body at will whenever and wherever he wanted, and he decided to ask her to marry him on one of those long drives to meet her. When he proposed, Marissa smiled coolly, completely nonplussed at his question, and simply said, "Yes."

In June after he graduated from N C State, he and Marissa were married in downtown Boone in a lavish and large ceremony. Then, the entire wedding party and the throngs of guests were treated to an outrageously expensive and decadent reception at Grandfather Mountain Golf & Country Club in Linville where her father was a member. For a simple Ashe County guy like Cal, the whole affair was over the top, and he kept telling himself to just survive the day so that he could get his wife into bed on their honeymoon.

His satisfaction, though, proved to be elusive that night and was a precursor of many of the nights to come. Marissa proceeded to get shit-faced at the reception, and he virtually carried her to the limo on their way to honeymoon suite. Once inside, she promptly passed out in her wedding gown. Cal undressed her and dumped her naked and reeking of liquor onto the bed. Then, exhausted and irritated, he traded his tuxedo for a tee shirt and jeans and went out on the deck to get some fresh air.

As he sat staring toward Grandfather Mountain, Cal tried to reassure himself that he had made the right decision to marry Marissa, but doubt had already seeped into his mind, even on that first night. His thoughts ran back to the reception and Leah Gibson. She was so lovely, ethereal and authentic. She was wearing pink, and her light green eyes were set off by her lightly bronzed skin. Her blond hair had been bleached by the sun, and underneath her neat pink hat, long, wild, and directionless curls framed her face naturally.

Cal could hardly take his eyes off of her, and several times she caught his stare and returned it, unflinching and calm. Leah did manage to smile at him as she embraced him in the receiving line, whispering in his ear, "Be happy, my friend."

She could have stabbed him in the heart less painfully. He felt Marissa watching him watch Leah, and when he turned to look at his new bride her dark eyes were angry and defiant. He walked over to her, wrapped his arms around her waist and kissed her deeply. She responded to his affection by rubbing up against him, stirring his arousal with her body as a promise of what awaited him, but the damage to her ego was done, and she began throwing back drinks like a sailor on shore leave.

Later, as Leah danced with every one of his fraternity brothers at the reception, he tried to quell the sick feeling in his gut. Cal wanted to throttle the lot of them with their lusty eyes and lecherous minds. Leah Gibson was too good for any of them. Most of all, she was too good for him, and as Cal sat watching Grandfather's profile fade into the first lonely night of his honeymoon, he realized that he had gotten exactly what he deserved but nothing close to what he had really wanted.

Cal leaned his head against the wall, shaking from his mind that inaugural nightmare in a long line of them during his marriage to Marissa. He didn't miss his ex-wife at all, and he was glad she was gone from his life. Now and, if he was truly honest, since he had seen her in that pink dress at his wedding, he wanted Leah Gibson with an almost feral desire.

Determined not to repeat his past mistakes with Leah this time, he vowed to show her that he didn't intend to settle for anything else. Cal would work to get what he really wanted this time whether he deserved her or not.

Chapter 29

The weather began deteriorating early Sunday morning, just in time for church. The snow started in earnest around 8 a.m. and by 9:30, the ground was already covered in a fluffy layer of white. Leah stood immobilized at the kitchen door, mesmerized by the size of the flakes as well as the way the wind gusts blowing up the mountain whipped the snow into white billowy pillows turning over in the air. Sure, Leah had seen snow, but not like this—outside was a virtual whiteout, and now she understood what Cal meant by "horizontal" snow.

She looked over at the outdoor thermometer on the wall—27 degrees. *Brrr*, Leah thought, and she shivered as she reached for her enormous down-quilted coat. Aunt Fi really didn't need to be going out in this despicable cold and snow, but Leah knew that wild horses couldn't keep her aunt from church. Aunt Fi had lived through 92 of these mountain winters.

Leah knew the five-minute drive to church would take fifteen this morning, and she was suddenly thankful that she had opted for her four-wheel-drive SUV in Virginia Beach over that sleek German car she had considered. Leah would drive them, and she walked to her purse on the counter to retrieve her keys to go warm up her vehicle.

The phone on the wall next to her purse rang loudly, startling her to the point that she dropped her keys. Leah picked up the receiver and leaned down to pick up her keys in one motion and answered, "Hello?"

"Leah?" the familiar voice on the other end asked.

"Hi, Mr. C," she said sweetly, "Lovely weather we're having this morning, huh?"

"No, but it is typical. Cal and I are leaving to come get you two girls for church. We'll be there in about five minutes," he finished.

Leah breathed a sigh of relief. She smiled and said, "Perfect! I really didn't want to navigate this much snow this soon. I'll let Aunt Fi know you're on your way. We'll be ready."

Just as she hung up the receiver, Aunt Fi came around the corner bundled from head to toe in winter garb. She had on a hat, scarf, an enormous coat, and a pair of snow boots with Sherpa lining at the top. Leah laughed, "You look warm."

"I look like the Michelin Man," Aunt Fi complained. "Are you ready?"

"I'm just going to put on my coat, hat and scarf," Leah replied. "The Cunningham men are on their way to retrieve us for church."

"Pshaw! We could have driven ourselves," Aunt Fi mildly protested, but then smiled into Leah's eyes and said, "But then you wouldn't get to sit really close to Cal."

"I'm sure he'll sit beside me in church," Leah said, ignoring her aunt's match-making designs as she put on her red wool hat and matching scarf then put on her big black coat.

Aunt Fi giggled then said conspiratorially, "That is decidedly *not* the same."

The Cunninghams pulled up beside the porch in Cal's four-wheel-drive old pickup truck. Leah sighed, and Aunt Fi giggled again as Mr. C got out of the passenger door to let them inside. Of course, Aunt Fi, with a twinkle in her eyes, insisted Leah get in first. She obliged. Mr. C then helped Aunt Fi climb in beside her before he finally got back inside and closed the door.

They were crammed in the truck's cab so tightly that Leah was virtually sitting in Cal's lap, and the thought made her stomach do a somersault. She looked up at him. He looked back at her and smiled, and Leah relaxed and leaned against him. She closed her eyes and breathed in his aftershave. He exuded sex appeal, and she silently scolded herself for thinking such unholy thoughts on the way to church.

Just in time, Aunt Fi broke the silence by saying, "I'm glad I used soap this morning, Tom."

"I'm glad you did too, Ms. Fiona," he laughed heartily. "What are you girls doing for lunch?" he asked.

"We're having green beans, stewed potatoes and fried chicken," she replied. "I made enough for all of us so I expect you to stay for Sunday dinner."

"You don't have to ask me twice," Mr. C answered good-naturedly.

Mr. C and her aunt began talking to each other about the weather while Cal and Leah continued the conversation about lunch—or at least she thought it was about lunch.

"When did you have time to cook all of that?" Cal asked Leah.

"I put the green beans and potatoes on to cook before I got into the shower. We peeled the potatoes last night. Aunt Fi fried the chicken while I was getting ready. All we have to do when we get home is put the rolls into the oven to bake," Leah said.

Cal smiled at their industrious natures. Leah and Aunt Fi were like his mom. They just enjoyed work. "What time did you get out of bed?" he inquired.

"Aunt Fi and I get up every morning at 6 a.m. We sure don't want to waste the morning. That's the best time of day," Leah said.

"I can think of a couple better times of day," he said quietly, and he gave her a smile so sexy that Leah blushed. Those unholy thoughts crept into her mind again, and she knew without a shadow of a doubt Cal could read them because he chuckled quietly then returned his eyes to the road.

Mercifully, they arrived at church, and Leah welcomed the blast of cold air that greeted her when she stepped outside. She felt the snowflakes on her face, and they melted instantly on her searing cheeks. She needed to get a grip on herself, she thought.

Cal sure wasn't helping. He parked the truck while she waited for him at the front door under the overhang of the church. The snow fell relentlessly, and as Cal walked from the parking lot to the sidewalk, large snowflakes clung to his coat and to his short sandy hair. Leah watched his gait and admired Cal's easygoing demeanor and his dashing good looks. He smiled warmly as he saw her watching him and put his hand in the small of her back as they walked into the sanctuary together. His touch electrified her, and she wondered if he could hear her breathing, shallow and fast.

As if she had never left, Leah walked without prompting to the pew where their families had sat for generations—on the right side of the church four rows from the back in the seats closest to the wall. In this small congregation, everybody had their place, their pew, their seat—it was a given. Today, though, the church was abuzz with excitement because Leah Gibson had returned home. The attention, love and kindness were humbling to Leah, and she was almost overwhelmed by the sheer magnitude of the congregation's welcome.

Today marked the second Sunday of the Advent, and the first two Advent candles were lit in observance. Leah absorbed the serenity of the sanctuary, the stirring words of the sermon, and the uplifting choruses of the Christmas carols, many of which she surprisingly still knew by heart, and as the service ended, she felt invigorated and energized. As Leah waited in the long line to thank and greet Pastor Canton, she sighed with contentment, and Cal put his arm around her spontaneously and naturally, pulling her close to him. She leaned her head into his chest and said, "I love this church, Cal. It feels like home."

"It *is* your home, Le," he whispered down to her ear. Leah smiled up at him and took his hand into her own, and they walked the rest of the way to the door in a comfortable silence.

After Leah had shaken Pastor Canton's hand and they had exchanged compliments with each other, she reached for the handle of the heavy, wooden door and pushed it open. The enormity of the snowfall stunned her, and Leah looked wide-eyed back at Cal. They had been in church less than two hours, and at least one foot of snow was already on the ground. Still, the same large, wet flakes fell steadily from the sky.

Cal walked alongside her. When he looked at her profile, he saw her amazement at the pile-up. "Pretty impressive, huh?" he asked. "I knew this storm was going to be a big one last night. I saw it coming over the western mountains like a big black wave," he said.

"How long is it forecasted to fall? How much snow are we going to get?" Leah asked in rapid succession.

"Well, I'm no weatherman," Cal said, "But I imagine we might get a couple of feet or so."

Leah's expression was one of shock, and Cal laughed at her surprise, finally remembering that she had never stayed in the High Country during the winter months. He wrapped his arm around her small shoulders and calmly said, "We handle snow fairly well up here in the wintertime, Le. Enjoy it! We'll be just fine." Then he promptly threw his head back, opened his mouth and stuck out his tongue to catch a mouthful of snowflakes.

"You're foolish, Cal Cunningham," Leah said with a laugh. They tromped through the snow to the truck, got inside the cab, and cranked it up to warm. Leah shivered with excitement, but Cal pulled her close to him, believing she was cold. She had no intention of telling him otherwise either.

He looked into her eyes, and she could see desire there. His blue eyes were dark like the sea, and Leah wasn't sure she was even breathing at this juncture. "You sure you want to go with me to Boone tomorrow in this weather?" he asked quietly.

"Wild horses couldn't keep me from going, Cal," she answered hoarsely.

"You're borrowing trouble, Le," he whispered, leaning closer to her so she could feel the warmth of his breath on her cheek. Leah knew he was no longer talking about the weather.

Undeterred, Leah looked up into his eyes, and without a blink, she said with certainty, "I love trouble, Cal."

Satisfied with her answer and sensing the need to tamper their mutual attraction momentarily, Cal simply smiled then backed the truck out of the parking lot to pick up Ms. Fi and his dad from the front of the church. He could think of many more appropriate places to continue this discussion later.

CHAPTER 30

After stuffing themselves completely at Sunday dinner, Leah felt the need to go for a walk, but as she stood looking out the window of the den, she was not even sure she could walk in snow this deep. She sighed.

Cal came over to her side and looked out at the sheer white landscape. He knew Leah was feeling cooped up. That feeling was common here in the mountains in the wintertime, especially if people couldn't or wouldn't get out of their houses. He wasn't one of those people, though. Cal loved the snow, the winter, and even now well into his 30s, he still played in it. Suddenly, he had an idea.

"Have you ever been cross-country skiing?" he asked Leah.

"No, but I snow ski. Is it about the same?" she inquired, interested.

"I'll tell you what—you go change into some ski bibs if you have some, and I'll go to my house and change then bring our equipment back here so we can try it. Ok?"

Leah couldn't contain her enthusiasm, and the smile on her face was one of pure excitement and joy. She reached up, put her arms around Cal's neck then promptly squealed into his ear. "Oh, Cal, I do have a pair of ski bibs. I'm so happy!"

"You're happy. I'm deaf," he remarked good-naturedly. "Now, go get ready. I'll be back in fifteen minutes or so."

Leah almost ran to her room to pull out her light pink ski bibs she had worn only a handful of times when she and the girls went skiing at Snowshoe over in West Virginia. She was an adequate skier like Toni, especially compared to Siobhan who was so graceful and smooth and Meg who bordered on the verge of being labeled a professional she was so good. The ski bibs brought back wonderful memories, and she hoped and prayed her friends were doing as well as they purported yesterday. Leah vowed to have Cal make a few pictures of her in this blizzard so she could send them to her girlfriends this week.

True to his word, Cal was back 15 minutes later, dressed in a navy blue ski suit that set off his bright blue eyes against his sandy hair, and Leah caught herself staring at him like a hormone-filled teenager. She silently scolded herself.

Cal took one look at Leah in her light pink bibs and almost came unraveled. *Why did she have to wear pink?* He was no longer certain this idea was a good one because he was no longer certain he could trust himself to show any restraint whatsoever.

Pulling himself together, he turned to his dad and said, "We're going to go skiing down the drive, across the meadow and back around to my house. Then, I'll bring Leah back home in my Jeep. You can take the truck home, Dad."

His father looked at him closely, then responded, "Be careful, son. I wouldn't want anything to happen to Leah. Ms. Fi wouldn't let you live it down if she got hurt."

Cal was no idiot. He knew for sure his dad was not talking about her physical well-being since Cal was not only an Eagle Scout, but also a very experienced outdoorsman who had lived in these mountains practically his entire life. No, his father was warning him about Leah in a much more important aspect—her heart. He answered sincerely, looking directly into his father's eye, "I promise to take good care of Leah, Dad."

For just a second more his father looked at him then nodded, sending them on their way with his blessing. Cal took a deep breath before he turned back around to Leah and asked, "Are you ready?"

Her smile was infectious, and he laughed deeply when she answered, "I was born ready, Cal Cunningham. Let's go!"

After a few minutes of fitting equipment, instructions on what to do, and pointing them in the direction they were going, Cal and Leah set off across the yard, down the hill, across the field, and finally out of site around the driveway. Mr. C and Aunt Fiona stood watching them at the window.

"She loves him, you know," Aunt Fi commented without the emotion she felt.

"Then you know the feeling is mutual, I guess, too," Mr. C answered her quietly.

"Neither one of them will admit it, though. Those two are stubborn as mules," she said.

"Wonder who they get *that* from?" he replied. Aunt Fi giggled, and he chuckled along with her. "They are perfect for each other, and always were," he added. "It's just a shame it took almost two decades, a bad marriage and the end of a career to get them together."

"God works in mysterious ways, Tom," Ms. Fiona said quietly.

"Indeed, He does," he answered. "Indeed, He does."

CHAPTER 31

Leah snapped off her skis then plopped onto the bank behind her, winded but exhilarated. She grinned up at Cal. His breathing was labored too. "I had no idea how hard this kind of skiing was. It's like work," she said.

"Yeah, but you love to work so I knew you'd like it," Cal commented. "It's not even cold out here now, is it?"

"No, I'm actually hot," Leah said then instantly regretted her choice of words.

They didn't escape Cal, though, and he squatted down beside her and answered in a faux-sexy voice, "You, my dear, are positively sizzling. Be careful before the snowmelt washes us away."

"You're positively full of crap," she countered playfully. "Perhaps the snowmelt will hose you off." Leah sighed contently. "This land is almost magical in the snow, Cal, isn't it?"

He carefully turned around beside her and leaned back with her into the bank, looking back across the meadow and up the mountain from where they came. The view was prettier than a postcard. "Snap a picture for me," she said, handing him her smart phone. Instead of snapping the view of the landscape, Cal first turned the camera toward her face, pink with exercise and glowing from satisfaction and happiness, and took her picture. Then, he snapped a picture of the view in front of them.

He then looked at the pictures, and stared at the image of Leah he had captured. He blond curls spilled out in every direction around her face, and her smile was one of genuine contentment. "You're just beautiful," Cal said quietly, "especially in pink."

Leah sat up, humbled by his kind words. She didn't know what to say, but she finally managed, "Thank you, Cal. Those are the nicest words I have heard in a long time."

"I doubt that, but you're welcome. I don't know if I've even told you yet that it is good to have you back home," he said.

"You haven't, but I'm glad you think so," Leah replied. "I've missed you for almost 20 years."

Cal leaned back against the snow, feeling like the wind had been knocked out of him. Now he was at a loss of words, and he closed his eyes for a moment. Finally, he answered her, "God, Leah, I feel bad enough without you reminding me how badly I screwed up."

"My comment wasn't intended to make you feel bad, Cal. We can't change the past," she said. "Let's just relish the day, ok?"

"No, I can't until I get a few things off my chest," he said, leaning up onto his elbows and turning to face her.

Leah sighed then asked, "What things, Cal?"

"You know what things," he said, then breathed deeply and continued, "First, I'm sorry I never told you I was afraid of what we might do when you were far too young and I was far too inexperienced to control myself the summer you arrived before I went off to school in Raleigh." Leah started to interrupt him, but Cal put his hand up to stop her so he could keep going. "Second, I made myself stay far away from you for the few years that followed because I thought you would outgrow me, wouldn't like me or would stay away forever once your grandmother died. Finally, I convinced myself that good looks and a hot body were enough to replace you when I met Marissa, and it was—until I saw you again after my wedding. It was too late then, Leah," Cal finished and he sighed loudly. "I'm just a screw up when it comes to you."

Leah looked at him silently and searched his eyes for sincerity. Finally, she said softly, "I've carried you with me my whole life, Cal, but it's not because you screwed up, it is simply that I was the right person for you at the wrong time. I so wanted to be that person for you, but I wasn't. Not then, anyway. Marissa—my polar opposite—was your choice, and I just couldn't come back and watch her live the life I wanted so I just didn't come back. I really can't complain, though, because I built a wonderful life in Virginia Beach with great friends. I honestly didn't even think much about Ashe County until I lost my career, my home and nearly my sanity over the last two years," Leah said. "Now I know what my life was missing all along was home—this home," and she spread her arms out wide to show him she meant here.

"I said it earlier, and I meant it—this *is* your home, Leah Gibson," Cal said, emphasizing her name.

"Yeah, well, it is Marissa's home too," she countered, "And when she comes back here—and she will—she'll be just as welcomed."

"*Bullshit!*" Cal answered sharply, and he pushed himself off of the snow. Leah was startled at his response, and she looked into his eyes, now angry and defiant. "She won't be welcome here by me, and don't you forget that," he said as he walked down toward the fence.

Leah sat up and watched him walk about twenty feet away. *What in the world is wrong with me,* she wondered. She shouldn't have brought Cal's ex-wife into this conversation, and she wasn't sure why she did. Now, he was upset, and she was sitting alone in the snow. "I'm not very good at this, Cal, and I sure haven't had much practice," she said across the distance between them.

Cal sighed, and he realized that she was trying to make peace again. As Cal started to turn around to tell her he wasn't very good at making amends either, he was hit by a rock-hard snowball in the right shoulder. Taken aback, he then was pelted in the face by another one as he faced her. Leah Gibson never ceased to surprise him, and Cal began laughing as his ran towards her, amid the continuing barrage of snowballs. When he reached her, she was laughing like a maniac, and so was he. He reached down and pushed snow all over her, covering her completely. Finally, he bent down beside her, grabbed her hand and pulled her up to him. With both of them laughing, covered head-to-toe in snow and breathing heavily, Cal said, "Truce?"

Leah answered breathlessly, "Truce!"

Without another word, Cal reached down and took her mouth with his. Leah moaned with desire, and it stoked the fire already burning deep inside him. He pulled her onto the ground beside him, and she moved closer, almost on top of him as he explored her mouth with his tongue. Cal was almost crazy with wanting her, but he knew they couldn't stay here. Gruffly, he said, "Come with me." Leah followed willingly.

He grabbed their ski equipment in his left hand, never letting her hand out of his right one, and he pulled her quickly toward his cabin where they could get out of the cold and snow. Once inside, he dropped the poles and skis by the door and turned his full attention back to her. Cal took her hand and led her toward the massive fireplace, burning hot with wood and embers. He unzipped her coat then unzipped his own and hung them on two pegs beside the fireplace. Next, he sat down on the hearth and removed his boots, and Leah sat beside him and did the same. Cal stood up and went over to the chest against the wall near the deck and took out two enormous quilts, brought them over and spread them out in front of the fire. Then, Cal stood in front of Leah, her green eyes dark with passion, her cheeks red from desire, and unbuckled her bibs and peeled them down her small, lean body. She stepped out of them, and Cal tossed them aside. He quickly shed his own then reached for the bottom of her turtleneck and stripped it slowly over her head.

Cal looked at the whole of her, and he felt like he just might self-combust from the heat of the desire inside him. He sat down quickly onto the quilt, and pulled Leah to him. She was even more beautiful, supple and sexy than that vision of her in the window he had carried with him all these years, and his yearning for her was almost uncontrollable.

He stripped off her pink bra and underwear, and he kissed every inch of her from her mouth to her neck, her breasts and her hips. Leah moaned with desire and reached down to pull his lips back to hers. When she whispered, "I've been waiting for you my whole life, Cal," he was lost, and he slipped into her so perfectly that he almost exploded with desire immediately just being inside her. Leah stopped him, though, by rolling him over onto his back, and she rocked back on top of him, lost in desire. He sat up and took her breast into his mouth, and she moaned again, her toned arms gripping him, wet with sweat. Cal rode with her to the top of the wave for seemingly hours at the crest, until they were both almost delirious, and until lights flashed, the walls echoed and earth moved as their passion erupted together. Cal held her on top of him and stroked her beautiful, wild blond curls, now wet with sweat. Leah rested her cheek on his chest, and let a tear of happiness escape from the side of her eye. She knew this is where she belonged, and she smiled as she listened to the rhythm of Cal's heartbeat, heavy and fast. They lay spent together and stayed wrapped in each other's arms until exhaustion led them into a deep, dreamless sleep.

CHAPTER 32

Christmas morning dawned clear, cold—and very early—at the Haas house in Virginia Beach. Siobhan's boys were growing up, but they still woke at the crack of dawn every year and stormed downstairs to see what Santa Claus had brought them and placed under the tree. She and Robert intended to treasure every year they had together with the boys, knowing that in the blink of an eye they would be out of the house, off to college and out on their own. Christmas was a special time.

They had long-standing, albeit strange, family traditions that made them laugh, drew them closer, and created excitement. The most revered and competitive was their Christmas pickle tradition. Each year, late at night on Christmas Eve, Siobhan would hide a pickle ornament among the branches of their tree. When the boys, including Robert, woke on Christmas morning, they would race downstairs to be the first to find the pickle and claim the mystery gift.

The mystery gift was always something silly, inexpensive and pickle-related, but it was proudly used, worn or displayed for the entire following year until the next Christmas's prize was claimed. Over the years, the gifts included a tumbler with a green pickle on it, a tee shirt with "Mt. Olive Pickles" written on it, a stress ball in the shape of a pickle, a big pickle-shaped pillow and a white toboggan with a green pickle patch sewed on the front. The rest of the family envied the winner, and when their friends or neighbors would ask why they donned pickle shirts, hats, cups, etc., the family would just smile. The pickle tradition was a Haas family secret, and they chose to let others think they were weird. The secrecy was half the fun.

This year, Siobhan had found a pickle key chain when they were on vacation on the Outer Banks. She quite honestly had forgotten all about buying the gift until she saw it. Now, Chase, her oldest son, was parading around the den, swinging the keychain on his index finger, the envy of the Haas boys because he located the pickle in the middle of the bottom branch of the Christmas tree this morning. Siobhan giggled. These were the "Kodak moments" of her life.

Robert was now in the kitchen cooking their traditional Christmas brunch of country ham, grits, and scrambled eggs. The boys drank freshly-squeezed orange juice, while Siobhan and Robert had coffee. The difference this year, though, was that she had absolutely zero appetite, and Siobhan knew that was a big departure from her normally robust desire to eat.

She had also noticed that she was losing weight, and that she really couldn't afford to drop another pound. Siobhan sighed. *This whole election crap isn't worth the stress or my health*, she thought to herself, but she knew there was no backing out at this point. She only had to survive until March and then she would be able to get on a more regular schedule—a schedule even better than her life in private practice with vacations, weekends, and holidays to spend with her boys. Oh, how she wanted that schedule.

Siobhan walked into the kitchen and up to Robert who was finishing up the eggs. Everything else was finished, and he had even set the dining table with their Christmas china and glasses. She wrapped her arms around his waist and kissed him in the middle of the back. "You're asking for trouble, lady," he said in a darkly sexy voice.

"I can't ask for something I already own," she retorted playfully. Robert turned in her embrace, wrapped his arms around her with the wooden spoon still in hands, and kissed her deeply.

"*You* must be Vixen, my petite reindeer," he said. "Go sit down, and I will call the boys. You must eat to keep up your strength for those reindeer games you promised to play with me later on." Siobhan laughed at his silliness. She was the luckiest woman in the world.

Siobhan's happiness made her think about the photograph Leah sent to Meg, Toni and her in her most recent e-mail. Leah was in her pink bibs in an enormous amount of snow leaned back against a bank. She had a huge smile on her face, and her cheeks were pink from the cold or exertion or both. Whatever the reason, Leah looked simply radiant, and Siobhan was certain she had never seen her lovelier, more relaxed or happier. Siobhan also knew that only one thing on this earth could cause such a transformation. Leah Gibson was in love.

The thought made Siobhan smile, then tear up—she missed her best friend terribly. She wiped her eyes as the Haas herd of men rounded the corner. Siobhan would call Leah later today to catch up, wish her best friend Merry Christmas, and get some answers about this Cal person. She wished she could see Leah as she talked, eager to see that same photographed smile in person, and Siobhan hoped that Leah's happiness would last until Meg and Courtney's ceremony in late March. Siobhan sighed. Sure, she had to survive until March to get through this awful election, but this morning, it was counting the days until the reunion with her friends that made the springtime seem an incredibly long way away.

CHAPTER 33

Meg walked with the tray of steaming hot green tea, English waffles and fresh raspberries to the master bedroom where Courtney was still sleeping. As she approached the gigantic bed, Meg smiled as her lover began to stir. She put the tray down on the edge of the nightstand then sat down on the bed beside Courtney.

For a few minutes, she just wanted to watch her sleep. Meg studied Courtney's face. She was peaceful, content, and still—almost like a photograph, and the thought made her think of the photo Leah sent via e-mail recently. Leah, though awake, had the same expression Courtney had this morning. Reclined against a huge, white mound of snow, Leah was as relaxed and happy as Meg had ever seen her. She wondered what or who prompted Leah's transformation. She also wondered who snapped the photo.

Meg tenderly reached over and combed one of Courtney's dark curls out of her still-not-open eyes and whispered, "Merry Christmas."

Courtney smiled, stretched slowly then sat up beside Meg and put her head on her shoulder. After a short pause or a few more winks, she answered, "Merry Christmas to you, too."

Without further adieu, Meg reached beside her and brought the tray to the bed. "I made us a real Christmas breakfast," she said.

"Oh Meg, you shouldn't have, but I'm glad you did! I am starving," Courtney laughed when she saw the ensemble of food. She added, "Red raspberries and green tea—how festive!"

Meg laughed at her excitement then crawled under the covers beside her. They ate, talked about the heinous weather—cold, wet, windy and cloudy—and reminisced about Christmases past. Finally, Meg slid a small gift wrapped in brown paper with a beautiful red and gold bow toward Courtney. Courtney took it with a squeal of excitement, and hugged it to her chest then leaned over and kissed Meg on the side of the mouth. Meg smiled then said, "Open it! You don't even know what it is yet, silly."

"I don't care! I'm just so happy," Courtney responded then continued, "But I have something for you first!" She rolled over to the edge of her side of the bed, opened the cabinet door to the small chest that served as a nightstand on her side of the bed and retrieved a flat, rectangular box wrapped in candy cane striped paper with a simple red and white bow on it. Now fully awake, Courtney bounced back up onto the bed and sat up with her legs crossed Indian style across from Meg. She was beaming from ear to ear. "I want you to open yours first," she said.

"Ok, but we could open them both at the same time," Meg offered. Courtney, still smiling, slowly shook her head "no." Meg relented and carefully opened her present. Now it was her time to squeal. "Courtney!" she gushed, "You got my magazine!"

"Not just the current New Yorker," Courtney said, "But a year's subscription so you can read them—no—pour over them until next Christmas!"

Meg's eyes filled with tears, and she reached over and held her smart, sweet and good Courtney. "You're the gift I cherish every day," she said hoarsely. "Thank you, Courtney." She let go of her embrace then clapped her hands together softly and said, "Now it's your turn—open it!"

Meg was suddenly filled with anxiety, wondering what Courtney would think, and she sighed as quietly as she could to keep her doubts at bay. Time seemed to move in slow motion as Courtney removed the bow, tore the paper, and opened the lid to the box. Meg only realized she was holding her breath when Courtney's eyes immediately welled up with tears and spilled in torrents onto her cheeks. Then she exhaled.

Courtney removed the two round-trip tickets to London, rifled through the literature about the 17th century hotel in Stratford on Avon already booked, and when she saw the two theater tickets for the Royal Shakespeare Theater, she completely broke down and cried. Flinging herself into Meg's arms, she sobbed great tears of joy, unable to form words.

Meg stroked her hair gently, smiling with great joy herself, and asked, "Do you like it?"

"Oh Meg, I love it, but it's so much—I mean—can we afford to do this?" she rambled.

"Courtney, I promise, we can afford it," Meg said, holding Courtney's hand in her own. "Besides," she continued, "I can't afford *not* to take my literature-crazy bride to the birthplace of William Shakespeare!"

Suddenly, Courtney squealed again, and Meg laughed and pulled her onto the bed beside her. "Merry Christmas," she whispered in her ear.

"Oh, it is! It is," Courtney sighed, and they lay wrapped in each other's arms as the snow fell gently down on the world outside, and they basked in the glow of their happiness on their world within.

CHAPTER 34

"Let me say for the record, a white Christmas is completely overrated," Toni purred from the sun porch of their rented cottage on the beach in Aruba. It was early on Christmas morning, and she and Carter sat reclined on a double beach lounger, coffee in hand, waiting for the sun to rise. She and Carter woke up early, and while the girls and her mother slept they decided to spend a few quiet moments alone together celebrating their first Christmas.

Carter took her coffee mug and put it down on the small table beside him and pulled her on top of him. He kissed Toni's smiling lips gently then more deeply as just her very presence fanned the flames of his desire. "It's getting hot out here," he whispered. She pressed herself against him more closely.

"I'm just warming up," Toni cooed.

Carter kissed her deeply then said, "Merry Christmas, Angel. You are the best gift I've ever been given."

"Oh, Carter, I feel the same way. I'm so glad we found each other. I'm just so happy," she replied. "Everybody should be so lucky."

The comment sent Toni's thoughts to her friends. She missed them, or at least being able to see each other regularly. They were all spread out now, and they were all busy living their lives. Sure, she and Siobhan had been able to steal a lunch together a several times over the last couple of weeks, but the euphoria and glee from their girl weekends, Mexican dinners and spa getaways was difficult to recapture over an hour long lunch.

Now, Meg was in the Capitol working like a slave in her new home while Siobhan had her hands full with the upcoming election for the district court bench. Leah was in the mountains of North Carolina with her 92-year-old aunt. Who knew what she was doing with the time on her hands, Toni thought. It was Christmas, and Leah was hundreds of miles removed from her life of the last decade. Toni hoped she wasn't alone. Meg had Courtney, Siobhan had Robert, and she had Carter. What did Leah have? Toni sighed hard, and Carter asked, "What are you thinking that caused that sigh?"

Toni said quietly, "Leah Gibson, my best friend in the world, is miles away in a new home without her friends or a job. It's Christmas, and I just hope she's not lonely or sad or . . . I don't know, Carter."

"Well, I certainly don't know Leah like you do," he answered, "but I know that she is a survivor, that she is with family and in the only real home she ever knew in her childhood. Those things have to count for something."

Toni leaned up onto her elbow and stared out across the ocean, pondering his observation and reconsidering her worry. Perhaps, Leah was fine, happy even. The photo she had recently sent of her in the snow had surprised, even shocked Toni. Leah had a faraway look in her eye, but one of peace and satisfaction, of happiness. What sparked that look? Toni then rephrased her rhetorical question. Who sparked that look?

She looked squarely at Carter who was looking at her, waiting for her to respond. Toni smiled and lay back down on his chest and held him tightly. Finally, she said, "Those things do matter. I just hope that she finds someone who thinks she matters more than anything else in the world. Leah Gibson, above anybody else, deserves nothing less."

CHAPTER 35

Leah stirred slowly on Christmas morning before sunrise. With her eyes still closed and her mind somewhere about halfway between sleep and wake, she greeted the morning with the same gentle smile that she wore to bed last night. Without leaving the warmth of her thick quilted bed, she looked up at the frosty window above her bed out of one eye. She was welcomed back to her high country home with a white Christmas, and Leah felt like a childlike excitement in her chest.

It was still dark outside, and Pander slept at her feet in a heap, exhausted from all of the excitement in the house last night preparing for the holiday celebration. Leah wrapped her arms around her waist, but the gesture proved to be an unfulfilling substitute for Cal's strong arms holding her close. She stretched slowly and opened her eyes. Was it possible to be any happier than she was this morning? Leah didn't think so.

She knew she was never going to go back to sleep so Leah decided to get out of bed, go downstairs and make a light breakfast for Aunt Fi and herself. As she padded down the steps, she simply absorbed the quiet, comfort and warmth of the house that was now her home. She brewed a pot of coffee, poured herself a huge mug full then walked softly to the den and turned on the multi-colored strands of Christmas lights on the tree.

The room was transformed, appearing both magical and spiritual, and Leah shivered at the sight. The myriad of colors shone on the walls, reflected off of the new blanket of snow stacked outside against the window, and sparkled against the shiny ornaments hanging on the tree. Leah lovingly touched the presents underneath as she sat cross-legged beside it with her back against the ottoman, and thought about the last month of her life.

She had no local friends, and she had no career. What Leah had now, though, was Cal Cunningham, the only man she had ever truly loved. She also had Aunt Fi, the only family she could call her own since her mother died. Amazingly, Leah was happier than she could remember being since she was a child.

Living with Aunt Fi was incredible. She was funny, industrious and loving, and she had opened up her home to her wayward great-niece Leah with no questions asked. In addition to all those wonderful traits, Aunt Fi was never judgmental—not of Leah or anyone else.

And Cal—oh, Cal—she couldn't get enough of him. Whenever Leah was around him or even when she thought of him, her stomach did flips. She was certain everybody could tell that she couldn't stop thinking about tearing his clothes off and making wild, passionate love to the man. Leah was sure she had never blushed as many times in her life combined as she had in the last couple of weeks. *I'm a shameless vamp*, Leah thought with a smile on her face.

She leaned her head back against the ottoman and closed her eyes. Last Christmas she was at Siobhan's—alone—celebrating with her friends and their families. Yes, she missed her friends terribly, but now Leah longed to see them so they could meet Cal, so she could tell them everything, so they could see how happy she was.

"Goodness gracious, gal," Aunt Fi said from behind her, "Santie Claus hasn't come to this house in years! Why're you up so early, Leah?"

Leah stood and walked over to her aunt and kissed her playfully on the cheek. She said, "I wasn't looking for Santa Claus, my dear, I was waiting on you to get up so we could eat breakfast then open presents."

"Well, the best present you can give me right now is a cup of that coffee," Aunt Fi replied.

Leah laughed and walked ahead of her to pull out a chair. Then, she reached into the cabinet and pulled a Christmas mug out, filled it to the top and handed it to her aunt. "Good to the last drop," Leah said. "What would you like for breakfast?"

Aunt Fi giggled and answered, "Oh no, I have a special surprise for us for breakfast, little one. It is a family tradition! Bet you didn't know we had any of those, huh?"

Leah was certain her mouth was hanging open from shock, but she finally managed, "Uh, no, I really didn't know we had any Christmas traditions—except Christmas Eve church service last night."

Aunt Fi sighed with pleasure and said, "Come over here for a minute and sit with me. I'll tell you all about our Cheese Cloud tradition," then she laughed a silly cackle for good measure.

"Cheese Cloud—what on earth is Cheese Cloud? I'm going to assume we eat it," Leah stated warily.

Aunt Fi got up and went to the refrigerator and pulled out a large dish with bread, milk, cheese and seasoned salt in it. She turned around with as much flourish as a 92-year-old could muster and said, "I present you with Cheese Cloud . . . even though it's not cooked yet." Without another word, she tottered over to the stove, turned it on the proper setting and walked back to the table to finish her coffee.

"Well, I've got to tell you, Aunt Fi—that was a letdown," Leah replied good-naturedly. "I was hoping for old family stories about making pastries or special Christmas tarts or you and Gran Belle trying to outdo each other."

Aunt Fi shook her head and laughed softly then said, "Cheese Cloud is as good as it gets. When Belle and I were little girls, Ma would always have Cheese Cloud baked and waiting on us when we got up on Christmas morning. Back then, Ma made the bread and the milk, butter and cheese were from our dairy farming neighbors down the street. We bartered beef for dairy. The only thing Ma bought was the seasoned salt. The dish was so good yet so simple that your grandmother and I never stopped making it. I'm glad I got to make it for you. I haven't made it since the Christmas before Belle died."

Leah was overcome by emotion, and she sat speechless looking at Aunt Fi, tears trickling down her cheeks. Finally, she responded, "Aunt Fi, that's one of the most beautiful Christmas stories I've ever heard. Thank you." She reached over and took her aunt's diminutive hand into her own. Aunt Fi squeezed her hand gently then got up to put their breakfast in the stove.

When she sat back down, her eyes were shiny with tears as well. She reached over for Leah's hand again then said, "God not only sent me the best present in the world, he sent me a Christmas miracle when you came home. You have made me the happiest old woman in these hills."

"Aunt Fi, I'm just sorry that I haven't come back before now," Leah confessed. "I'm a pretty lousy niece since I didn't visit you for almost 15 years."

"Nonsense," Aunt Fi protested. "I didn't want you to come for a visit. I wanted you to come home—and you did. God has a way with timing things that we can't understand. You weren't ready to come home, but maybe I wasn't ready for you either. I know one thing for sure—Cal Cunningham wasn't man enough for you until now," she added and giggled conspiratorially.

"I don't know about that, but I do know I never got him out of my system, got over him or stopped thinking about him," Leah said. "I just never could understand how he could get over me, why he didn't wait for me, or why he didn't want me." Leah sighed heavily.

Aunt Fi didn't miss a beat when she answered, "Oh, those are easy questions to answer, Leah. Men are stupid. Well, they are idiots until they turn about 30 anyway," she said lively. "That boy loved you even when he married that dreadful girl from Boone. Only a fool could miss how he stared at you on his own wedding day. Cal just got sideways with that one. You were gone, and she was here. She put out, and he loved sex. He just thought that meant he loved her. See, men are stupid," Aunt Fi finished then got up to check on their Christmas Cheese Cloud. When she sat back down, she looked over at a rather shell-shocked Leah and the look made Aunt Fi laugh. She asked Leah, "Isn't it one of the great mysteries why I never married?"

Leah laughed with her then replied, "I think it is a mystery, Aunt Fi. You are so smart, hard-working and good—and you are one of the most beautiful women I've ever known. Did you not ever meet Mr. Wonderful?"

"You my dear are either blind or a liar, but thank you. Oh, my youth was such a long time ago, you don't want to hear about ancient times, my dear," Aunt Fi answered softly.

"Oh, but I do! There's nothing I would rather hear from you than our history, your history, my family history," Leah implored her gently.

Aunt Fi started to get up, but Leah stopped her. Instead, Leah got up from the table, put on the thick homemade oven mitt and pulled the aromatic and fluffy Cheese Cloud from the oven and put it on the table between their seats. Simultaneously, they inhaled deeply then laughed because they were so much alike. Leah got two Christmas plates off the counter, two forks and a serving spoon and refilled their coffee mugs then she sat back down at the table.

As she spooned each of them a serving of breakfast, she insisted again by saying, "Tell me, Aunt Fi."

Aunt Fi shook her head softly, a tender smile on her lips. Finally, she began, "Oh, my dear, I haven't even said his name in almost twenty years—James Cecil Gibson . . . Jaycee Gibson to all of us."

"*Gibson*? As in Leah Gibson," Leah inquired curiously.

"Yes, the same—Jaycee was your grandfather's older brother, and he was my first and only love. We met at a corn shucking of all places," Aunt Fi chuckled. She had a faraway look in her eyes, but she continued, "I knew the second I saw him he was the one for me and I for him, and I told Belle so that very night."

"Tell me about him, Aunt Fi," Leah said.

"Oh, he was young and so handsome. He was tall, and when he stood beside me, we looked absolutely ridiculous together," she said. "But he had this way of taking the ridiculous and making it special. He would tell me we fit each other because we were like two oddly cut pieces of the same log, him too long, me too short so together we were just right." She paused to sigh, obviously seeing him in her mind's eye. "He had this gorgeous dark hair that hung thick and straight, and he parted it down the middle. When all the other boys were loading their locks up with lard, Jaycee let his hang loose and wild and free—that was just his way.

"He was strong too, just like your young Cal, and he loved this land. Jaycee and your grandfather, George, bought this farm with the intention of growing burley tobacco, but then the war came calling," Aunt Fi said quietly. "Your grandfather wanted to enlist, but Jaycee convinced him that he should enlist first since he was older, and that one of them had to stay at the farm. So, that's what he did.

"I remember him coming to the house the day he enlisted like it was yesterday. It was January, but it wasn't really cold, and he asked my mother if he could take me for a walk. I watched Ma look him in the eye, and she saw that he loved me so she said yes. Mind you, Ma never said yes to anything we thought was fun since that was the devil's handiwork to her. Anyway, we walked down the mountain and over to this outcropping of rocks above a little run of rapids in Buffalo Creek. He brought a blanket and spread it out on the grass near the creek bank. There, he told me he enlisted, and that he wanted to serve his country, that he felt like it was his duty. It was a different age, and I knew he had to go to war, but I was scared, and I told him so.

"Jaycee held me against his chest and reassured me over and over that my tears and fears were silly and that when he came back we would be married. He turned me around to look up the hollow across the meadow to where his farm was. He told me to close my eyes and when I did he described our future home in such detail and with such feeling that I could see it in my mind. Then, he took this beautiful gold band out of his pocket and placed it on my ring finger." Pausing for a moment, Aunt Fi sighed with nostalgia, but not sadness then she continued, "He said to me, 'Fiona, with this ring I thee wed.' Well, I have never been so speechless in my entire life, child. Finally, though, I found my voice and I answered him, 'James Cecil, with this ring I thee wed.' So the way we saw it, we were man and wife before God and each other. We pledged our eternal, undying love for each other that evening and consummated our marriage. We knew we didn't need a piece of paper to make our union official.

"Jaycee shipped off the next morning, ultimately headed to fight the Japanese in the Pacific as a Marine. Belle and George drove us to the train station in Jefferson. He and George shook hands, and Jaycee gave Belle a hug. Finally, he turned back to me, and I could see in his eyes that he didn't want to leave me, but I knew he had to go so I stepped right over to him and kissed him passionately and unabashedly—he was my husband, after all. As the train pulled away from the station, I stood on the platform and waved goodbye to him.

I remember standing there looking down the tracks long after the train had disappeared around the mountainside, pretending to still see his face looking and smiling at me.

He wrote to me every other day, and I did the same. The first letter he sent me included a picture of him in his uniform. Oh, Jaycee Gibson was one handsome soldier, Leah. Those letters were my life, my solace and my sanity in 1942. I raced to the mailbox every day, hoping for a letter to read and re-read again and again.

"Then, in the middle of August of 1942, the letters just stopped. After the first couple days, Ma and Belle tried to assure me that the postal service was simply unreliable in the field, on the ship from the other side of the world. After a week, I knew something awful had happened, and I was simply inconsolable. Belle and George encouraged me to pray, to hope and to believe. Ma would just pat me on the hand. Finally, on August 29, two uniformed soldiers pulled up to George's house and got out of the car. Belle and I were in the kitchen canning figs and pickling beets while George was in the shed sharpening his plough. Well, the gentlemen saw George first and approached him at the door. As they walked to the front porch slowly and solemnly, Belle saw them before I did, and this small whimper, almost a yelp, escaped from her throat.

"When I turned around to see what had got into her, I saw them too, and I simply dissolved onto the nearest chair, my head spinning and my extremities numb. One of the men was a chaplain, and as George came to the door frame of the kitchen, his eyes were shiny with tears, welled up and threatening to spill over. He said quietly, 'Fi, Jaycee was killed in battle at Guadalcanal on August 8.' Unable to say anything else, he simply bowed his head and leaned against the door frame for support.

"The chaplain came over as I wept at the kitchen table and placed his hand on my shoulder. Beside me, he gently put the parcel with all of Jaycee's personal belongings and said sincerely, 'We truly are sorry for your loss. Sergeant James Cecil Gibson died honorably serving his country. He was a brave soldier.'

"I read his journal and all of our letters incessantly. His entries about the war were awful, but he always found something beautiful to say before he went to sleep each night. I would conjure up his face as I read his words, and through my tears, I felt oddly comforted. I honestly believe his words to me and our expressions of love for each other sustained me through the funeral and the dark months ahead. I loved him in a way that was irreplaceable, and I never regretted my decision to stay single. Jaycee Gibson was the one true love of my life. Of course, I believe he's waiting on me in heaven, along with Belle and George," Aunt Fi finished, and looked over at Leah who was overcome by emotion so great that her tears streamed steadily down her cheeks, under her chin and onto the table. Aunt Fi patted her hand, "I'm sorry, my dear—please forgive the musings of a sentimental old lady on Christmas morning."

"Oh, Aunt Fi, you are not an old lady—you are an amazing, strong, inspiring woman," Leah said, sniffling her tears away. "Thank you so much for sharing that story with me. I've always admired you, and now I'm simply in awe of you."

"Pshaw! Eat the rest of that Cheese Cloud before it gets cold," Aunt Fi insisted. "Then we can call the Cunningham men-folks and get them over here to eat the rest of it and open presents."

"This stuff is incredible," Leah said as she stuffed her mouth with the last bite of the Christmas morning delicacy. "I've got to make sure I know how to make it for us next year."

Aunt Fi took the last bite of her breakfast onto her fork and put it into her mouth then she smiled and said, "This tradition never got old like I did."

Leah smiled as she stood and collected the plates and forks and took them to the sink. She told Aunt Fi to go get comfortable in the den. After she washed up the dishes, refilled her coffee mug with the remaining coffee, and covered the rest of the Cheese Cloud, she called Mr. C. He answered on the first ring and said, "Merry Christmas!"

"Merry Christmas, Mr. C! Are you ready to come eat breakfast and open your gifts? I know you have been good this year. It is Cal Cunningham I am not so sure made Santa's list," she teased.

"Oh, he's here—worse than a five-year-old, Leah. He's outside at the shed just now. We'll be there in about 15 minutes," Mr. C finished.

Leah was positively giddy with excitement as she waited, and she retreated into the den with Aunt Fi. She sighed with delight, and Aunt Fi laughed softly. "He'll be here in a minute, my dear."

"I know," Leah said wistfully, "I was just thinking that this is the best Christmas morning I have ever had. This house is almost magical this time of year, Aunt Fi. I'm so glad you invited me to stay."

"Don't be silly, child. This house belongs to you, and it is and always has been your home. I am just thankful you figured that fact out before I was dead and gone," Aunt Fi said.

The Cunninghams drove up outside as if on cue. Leah stood and had to restrain herself from running to the door. She opened the door for the present-laden men and offered to help them. Of course, they protested mightily, and Cal accused her playfully of trying to figure out what was inside the presents. Leah rolled her eyes and Cal planted a kiss on the side of her mouth. She just smiled and held the door as they came in from the cold.

While Mr. C went into the den with Aunt Fi, Cal stayed in the kitchen with Leah and stole up behind her as she made a fresh pot of coffee. He wrapped his arms around her waist and leaned down to kiss the back of her neck. Leah thoughts strayed to the unholy, and she leaned back into him, resting her head under his chin. When she turned on the coffee to brew, she turned around and put her arms up around his neck.

"Are you trying to warm up the kitchen," she asked provocatively.

Cal leaned down to her ear and growled lowly then answered, "I'm trying to keep from burning it down."

Leah thought she would self-combust with desire, but she knew the kitchen was not the place for such frolic either. She kissed him then said, "Keep that appetite for later, Tiger."

She shooed Cal to the den with his father and Aunt Fi then she spooned generous portions of Cheese Cloud onto plates and warmed them quickly in the microwave. Leah carried the men's plates to the den so they could eat and talk easily and comfortably and so Aunt Fi wouldn't have to get back up to go to the kitchen.

When she walked into the room, the others were whispering conspiratorially, and Leah cocked an eyebrow in their direction and said, "Do tell."

"Nothing to tell," Aunt Fi said. "We were just discussing your Christmas presents. Wait a minute—where's the other family member?"

Cal and his dad and Leah exchanged looks with each other, all confused by Aunt Fi's question. "Who do you mean, Aunt Fi?" Leah asked.

"You're a bad parent, Leah! Santa's going to remember your lapse. Where is Pander?" Aunt Fi asked.

Leah laughed then answered, "I'm sure she is still chasing kitties in her dreams. She was exhausted from all of the festivities last night. My furry girl didn't budge when I got out of bed this morning. I'll wake her up." Leah walked to the foot of the stairs and called, "Pander, come on, girl! It is time for breakfast!" Seconds later, the "click-click-click" of her dog's feet on the hardwood floors could be heard before she began barking and barreling down the steps, obviously famished.

After everybody had eaten and the dishes had been cleared, Cal handed out presents to everybody. Once the base of the Christmas tree was emptied of gifts, they took turns opening them. Aunt Fi went first.

Mr. C gave her some beautiful white bath towels and a bottle of her favorite cologne from Hilda down at the local drugstore. Cal gave her a new coffee mug with a picture of the church on it. She opened Leah's gifts last, and when she saw them, she gasped with surprise. When she found her voice, she said, "Oh my dear, wherever did you find these? I haven't seen them for probably forty years!"

Leah smiled broadly and volunteered, "I went through the hall closet while you were at the doctor's office with Mr. C, and I found them in a box. The photographs were worn, but they were so beautiful and fun that I knew you would enjoy looking at them."

"Oh, I do," Aunt Fi said as she held the stretched-canvas pictures toward Cal and Mr. C. The picture on her left was of a much younger Fi and Belle, probably from the 30's grinning and hugging each other in front of an old barn. The other picture was of the farm from the meadow below up the hill. The house was new and gleamed against the green of the mountains behind it. Made in the spring, all of the trees were in full bloom. "You've got work to do this afternoon, Tom. These pictures have to be put up on my wall," Aunt Fi said.

"Yes ma'am, they are too beautiful to put anywhere else," Mr. C answered.

Mr. C went next. Aunt Fi gave him an entire box of canned goodies—vegetable soup, pickled beets, apple butter, fig preserves and yellow squash. He exclaimed, "Yippee! I hit the jackpot!" Leah and Aunt Fi laughed at his excitement.

Next he opened the big box from Leah. When he saw the size of it, he told Cal, "I told you I had been very good this year." Cal snorted and rolled his eyes. When Mr. C pulled out the North Carolina State University blanket, he was speechless, though, and Cal was obviously envious of the gift. Mr. C picked it up and looked at every square. Finally, he answered, "My dear, you have touched my heart. I love it." He stood and kissed Leah on the cheek. She beamed.

Mr. C held the blanket on his lap and shot Cal a warning, "Don't you even think about using my blanket, son. Boys have been disowned for lesser transgressions." Leah giggled at his melodrama.

Cal went next to open his gifts. Aunt Fi gave him a homemade cane basket for his kindling. He knew the gift took many days and nights of work, but he loved it. Cal reached over and kissed Aunt Fi on the cheek. Leah would have sworn Aunt Fi blushed.

Next, he pulled the gift from Leah toward him. His gift was large, too. *Man, it is heavy,* he thought, and he tried not to sigh with sadness that he didn't get a blanket. When he pulled off the paper and bow, he opened the lid to find a bag of rocks on top of some paper. Leah was chuckling, and Cal was confused. He took the rocks off of the paper then removed the paper. Underneath, a soft, red and black material greeted him and Cal let out a "Woo-hoo!" as he pulled out his own N.C. State blanket. He playfully replied to his father, "I don't need to use your blanket because I have my own!"

Cal took the blanket and wrapped it around Leah's shoulders, causing her to say, "I'm tainted! It was hard enough to sew all of those vile pieces together. Keep your blanket to yourself, mister." Cal pulled the blanket with Leah in it toward him and kissed her squarely on the lips. She smiled into his eyes. *He likes it,* she thought.

"I love it," Cal said genuinely. "It's your turn now!"

"No, first, let's give Pander her presents," Leah implored, and at the sound of her name, her dog jumped up from beside Aunt Fi's feet. Leah gave Pander a huge bone that Aunt Fi ordered from the butcher, and she slipped a new sweater over the mildly protesting beagle's head. Pander was obviously more interested in the bone, and she pulled the big bone back to her spot at Aunt Fi's feet. "Why, you're not my dog at all," Leah cried.

Aunt Fi piped up, "That's right—Pander's my girl now!"

Leah faked a sigh with a sadness she sure didn't feel then squealed, "My turn!"

First, she opened a square box just smaller than a shoe box that was wrapped lovingly in brown paper with a big green bow from Aunt Fi. As she pulled the paper away, Leah held a beautiful wooden box with a mother-of-pearl inlay on the top. She opened the lid to find about 25 recipe cards handwritten by Aunt Fi. Tears filled Leah's eyes as she noticed that Aunt Fi had put the recipe for Cheese Cloud on top. Leah got up and hugged her aunt's neck and kissed her on the cheek. Aunt Fi smiled then said, "Now you don't have any excuses to keep you from making me anything I ask for to eat!"

Leah laughed and replied, "I finally have a place for all of those other recipe cards you sent me over the years. Aunt Fi, I love it."

Next, Leah opened a small box from Cal. Inside, Leah discovered beautiful Carolina Blue stone earrings. She grinned and said, "See, you are coming around!"

"Over my dead body," Cal chuckled.

Last, Leah picked up an envelope with her name on it. Inside, she recognized Mr. C's handwriting on the note which read, "I couldn't wrap the blasted things so they are on the bed of the truck. Enjoy!"

Excited, Leah leaped up, grabbed Cal's hand and dragged him outside to the truck. When she got close enough to see inside the bed of the truck, she screamed with joy. Mr. C had made her two window boxes for her potting shed. He had painted them white so that the flowers in full bloom would not be overpowered by the paint. She could not have been happier, and Leah jumped up and down then wrapped her arms around Cal's neck and planted a kiss on his smiling mouth.

"Those are from dad," he laughed and continued, "But don't go hugging and kissing on him this way or he'll likely have to be airlifted to the hospital. I'm glad you like everything, Leah. I do have one more gift for you, though."

Leah said, "Cal, the earrings are enough!"

"You haven't seen what I got you yet," he responded. "You might not like it."

"Don't be silly," Leah said, "I like everything."

They walked hand-in-hand to the cab of the truck where Cal reached in and retrieved a rather large gift, wrapped in red and green foil with a huge red bow. He put it under his arm and grabbed her hand then led her toward their stump chair. As they sat down, Cal leaned against the chair back and pulled Leah down to sit in front of him. Quietly, he said, "Open it."

She did, tearing the paper down the back and sliding the paper off of the box. Finally, she broke the tape holding the sides of the box and opened the lid. Once she pulled the tissue paper aside, Leah lifted out a soft pink fleece dress with a Johnny collar with a light blue and pink pattern that matched the turn-back sleeve cuffs. It was stunningly beautiful and Leah had never seen anything quite like it. She would have bought this dress any day of any week of any year in any boutique. She whispered, "Oh my goodness, Cal. This is the prettiest dress I have ever seen."

Cal smiled and pulled her back against him then he said, "No, it is not the prettiest, but it came the closest to capturing the vision that you were in that pink dress fifteen years ago when I saw you last. I have never forgotten how ethereal you looked in pink. I had Lettie McGowan make this for you. I picked out the fabric and told her what I wanted. Ms. Fi gave me your size."

Leah was overwhelmed at his thoughtfulness, and she hugged the dress to her chest. She was overcome by emotion and turned into Cal's arms. "I don't know what to say, Cal. Thank you for the best Christmas of my life," she said through her tears of joy.

"Merry Christmas, Angel," Cal whispered into her head of curls. "I hope this is first in a long line of best Christmases I get to spend with you."

CHAPTER 36

Marissa Montgomery passed the sign that read "Welcome to West Jefferson" on a gray, blustery March morning with a sigh of disgust. As she fully expected, nothing in this boring, little town had changed. *I might as well be driving through a cemetery*, she thought.

She had always hated the monotony and the quaintness of the town. While the other townspeople deemed their involvement in other people's lives as "neighborly" or "helpful," Marissa knew they really just wanted to stick their noses into everybody else's business, especially hers.

The fact that she was here again made her stomach turn. She sighed loudly. Marissa already yearned for the excitement and the pulse of Nashville. She longed for the personal anonymity of the big city at the same time she dreamed of fame and fortune. *Thank God my stay in this dead little town is only temporary*, she mused.

As she rolled down the quiet streets of West Jefferson, she passed the hardware store. Oh, how she despised that hole in the wall! Marissa knew she had given the best years of her life to that dump, all the while saving enough money for her shot at stardom. Well, she had learned her lesson. This time, she would move in then move out quickly, collecting her inheritance from her recently-departed daddy's estate as soon as she reconciled with Cal Cunningham. Why her dear old dad made that demand was beyond her. He was never really that fond of Cal. Her late father probably just wanted her to come back home to the hills, but Marissa knew if she stayed here she would be as dead as he was. She intended to play the role of her life as the penitent, prodigal wife, though. Then, in less than fifteen minutes after the cold, hard cash her father bequeathed to her was in her possession, Marissa Montgomery was going to blow out of this town like a tornado.

She had no intention of being married again, especially to Country Cal, but she did admittedly get turned on by the thought of having hot, crazy sex with him. He was and always had been good in the sack, and Marissa should know since she was almost an expert. She had had her share of one-night stands, often bartering sex for a place to sleep or engaging in groupie sex hoping it would boost her singing career in Nashville, but Marissa was always left unfulfilled and empty.

She had also resorted to using sex as a weapon. Once, when a record producer told her that she had to put out before he would listen to her sing, she did—only to discover that the bastard had given her crabs and then refused to let her into his studio. About a year later, Marissa ran into him again out with his friends. When she saw the wedding ring on his finger, she saw an opportunity for payback. Turning on the sex appeal, she fell all over him and kept the liquor flowing. Finally, she managed to get him to her hotel room and while he was in the bathroom, she took his cell phone, dialed his home and pressed "send" just as he came running to her seductive beckoning from the bed. After a very loud, albeit short, roll in the sheets, Marissa knew she had completed her revenge. When he discovered what she had done, it was too late, and Marissa simply laughed at him as he skulked out of her room to go beg for forgiveness. He was pitiful.

Not that she wanted to hurt Cal. Unfortunately, he was just a means to an end, just an obstacle in her quest for the life she truly deserved. Her father's estate would ensure her future. She only had to meet the requirement in his will of "reconciling" with her estranged husband. In Marissa's interpretation and that of her attorney, she only had to try, not to succeed, and try is all she intended to do.

While March had brought warmer weather to Nashville causing daffodils to spring up and trees to bloom almost overnight, the North Carolina High Country was still in hibernation, frozen and gray. Marissa was sure there was not enough moisturizer in a five-county area to keep her skin from getting dry and flaky.

She looked at her watch. It was only 6 a.m., and on a late winter Wednesday, the town had yet to stir into its regular, slow pace. She would just drive on over to Cal's house and surprise him—and she was certain that is exactly what he would be. Marissa wondered if he was still in bed or at least still in his boxer shorts, and the memory of Cal's body made her hot. She pushed harder on the car's accelerator then opened her driver's window slightly to cool down. Marissa smiled as she turned onto Buffalo Road. Reconciling had its benefits.

CHAPTER 37

Leah woke early on Wednesday, excited that she had a meeting at the Ashe County Agricultural Extension Agency with its director about an business idea that had been circulating in her mind now for a couple of months. The last frost would likely be gone in just over a month, and Leah was anxious to plant the various gardens that she and Aunt Fi had planned.

They had laid out an herb garden, a vegetable garden and a large cut flower garden. In January, she and Aunt Fi had planted a myriad of bulbs in the window boxes at the potting shed. In addition, Cal had taken extra care with the orchard, pruning the trees last year after they had stopped bearing fruit and cutting back the berry bushes and grapevines. Leah said another prayer for a bountiful season as she sat down at the computer to go over her projections, business plan and resume' one last time.

In January, she finally got internet service at the farm house. Aunt Fi didn't know what the internet was, but she told Leah that if she needed something to help them stay organized and more easily order plants and supplies then it was worth the investment. To help pay the bill, Leah was working with Cal at the hardware store three days a week, Monday, Wednesday and Friday, from 10 to 2 during the week and other times when he needed her to fill in for him and the two others employees. Mr. C stayed with Aunt Fi when she was at work.

Leah reviewed the spreadsheets one last time, and satisfied they were like she wanted them, she printed them and put them in her portfolio folder. Aunt Fi was still asleep, and Leah quickly left her a note that she had left her some fresh coffee in the pot. She checked her make-up and smoothed her skirt then Leah grabbed her purse and headed to meet Charles Moretz in town.

As she passed Cal's house, she noticed a car in his driveway, and Leah wondered who would be at his house this early on a Wednesday morning. Cal was a pillar in the community, and people relied on him for just about everything. While his dependability kept him busy and profitable at the hardware store, it also infringed upon his privacy more than he liked. Leah smiled as she thought about him being grouchy for having to get up even earlier than usual. She was certain he would tell her all about it today at the hardware store.

She drove the short distance into town, noticing along the way that the trees were finally beginning to bud. Leah sighed with delight. She had always loved the springtime and its promise of new life, new beginnings. This year, the spring was even more special since the new life and new beginning it heralded was hers.

At just before 7 a.m., Leah turned into the parking lot of the agency. As early as it was, the lights inside the one-level brick building were already on. She was grateful that Mr. Moretz had agreed to meet her before regular business hours so she could get back to the farmhouse to check on Aunt Fi then get to the hardware store by 10. As she approached the door, Leah realized that she was nervous, so she took two deep breaths to calm herself. Telling herself that she had a solid business plan, she knocked on the wooden door.

When the door opened, Leah was surprised to see a man in his late 30's, not the weathered old farmer she expected. When he smiled, he was handsome, and he instantly set her at ease. Leah asked cheerfully, "Are you Mr. Moretz?"

He laughed heartily then answered, "Lord, no! I'm Charles—Chip when you get to know me better. Mr. Moretz is my dad! Come on in! I'm sorry I'm so excited, but when I got your e-mail describing your plan I envisioned an old maid! You are Leah Gibson, right?"

Leah smiled broadly. She already liked Chip Moretz. She replied to him, "I am Leah Gibson. So you didn't like my plan?"

"No! I didn't say I didn't like it. I think it is interesting, but you are going to have to tell me more about it. When did you learn to garden, can, cook, sew, quilt and crochet? You must have started in the cradle, my child," he said playfully.

Leah nodded then answered, "It wasn't long after the cradle, Chip. My grandmother and great-aunt taught me all of these wonderful things in the summers from the time I was six or so until I went off to college. I just took a more than decade-long detour into banking before I figured out that was not the smartest career choice."

"Nonsense," he responded enthusiastically, "You could never have put together this package without that background. Your projections of income and expenses and your cost estimates are sound, even conservative, but your business description sells the idea. Tell me all the details."

For the next few minutes, Leah elaborated on all of her plans for her farm-based business, and when Chip said he loved it, Leah was giddy. "Really?" she asked. "I'm thrilled to hear you say so. I have a tight-knit group of girlfriends that I believe would love to vacation in our lovely mountain paradise as a group. If I kept the wine flowing, they would love to learn skills they could take back home with them," Leah stated. "As a matter-of-fact, I intend to make my circle of friends my guinea pigs!"

Chip laughed. "Well, I can't think of anybody better than friends to test the idea," he said. "Just think, they will either go home with new skills or one hell of a hangover or both!"

Leah laughed with him. For the first time in many months, even years, she had a way forward. She would run this whole idea by Aunt Fi then Cal and then Mr. C. With their help, Leah Gibson might finally get on her feet financially and at the same time love her work. This business would be her life, and she realized she wanted it far more than any success she had ever enjoyed as a banker.

Chip smiled at her and asked, "Would you like to go get a cup of coffee, Leah?"

Leah smiled back then looked at her watch. It was already almost 8 a.m., and she needed to get back to check on Aunt Fi then get to work. She sighed then said, "Oh Chip, I'd love to go, but I need to get back to the farm and check on my aunt. Can I have a rain check? I appreciate your interest, and as this plan progresses, I'd love your feedback."

"You bet, Leah," Chip answered. "Now, go! Your aunt needs you and I need another cup of coffee. I'll see you soon!"

CHAPTER 38

Siobhan let the hot water from the showerhead flow down her body. The wet heat soothed her, and she knew if she kept her eyes closed too long, she might just fall asleep standing up. She was exhausted, but Siobhan was elated. Last night, after all the election votes were tallied, she had been declared the winner of the hard-fought race for a seat on the district court bench. Today, she got to go the courthouse and check out her chambers. Siobhan was excited about the day as well as very thankful she didn't have a calendar call as an attorney this morning. At least for four more years, those days were over.

Both the campaigning for election and the brutal winter had taken a toll on her, and Siobhan had ignored her health by not exercising regularly, not eating well and not getting enough sleep. She looked gaunt, sallow and soft—none of which she considered to be good. Siobhan had also noticed concern etched on Robert's face every time he looked at her.

She sighed and picked up the jar of bath salts Leah had given her for Christmas and opened the lid. The lemon scent filled the air, and Siobhan breathed in the aroma with delight. Siobhan conjured up her best friend's smiling face. She couldn't wait to see Leah next month over Spring Break in Washington DC for Courtney and Meg's civil union ceremony. Just the thought of Leah Gibson made her grin, and through their exchange of e-mails and photographs, she had seen a real transformation in her best friend in just over four months' time. Siobhan knew the mysterious Cal had something to do with Leah's happiness.

She shook a tablespoon of the salts onto her saturated washcloth and smoothed it over her arms, neck, stomach, legs and chest. Then Siobhan started at her neck and slowly worked the salt over her skin to rejuvenate and soften her skin. She had almost depleted her supply from Christmas and used it stingily to ensure she didn't run out of the miracle product until she got more from Leah. Siobhan had already e-mailed Leah and requested more lemon, mint and vanilla—the salts were that good!

As she finished her legs and stomach, she worked the last of the salt on her chest and massaged it around her breasts. As much weight as she had lost, her breasts were still almost freakishly large, and Siobhan snickered thinking about Robert long ago dubbing them her "twins." Oh how she loved that crazy fool of a husband.

Happy and refreshed, she hung the washcloth over the towel bar. Finally, Siobhan ran her hands over her body as she turned around to rinse off, feeling the smooth, slick residue of the salt on her skin. Suddenly her right thumb hit a sore spot on her left breast, making her jump and wince in pain. In that instant, time moved in slow motion, and her breathing became heavy. Forcing herself to carefully try to touch the spot again, Siobhan found it by the hard pebble-like bump under her skin in the heavy flesh at the bottom of her breast. She felt dizzy. She felt sick. She leaned against the shower wall.

Siobhan's hands were shaking, and she was completely immobilized with fear. She wanted to cry out to Robert, to God, but she couldn't move, couldn't make a sound. The water continued to flow hot over her skin, but she was cold and shivering, terror seizing her body as clarity seized her mind. She started crying then. Having just been declared the victor in the exhausting battle with her political opponent, Siobhan realized that her real fight might just be beginning. The outcome of this fight, though, would not determine what she did in the foreseeable future, but whether or not she would have one.

CHAPTER 39

Leah turned off of Buffalo Road onto the long, winding road up into the hollow. As she drove past the driveway to Cal's house, she noticed that the stranger's car was still there. Cal's pickup was too. Leah wondered what was going on. She pulled her cell phone out of her purse, quickly looking to see whether or not he had called her. She sighed with disappointment. He had not called. It was a few minutes after 8 a.m.

The morning was chilly but clear, and as Leah drove, she noticed vestiges of spring on the hills as the dogwoods leaves had begun to sprout in just the last week or so. The remaining snow from the particularly cold winter was now pushed back into the deeper shadows and crevices. She pulled up in front of the farmhouse, got out and first walked to the potting shed. She smiled as she peeked into the window boxes Mr. C had made. The green tips of the tulips she planted in January were just beginning to push through the soil, and Leah knew that they would be in full bloom next month for Easter.

Climbing up the steps to the front porch, Leah almost danced to the front door before she remembered that it was still early and Aunt Fi might be sleeping. Gingerly opening the door, she put her portfolio on the kitchen table and took off her coat. The house was quiet except for the ticking sound of the mantel clock from the den.

Leah poured herself a cup of coffee from the still-warm pot she made before she went to her appointment and sat down at the kitchen table. She let her mind wander to her business plan to open and operate a women's "farm and frolic getaway" at the Gibson homestead. The week-long getaway would include days devoted to organic gardening, canning, crocheting, quilting and cooking and nights dedicated to lots of wine, great food and spa services Leah intended to bring in to pamper the guests. These services included manicures and pedicures, facials and massages. She could accommodate up to six guests for five days and she intended to pilot the getaway for eight weeks this summer, the first of which she would host her girlfriends in June. None of the instruction would be intended to make the participants experts, but instead, pique their interest in various green and ecologically sound practices. Each of the women would go home with something they made during the week—a supply of canned vegetables, a container herb garden or a lap quilt. Leah hoped the fun they had would lure them back the next year, hopefully with more of their friends in tow.

Granted, she still had some finer details to work out, but Leah was certain there were other women like her who had an interest in farm and sustainability practices that could be duplicated and transported back to the participants' suburban homes. At least, she hoped so.

She looked at her watch. It was nearing 8:30, and she needed to get changed and ready for work at the hardware store. Leah also needed to take Pander outside for a short walk since Aunt Fi was sleeping in this morning.

She stretched as she rose from the chair then walked over to the coffeepot and filled her mug with more coffee after checking to make sure there was enough for Aunt Fi to have a cup. Leah considered making some dried apple jack pies for her aunt on this chilly March morning, but she knew she'd never hear the end of Aunt Fi's complaining about being fussed over if she did. Instead, she reached up and grabbed the cereal out of the cupboard then went to the freezer and measured out ½ cup of frozen blueberries and took them to the sink to quick-thaw them under cool water. After she put them beside the bowl, spoon and cereal, Leah went upstairs.

Pander was probably crossing all four of her legs at this point since her beagle companion normally went for her morning jaunt around 7. Leah was surprised that her furry friend had not bounded down the stairs and begged her to go. Pander usually let her get about two steps up before she came around the corner and waited for Leah at the top of the stairs, but this morning nearing the top of the stairs, Pander was nowhere to be seen. Perhaps, she too had decided to sleep in!

Leah grabbed the banister at the top and turned left to go into her room, but Pander wasn't there. Turning around in her doorway, she peered to the other end of the upstairs hallway toward Aunt Fi's bedroom. The door was open about as wide as Pander. Her dog thought she owned this house now, and Leah knew she had made herself at home at the foot of Aunt Fi's bed since she left Pander all alone early this morning. Leah sighed and walked as quietly as possible with her boots down the hardwood hallway.

Walking to the door, Leah smelled the chocolate mint that Aunt Fi kept on her window sill. The aroma was soothing and inviting, and it always made Leah smile. She pushed the door open a little more and stuck her head in around the door. Pander was on the bed beside Aunt Fi, her head resting on Aunt Fi's thigh. The dog saw Leah, but she didn't move.

Fear suddenly filled her, and Leah felt like she might be sick as she slowly pushed the door aside and walked toward the bed. Still, Pander didn't move and neither did Aunt Fi. Leah was having a difficult time swallowing and her breathing came in gulps. Her legs felt like lead, but they propelled her nonetheless to the bedside.

Great tears welled in her eyes as she crumbled onto the bed beside Pander. In her aunt's hands was a faded, frayed black-and-white picture of a dark-haired young man smiling confidently into the camera. Leah knew it was Jaycee Gibson even though she had never seen his picture before. Visibly shaking and on the verge of falling to pieces, Leah touched her aunt's hands and, finding them cool to the touch, put her head into her hands and sobbed uncontrollably, unable to stop, unable to leave Aunt Fi's side. Pander, too, was obviously grieving, and she climbed into Leah's lap as she cried.

An indeterminate amount of time passed. With her eyes swollen and throat raw, Leah woodenly rose with Pander and walked to the bathroom. She washed her face and took Pander outside to relieve herself then came back to the house to figure out who to call. She picked up the telephone and called Mr. C first. He answered on the second ring.

Unable to verbalize the situation, Leah simply said, "Mr. C, p-please come," into the receiver as she began crying again.

She knew immediately that he understood when he answered solemnly, "I'll be right there, my child."

Sitting on the front porch with Pander in her arms, numb to the cold and the wind, Leah grappled with the emotions that bombarded her from every direction. She felt aimless, bereft and empty. *How will I manage without her?* Leah asked herself.

Mr. C pulled up in front of the house and walked over to her. She stood as he came up the steps, and he pulled her into a fatherly hug. Leah cried unabashedly for her loss and tried to comfort her aunt's closest friend too. Her passing would be hard on Mr. C.

He held her at arm's length then took his thumb and wiped a tear from her cheek. He smiled sadly and said, "Fiona was a remarkable woman, my dear, and she lived a long, productive, giving life. She will be missed by all of us, especially you, but I believe she is in a better place now."

Leah sniffled and shook her head as she remarked honestly, "I believe that too."

They walked into the house silently and went upstairs. Entering her room again, Leah stood at the foot of the bed and looked at her aunt. Her white hair was combed, and it hung loose around her face. Her face was serene, and she looked almost like she was sleeping. Leah took the picture of Jaycee from her hands and gently put it on the bedside table.

Mr. C walked up beside her and put his hand on her shoulder. Reverently, he whispered, "Why don't you walk down to Cal's while I tend to the ambulance and coroner, Leah?"

She returned his whisper by answering simply, "Ok."

Leah grabbed her coat and coaxed Pander to come walk with her down the winding path to Cal's house. The morning chill was waning even though the sun was just beginning to peek above Mount Jefferson in the east. She moved without urgency, her thoughts racing in every direction. As her legs carried her effortlessly across the bumpy path, her emotions seemed to have retreated, lurking somewhere deep inside her, waiting to attack without warning.

As she walked up the flagstone path to the kitchen door, Leah noticed the same strange car parked under the trees just out of the path of the driveway. The car was just an observation, though, and in her current state, it didn't even provoke any curiosity on her part. She picked up Pander and knocked on the door.

A quiet peace settled over Leah, and she took a deep, calming breath as she heard footsteps coming to the door. Cal would reassure her that everything was going to be alright, that she could go on, that there was still a place for her here. Leah realized she needed that reassurance.

As the door knob turned and the door opened, she relaxed even if she was unable to force a smile. The feeling was short-lived, though, and Leah put her hand up to the door frame to steady herself. As the deafening silence filled the space in between them, Leah finally managed, "Where's Cal?"

With her best syrupy voice and a well-practiced sultry look on her face, Marissa answered, "Well, little Leah! It's super to see you again. I'll tell him you came by. My Cal is still in the shower."

Without another word, Leah turned and walked back the way she came. She didn't remember the walk up the hill or going across the yard, but she somehow made her way to the stump chair nonetheless. Leaned against the back, Leah sat staring blankly across the valley, numb to time and her surroundings. Only when Pander jumped from her lap and began walking around the edge of the wood did she get up and make her way back to the farmhouse.

She noticed that the ambulance was gone and so was Mr. C., and as she climbed the steps, crossed the front porch and walked into the kitchen, Leah dissolved in a heap onto the kitchen floor, her back against the door. She watched as Pander slowly walked to the den, jumped up on the couch where Aunt Fi always sat and curled up with her head on her paws. Pander sighed and that sadness breached the wall around Leah's heart. Unable to stop the onslaught, Leah fell over on her side and let all of her emotions flow out of her in torrents of tears and heart-breaking sobs until she lay spent and tired on the kitchen floor. Leah felt incapable of coherent thought and her arms, legs and torso felt like they had liquefied and rendered her unable to move. Unable to muster the strength to do anything else, Leah simply closed her eyes and let exhaustion take her into a world that was dark and dreamless.

CHAPTER 40

Cal was in a particularly bad mood when he arrived at the hardware store at 9:30 in the morning. His day had gotten off to an unbelievably bad start and nothing since then had gotten any better. An hour later than his usual morning arrival, Cal knew that now he wouldn't have time to review the inventory or check on his weekly order. *Damn Marissa,* he thought.

Walking past the mirrored wall where the light bulbs were displayed, he caught a glimpse of his reflection—scowling and angry. Cal sighed, trying to shake off his mood as he headed to the office to see Leah. Perhaps she could shed a little sunshine into his life this morning, and thaw the cold that the Ice Queen herself, otherwise known as his rotten ex-wife, brought into his house this morning.

When he opened the office door, he noticed that the light was off. Cal looked at his watch. It was after 9:30. He wondered where Leah was this morning. She was usually an hour or more early when she helped him out on Mondays, Wednesdays and Fridays from 10 am to 2 pm. He took his coat off then sat down at the desk and called her cell phone. Leah didn't answer. Then, he called the farmhouse. The phone rang four times before the machine picked up. Now he was really worried. His dad should have been there by now to stay with Ms. Fi.

Tapping his fingers on the desk, Cal wondered what was going on. Finally, he called his dad's mobile. After the first ring, his father answered, "Hello?"

Cal breathed a sigh of relief. "Hey Dad, are you at Ms. Fi's yet? Leah's not here at work yet, and I was wondering if you'd seen here."

A long silence greeted Cal. Finally, his dad answered, "No, son, I'm not at Ms. Fi's anymore. Leah walked down to your house over an hour ago to see you and tell you the news herself."

Feeling as if he had had the wind knocked out of him, Cal momentarily was stunned into silence before he mumbled, "What news, Dad?"

He heard his father sigh heavily then his replied, "Cal, Leah found Ms. Fi dead in her bedroom this morning after she got back from an early morning appointment. Leah is not coming into work today, son. I'm not sure where she is, but I know she doesn't need to be all alone right now. I'm going to go check on her."

"Dad, wait," Cal said as he stood up at his desk and put back on his coat. "Let me go. I want to make sure she is alright."

He walked to the front counter and told Betty that he had to leave and that Leah wouldn't be in the rest of the week. He told her what happened, and Cal asked her to let the staff know that he would probably be out of the store for most of the week too. Betty nodded solemnly, and answered sympathetically, "I'll take care of everything here, Cal. Just go."

He mumbled a thank you and walked out to his truck to go find Leah. Cal thought diligently about the morning, and he wondered where everything got so off track. Why did Leah not come to his house this morning? Why did she not call him instead of his dad? Where had she gone this morning so early? Cal's mind raced around and around with questions.

He drove as fast as he safely could out of town and around the winding bends on Buffalo Road. Finally, he turned onto the hollow road, and he let out a loud, audible sigh of relief. Cal passed his driveway, and he scowled when he saw Marissa's car still there. Dealing with her crap was the last thing he needed right now. He had made his feelings abundantly clear this morning when he told her to leave and not come back ever again. She, of course ever the actress, had boo-hooed and sobbed and begged him to give her another chance. *When hell freezes over,* he thought.

He turned into the driveway leading to the Gibson farmhouse. Relief flooded over Cal when he saw Leah's vehicle parked beside the potting shed. He looked at his watch. It was only 10:15 a.m. How could it only be 10:15? Today felt like it was already in its 25th hour. He pulled his truck beside Leah's SUV, parked then walked toward the front door. Cal looked at the farmhouse, already sensing the enormity of the loss of Ms. Fi's feisty presence, and his heart almost broke for the love of his life. After the two of them just re-connected after almost fifteen years only months ago, the loss now felt almost unjust, and it joined a long line of injustices Leah had suffered over the last two years. Ms. Fi was all the family Leah Gibson had in the world, and that fact affected him profoundly since his father was his only living relative now. *Thank God we have each other*, Cal thought.

He went to the door and knocked lightly. He looked through the small space between the two curtains on the door. He saw Pander come to the door, but she didn't bark. Perhaps, Leah was asleep in the den. Maybe she was upstairs. Cal wasn't sure, but he couldn't see her through the semi-sheer door coverings.

He sighed and wondered whether he should knock again, knock harder or just come back later. Cal stood forlornly considering his options when suddenly a shadow rose up and covered the window of the front door. Startled, he struggled to regain his composure at the same time he tried to figure out what or who was at the door and from where the shadowy figure had come. Looking more closely at the shape, Cal realized it was Leah.

Now thoroughly confused, he waited patiently for her to open the door. When she did, Cal looked at her face, and noticed that her eyes were swollen and her cheeks were red. She had been crying, all alone here at the farmhouse. He felt thoroughly awful, and he reached for her, pulling her to his chest to hold her against him.

Leah didn't speak. Instead, she just clung to him, distraught and dazed. She no longer had the energy to cry, but she felt aimless, and the clear lack of direction frightened her and caused her to shiver. Cal figured she might be cool as they stood on the threshold of the door, so he took her hand and led her inside to the den. Pander, obviously still in mourning without Aunt Fi, barely moved as they entered the room.

Cal sighed and said gently, "Leah, I'm so sorry about Ms. Fi, and I am even sorrier that I had to find out from my dad. Why didn't you call me or come tell me?"

Leah stared at him, unblinking. Silence filled the whole of the room until it roared in her ears. Without any preamble or detail, she simply answered, "I did."

Confused, Cal looked at her, searching her face for clarity. He got none. He stuttered, "I . . . I don't understand . . ."

Leah felt frustration, maybe even anger, rising in her throat, and she forced herself to tamp it down by taking a deep breath. She leaned back onto the couch and pulled her legs up to her chest, retreating from his grasp. Finally, she responded in a rush of words that filled the room and hung heavy in the air. "I saw a strange car at your house this morning around 6:45 on my way to meet with Chip Moretz. Then, when I came back by a little after 8:00 it was still there so I sat here at the table and worked on a couple of spreadsheets that I've been putting together until a little after 8:30. When I walked upstairs to take P-pander out, she was in Aunt Fi's room." Leah took a gulp of breath, feeling emotion starting to well back up inside her. She continued more softly, "I knew immediately something was wrong. Pander wouldn't leave her side. Aunt Fi was already gone." Tears rolled steadily down her cheeks. Leah wiped them away with the back of her hand. She added, "I called your dad first because he was getting ready to come over anyway. When I talked to him, he . . . he just knew. When he got here, he called the coroner and the ambulance, but he told them not to bother with the lights or the siren so they didn't. Then, he told me to walk down to tell you, so I did." She stopped there and just studied his face.

Still obviously confused, Cal questioned uncertainly, "What stopped you from walking down to the house? Why didn't you come tell me?"

Succinctly, Leah answered again, "I did."

"When?" he asked flabbergasted.

Pausing like she was trying to figure how best to answer his question, she could barely contain her anger or disgust—whatever it was—when she finally replied, "You were *still* in the shower or let's quote it exactly—'My Cal is still in the shower.' So, again, let me reiterate—I *did* walk down to tell you." Finishing her story, she felt deflated and numb, and the expression of emotion left her exhausted again.

Cal, on the other hand, felt anger rising in his chest, and he sat back beside her on the couch as he let his rage toward his ex-wife simmer momentarily so it wouldn't spew out so vehemently. "Marissa had no right . . . she showed up unexpectedly, and in less than a couple of hours here, she's already causing trouble. She's just no good, rotten . . . I'm so sorry, Leah," he said sincerely. "When you needed me, I wasn't there for you. Will you forgive me?"

Leah rested her head on his shoulder and slipped her arms around his waist as her tears continued to run unabated down her cheeks. "I already have, but I won't lie—I felt like I had finished in second place again. After I left your house, I came back here to this empty house, and I felt all alone in the world, disconnected from everyone and everything, like I don't belong anywhere. I fell asleep exhausted on the kitchen floor, for heaven's sake. I'm so tired of living my life in limbo," Leah rambled.

"God, Leah! You won't ever have to live in limbo again. You belong with me. You, honest to God, always did—I was just too stupid to realize it until after I made the biggest mistake of my life by marrying Marissa. You are home, and I'll be damned if I am going to let Marissa or anyone or anything keep us apart again, okay?" Cal implored passionately. "Where does she get off calling me hers? I've never been hers. What is her problem?" he asked.

Leah smiled then answered, "Oh, that's easy. Marissa is just a crazy bitch, Cal." She laughed heartily at her summation, and she suddenly felt like the weight of the world had been lifted from her shoulders. Cal laughed too, and feeling an incredible peace descend upon her, Leah had no doubt that Aunt Fi was watching her from a much better place, chuckling with delight and nodding in agreement.

CHAPTER 41

Toni sat staring at the computer screen in her office, waiting for it to come on so she could check her e-mail. She was having trouble waking up this morning, and she thought seriously about going to get a cup of coffee from the cafeteria, even though the brew was heinous tasting and thick enough to patch holes in the interstate. Gross. Toni wasn't *that* sleepy.

After her computer roared to life, she jumped right into her work, and less than two hours later, she was up to date on all of her reports, e-mails and their patients' electronic medical records. She sighed with a sense of accomplishment, and Toni decided to go visit with some of the patients on the floor for a few minutes.

As she stood to go, her telephone rang and she walked around her chair to answer it. "Good morning—this is Toni," she said cheerfully.

"Hey you," Siobhan said softly in her ear. Sensing stress or something amiss, Toni sat down in her chair.

"Siobhan, congratulations my honorable friend," she said with a happiness that seemed somewhat out of place. Then she continued more soberly, "How are you? I've missed you!"

"Oh, Toni, I've missed you too. Are you tied up right now? Did I catch you at a bad time?" she asked in rapid succession.

"No, I just finished up my office work. I've got plenty of time to talk," she answered. "What's up, Sio?"

Toni heard Siobhan sigh into the receiver, and she felt a pit form in her stomach, confirming her sense that something was wrong. After a silent couple of seconds, Siobhan responded very quietly. "Toni, I found a lump in my left breast this morning, and I'm scared to death. I . . . I don't know what to do . . . who to call . . . I . . . just needed to hear your voice, I . . .," she trailed off, obviously uncertain and afraid.

"Siobhan, where are you right now?" Toni asked.

"I'm at the courthouse sitting in my soon-to-be chambers. Robert was gone this morning when I got out of the shower, and I didn't want to alarm the boys as they were heading to school. I left Robert a message to call me ASAP, but I don't want to be alone," she said through her sobs and sniffles.

"I'll be there in 10 minutes, your honor," Toni said with an encouraging smile in her voice. "Walk down to the Dunkin' Donuts and get each of us a large hazelnut coffee. I'll meet you in the courthouse lobby then you can escort me to your new digs and show me around."

Siobhan instantly felt better and said, "Thank you, Toni. I'll see you in 10." Charged with a task, she dried her eyes, wiped her nose then grabbed her purse and left in pursuit of two cups of the finest coffee in town.

Chapter 42

Later that afternoon, Leah finally had the chance to sit down at her computer and compose an e-mail to her friends to tell them about her Aunt Fi's passing. The day seemed to stretch on forever, like some kind of awful time warp. She, Cal and Mr. C met with the funeral home and Pastor Canton at the church. They would hold a visitation at the funeral home on Friday evening and have the funeral on Saturday afternoon. Afterward, Leah went to the farmhouse while Mr. C went to the florist after insisting that Leah let him buy the casket spray for Aunt Fi. Cal went to make sure Marissa had hit the road back to Nashville or Boone or anywhere besides Ashe County.

Leah opened up her e-mail and immediately realized that she forgot to call Siobhan to find out the outcome of her election. Too late—the most recent e-mail was from Robert—late last night and the reference line said, "SHE WON!" Leah smiled broadly. Siobhan was going to make a great judge.

She typed and sent a simple e-mail to Meg, Siobhan and Toni telling them that Aunt Fi died early this morning. Leah told them that she was all but sleepwalking right now, but she wanted to let them know about Aunt Fi's funeral arrangements. She finished the e-mail by letting them know that she missed them fiercely and would call each of them this evening to talk more. Leah hit "send" and shut down her computer.

She let her mind wander to Aunt Fi, and she couldn't help but smile. She thought about all of the old hymns they used to sing together when they were stringing beans, shucking corn or crocheting when she used to visit as a child. Leah had promised the minister she would have a list tomorrow of her aunt's favorite songs for the service. She knew "Amazing Grace" and "Nearer, My God to Thee" would be included.

Leah sighed when she thought of how little she knew about the property, Aunt Fi's finances and the basics of operating the farm, and she felt a little overwhelmed thinking about it all. She took a deep breath. Today was not the day to worry about all of those things. In addition to the music for the service, Leah was also tasked with finding the perfect dress for Aunt Fi to wear for her visitation at the funeral home and sitting here at the kitchen table alternately reminiscing and worrying was not getting the job done.

Leah walked upstairs to Aunt Fi's room. Again, the smell of chocolate mint greeted her and uplifted her dampened spirits before she ever got into the bedroom. Smiling, Leah went inside and walked over to the edge of the bed. Mr. C had stripped the linens off and the mattress looked stark and out of place in Aunt Fi's neat and orderly room. Leah promptly walked out to the linen closet in the hall, pulled out a clean set of white sheets and a colorful quilt and made the bed. The sheets smelled of lavender, and Leah reminisced about making tiny little pillow cases with Aunt Fi and Gran Belle in which they would place the fragrant dried flowers to keep their linens smelling fresh year-round.

So many memories, Leah thought, and she considered herself incredibly fortunate to have been blessed with such loving, kind and industrious role models. She wandered around the room casually for a few minutes, opening the Bible on the nightstand to a bookmark in Exodus, admiring the placement of the canvas picture she had made for Aunt Fi hanging on the wall opposite the bed, picking up the faded photograph of Jaycee Gibson, and touching the ivory brush and comb set that graced the top of Aunt Fi's vanity. The stillness of the room made Leah's heart ache, and she felt lonely and even a little guilty for snooping.

Sighing to shake away her sadness, Leah went to the closet and opened the door. She turned on the overhead light, and was greeted with the neatest closet she had ever seen—by far and bar none. The modest amount of clothing hanging there was organized by clothing type and color—shirts, pants, skirts, dresses and coats. Even the shoes were in order, stacked neatly in their boxes against the back wall of the closet. Leah couldn't help but smile. Her Aunt Fi was an amazing woman.

Leah looked through the dresses hanging on the far right side of the closet. At the very end was a garment bag with a piece of paper pinned to the front. She took the bag off of the rod and pulled it out to see it more closely. The paper had a handwritten label that simply read "Special" in Aunt Fi's handwriting. As Leah unzipped the front of the bag to see what was inside, a beautiful rose-colored suit was exposed. It was stunning and absolutely as promised—special. She removed it completely from the garment bag and put the suit onto the bed. Underneath the suit was a lovely white cotton shirt with small hand-embroidered roses on the placket and the straight collar. Leah was overcome with emotion when she realized that, once again, her Aunt Fi had thought of everything.

With the task of finding her aunt's final outfit complete, Leah decided to explore the rest of the contents of the closet. No longer feeling guilty or as if she was intruding, Leah was growing to believe that Aunt Fi had designed the contents of her closet as a welcome to her niece to explore, understand and appreciate. She pulled three boxes from the front of the top shelf, sat down cross-legged on the floor and opened the lid on the first one.

Inside, Leah found all kinds of family treasures neatly organized and labeled. The trove included her mother's birth certificate, her grandparents' and parents' marriage licenses, death notices for her great-grandparents, Jaycee's enlistment papers, all of their love letters, the letter of condolence from Major General Alexander Vandergrift as well as family photographs from almost one hundred years. Leah was mesmerized, and she went through each piece of her family's history with care.

Now fully ensconced, Leah moved to the second box where she found every imaginable piece of documentation related to the farm—deeds, tax records, farm and property insurance policies, invoices from machinery purchases, ledgers of tobacco harvests, sales, and labor costs, and a big binder of bank statements labeled "farm account," the most recent of which was dated last month. Leah was a stickler for good accounting and record-keeping, and she smiled as she realized that the trait was obviously genetic. She looked at the balance in the account then rubbed her eyes and looked again. She put the binder down momentarily and gasped for the breath that seemed to have been knocked out of her. The account had over $70,000 in it. *How was that much savings possible?*

As Leah pulled the third box toward her to open, her head was reeling. She sighed with anticipation as she lifted the lid. The box contained four binders, each labeled with a general description of what was contained within. The labels read "Legal Documents," "Bank Statements," "Stock Certificates," and "Personal Information." Only after Leah exhaled loudly did she realize that she had been holding her breath.

She opened the binder with the bank statements inside. Each account was separated with a tabbed divider. Leah counted six accounts by the number of tabs. She opened the first tab and mumbled, "Holy Cow," followed by similar outbursts after she read the subsequent statements in the binder. Now almost in a daze, she leafed through the stock certificates, legal documents that included the wills, trusts and estate documents from her grandparents, and her great-grandparents. The total estate was more than $1 million. Leah felt faint, and she leaned back against the foot of Aunt Fi's bed as she tried to fathom everything. In the smallest binder labeled "Personal Information," Leah found a copy of Aunt Fi's last will and testament. An envelope was attached to the front addressed "Leah," and she numbly unfastened it and opened it. In Aunt Fi's unmistakable handwriting she read:

My dear Leah,

> *As you are reading this letter, I know you are grieving my death. Please don't, my child. I have lived a great, long life, and I wish you the same longevity as long as you have happiness, your health and loved ones around you as I have had. Having you, your mother and your grandmother in my life have been some of the greatest of my life's joys. We loved each other unconditionally, lived our lives fully and learned to revel in the simple pleasures all around us on this patch of God's beautiful earth.*
>
> *Your grandfather was an astute businessman, and after his brother and my true love died, he invested heavily in sound, understandable things that allowed us to live our simple lives financially secure. Your mother made us promise to let you live your life on your own, never knowing the financial times that you would face would be so devastating to you. I wish you had*

confided in me, for I would have helped you through with much less pain and loss than you have suffered in the last couple of years. I am not sad, though, that your circumstances brought you home to me. I have prayed for your return since you left after your grandmother's death. This farm, this house, this land—this is your home, Leah.

Your love of everything here made my last days so joyful, and I am excited for the plans you will see to fruition as you move forward with your vision of what this farm will be for our next generation. Treat it with the love you have in your heart, and you will be rewarded with the beauty and bounty it will provide.

I know you are afraid of many things right now—failure, loneliness and uncertainty. Know that all of us who have come before you stood on this land with those same fears facing us. Persevere, my child, and know that just like jams and jellies we so lovingly preserve in mason jars, you have good canned inside you that is no less sweet and pure. You carry and preserve the best from all the generations of us who were lucky enough to have been granted a life on this piece of paradise. That goodness is an indelible part of who you are and it will be there for future generations to discover when you open up and share it with them.

Angels are watching you, Leah. You'll feel us in the breeze, see us in the flowers, taste us in the fruits, and find us in all of the beautiful places you know and have yet to discover in our idyllic mountain hollow. Lean on your memories to sustain you, to comfort you and to give you strength in the days to come, but don't forget to rely on the people still with you for help either. Tom and Cal Cunningham are life-long friends. Trust them and open your heart to them for support. They will not let you down.

Take all of this information to Matthew Brown, our family attorney, and he will help guide you through all of the legal and estate necessities along with Tom. You have a life to live. Get to work!

Love,
Aunt Fi

Leah hugged the letter to her heart as she let her hot, salty tears cleanse her sorrow, soothe her fears and touch her heart. She felt oddly comforted in Aunt Fi's room and she reached over and carefully packed the contents back inside the box. Then she stood, replaced the boxes back on the top shelf, turned off the closet light and closed the door. Leah gently zipped the suit and shirt back inside the garment bag and took it with her as she headed back downstairs. She had to find the right hymns for Aunt Fi's funeral service, take Pander for a walk, and call Mr. C. Leah smiled as she composed her mental list. She had to get to work.

CHAPTER 43

The day of Aunt Fi's funeral service was one of those extraordinary spring days that you want to relive over and over, especially after this most recent cold and wet winter in the High Country. The brilliant blue sky was virtually cloudless, and a warm southwest breeze whispered through the newly budding trees. As expected, the Buffalo Creek United Methodist Church was filled to capacity with friends from every phase of Aunt Fi's long and gracious life, and Leah was touched by their words of kindness and stories of her aunt's positive impact on their lives. What could have been a sad, morose affair was instead a true celebration of Aunt Fi, and Leah left the church moved, inspired and humbled by the blessing of her Aunt Fi's remarkable influence in her life.

Cal had stood steadfastly at her side through the visitation at the funeral home last night and at the church today. Mr. C shared stories of Ms. Fi that had every person in attendance laughing, smiling and nodding their agreement. This funeral was a dry-eyed affair, and Leah knew Aunt Fi wouldn't have had it any other way.

Walking arm and arm through the cemetery after the service, Cal leaned his head down to hers and asked Leah, "How are you doing?"

She smiled up at him and answered, "I'm fine, but I am sure going to be lonely without her."

Cal nodded then said, "Yes, but you still have Dad and me and the rest of your friends and neighbors. Besides, Ms. Fi is going to be everywhere and in everything around the farm."

"I know," Leah sighed with a smile, "But I have so much to learn! She knew more about that farm than anybody, and all the books and articles I read just seem to pale in comparison to her knowledge."

"Now that's absolutely true," he said, "But she had to learn all of that knowledge too. I know you may find this hard to believe, but the rest of us weren't blessed at birth with farm expertise." Cal put his arm around her slim shoulders and hugged Leah to his side.

Leah leaned into him and laughed, "Why, I thought all you NC State students had to be blessed by the Holy Ghost prior to admission to the Ag program there."

He chuckled in response and said, "We do, but as a bonus we get to spend four years enjoying the beat-down our Wolfpack puts on those dastardly Tarheels."

"Lord, help him," Leah said to the sky. "It's too bad you have had so little enjoyment over the last couple of decades. Maybe that's why you've always been so grouchy."

"I'm not grouchy! I'm just cool," he teased.

Leah loved Cal's playful side, and she couldn't help being turned on by his sheer proximity. She said, "Well, now that's a disappointment. I like you so much better when you're . . . hot."

Cal leaned a little closer and uttered a low, sexy growl in her ear. Leah felt like she would burst into flames, and as they passed the church and arrived at Cal's truck, she silently hoped that her desire wouldn't doom her to hell. She chose to think it wouldn't and refocused on Cal as he got into the cab beside her.

He turned to her, breathing noticeably harder than he had been a few minutes earlier, with eyes that were just short of feral. Cal asked hoarsely, "Can I take you home with me?"

Leah leaned over to his ear and answered in a quiet, but sultry, voice, "You can take me anywhere, Cal Cunningham."

"I intend to take you everywhere, Leah Gibson," he responded, "So let's get started."

Now almost breathless, Leah simply nodded, her eyes meeting his, and put her hand in the air like a starting pistol and said, "Pow."

CHAPTER 44

Meg had awakened early on Saturday morning with a bad feeling that kept her from falling back to sleep, and even now late in the afternoon persisted. She didn't feel bad—she just felt troubled, an uneasy coil deep in her gut. Courtney had asked her several times during the day what was wrong, and each time Meg had responded honestly, "I don't know."

She did know not to ignore her gut because it had never failed her in her entire life. It foretold of the events of 9/11 when she was supposed to go stay with her college friend, Hannah, for a week. Meg and Hannah had made all kinds of plans by telephone—a Yankees game, "Phantom of the Opera," and dinner at Angelo's, but she just couldn't shake a bad feeling about the trip. That first week of September, Meg would wake in the middle of the night with the words, "Don't go," reverberating in her head. She delayed buying her plane tickets and made all kinds of excuses about why she was so non-committal. In the end, Meg's decision not to go was one of the best of her life. Hannah, who was employed by Pitney-Bowes in the south tower of the World Trade Center on the 63rd floor, barely escaped with her life and her apartment was covered in ash and dust, even though it was blocks from the financial district in Manhattan.

Meg sighed out loud, and Courtney looked up from her book with concern. She asked, "Meg, are you okay?"

"I don't know, *Cherie*," she answered softly. "I have a sense that something is terribly wrong somewhere."

Courtney trusted Meg's second sense too because she had seen it in action. Meg had bailed out of a golf game with two clients and a co-worker about four years ago, claiming she had a terrible migraine. The truth was that she had a foreboding of trouble. The co-worker had another sales representative take her place, and the foursome teed off that April afternoon. Seven holes into the round, a severe thunderstorm rolled up and the four golfers took cover under the eaves of a work shed. It wasn't enough. A bolt of lightning struck a huge long leaf pine tree only feet from where they stood. Meg's co-worker fill-in was killed and one of the clients was severely injured.

Courtney offered, "Why don't you check your e-mail? Maybe you'll find the answer there."

Meg considered this suggestion then said, "That's a good idea. I think I will." As she walked past Courtney, she squeezed her shoulder. Courtney was so smart, and she knew Meg so well. Meg just wished she had thought to check her messages earlier, somehow sensing she might find the source of her concern there.

Sure enough, she had an e-mail from Siobhan asking if she would be available to talk by phone tonight at 6 p.m. Meg quickly replied that she would not only be available, she would be anxiously awaiting Siobhan's call. Meg looked at the clock on computer. It was only 4 p.m. She had to wait another couple of hours.

Siobhan had called Meg late Wednesday afternoon to talk. After the e-mail Tuesday night from Robert, Meg was certain the call was simply to share the celebration of Siobhan's victory for a seat on the bench in Virginia Beach. The initial elation of hearing Siobhan's voice was immediately replaced with fear for her good friend's life. Siobhan called with Toni from her office to tell her that she had found a lump in her breast. She was frightened, and Siobhan was uncertain as to what the discovery meant to her brand-new career as a judge, her family, her body and her sanity. What was never in doubt, though, was her resolve to overcome any obstacle with the incredible support of good friends in place. Siobhan was calling on that support on day one. Meg reinforced that she expected to see Siobhan and Robert in about a month in DC, and she asked Siobhan to call her when she knew more. Meg was certain that was the reason for the follow up call, and she had a feeling that the news from Virginia Beach was going to be encouraging so the nagging feeling in her gut didn't feel related to Siobhan.

Perhaps the out-of-sorts feeling she had was simply a guilty conscience because Meg had been unable to break away to get to Leah's side for her aunt's funeral today. Leah sent her closest friends a heart-breaking e-mail on Wednesday informing them of her loss, but all the funeral arrangements were finalized so quickly that none of them were able to rearrange their schedules to manage the trip today. Meg felt horrible about Leah being all alone—again—during one of her darkest hours, and Leah Gibson had had enough dark hours in the last two years for several lifetimes. Meg took solace, though, in the peace she heard in Leah's voice when they talked and the happiness that seemed to emanate from the pictures she sent. Leah was obviously very much at home.

Meg sighed. She sent Leah a beautiful miniature gardenia, hoping her best friend would plant it in a special place to honor the memory of her aunt. She was certain Leah would nurture and tend it with great care, and Meg conjured up Leah in her mountain garden, happy and fulfilled. Meg smiled as she continued to watch Leah in her daydream. In her vision, Leah walked toward a lovely farmhouse with a wooded hillside at her back before she suddenly looked over her shoulder, fear flashing across her face. The gesture startled Meg out of a trance and instantly wiped the smile off her face.

Her heart was racing now, and the concern in her gut had escalated to full-blown terror. Meg knew what she just experienced was no daydream. It was a premonition, and it sent chills down Meg's spine as she understood its meaning—Leah Gibson was alone again and her dark days weren't over yet.

CHAPTER 45

Leah telephoned Siobhan Saturday evening after she and Cal spent the afternoon together. Cal took her home to the farmhouse so she could check phone messages, her e-mail and send some thank-you notes. She asked Cal to stay the night, but he decided to let her have some quiet time at her home. He promised to check on her before he turned in for the night.

Leah and Siobhan talked for an hour. They laughed, cried, comforted and reassured each other. Siobhan told her about finding the lump, telling Robert and her boys, holding hands with Toni as they rode over to the hospital together for the biopsy, and the results. Siobhan had breast cancer—stage three, but it had not metastasized. She was due to have a lumpectomy on Tuesday and would begin chemotherapy immediately. She told Leah that she felt strong and that neither hell nor high water would keep her from going to their trip to the Capitol in April.

Leah could hear Siobhan's determination, and she felt a cautious optimism about her best friend's prognosis. She told Siobhan about the beautiful weather for Aunt Fi's funeral and how she could see her aunt in all of the signs of spring. Leah missed her aunt already, and she confided in Siobhan that she was afraid that she might not be able to manage the farm. She then told her about the small fortune she had discovered, and asked for Siobhan's advice.

After what was likely a stunned silence, Siobhan cautioned her to be careful not to tell anybody but those she knew well and trusted. Leah promised her she would rely only on Cal and Tom Cunningham and Aunt Fi's attorney. Siobhan sighed with relief then said sincerely, "Nobody deserves a windfall more than you, my girl. What are your plans?"

For the next twenty-five minutes, Leah enthusiastically told her best friend in the world about her idea to attract women to the hollow to learn some homemaking skills while they relaxed and were pampered over wine and among friends. Leah detailed the activities she had planned like container gardening, water bath canning and quilting followed by experts to provide massages, manicures and pedicures and facials. Siobhan was excited and asked Leah when she could come. Leah responded, "I want you, Toni and Meg to be my first guests—my guinea pigs of sorts."

Siobhan laughed and answered, "I accept on behalf of all of us. When can we come?"

Leah replied, "I was thinking the first week in June would be wonderful. Meg and Courtney will be married, we can consider it a bachelorette party for Toni before her July 4th nuptials, and you, my dear, will be through your chemotherapy. What do you think?"

"I think I'll go mark it on my calendar. So when are you going up to Washington? Are you coming alone? I think Robert and I are going to ride up with Toni and Carter," Siobhan fired at her.

Leah sighed and realized she might as well go ahead and let the proverbial cat out of the bag. She said, "I have asked a friend of mine to go with me to Washington."

Siobhan squealed with delight and asked, "Is this friend the mysterious Cal Cunningham?"

Trying not to be prickly, Leah decided to play along instead of playing defense. She simply said, "My friend wouldn't be a mystery if I told you anything further."

"That sucks," Siobhan said, faking irritation before she laughed. "I don't care if you bring the farmer in the dell."

"That's about right," Leah joked, prompting Siobhan to laugh harder.

Finally, Siobhan said, "I so needed this conversation, Leah. You mean the world to me, and I love you."

"I love you too," Leah replied softly the added, "And I miss you. Are you sure you're going to be okay? I'm worried about you, Sio."

"Well, I'm worried about me too," Siobhan said, "But I can get through this ordeal. What about you? Are you going to be alright in that house all alone?"

"I've got more than my hand to keep me company these days," Leah deadpanned and in seconds, she and Siobhan dissolved into a fit of hysterics that lasted for the next ten minutes and left them unable to control their laughter even long after they ended the call.

CHAPTER 46

Marissa sat on the enormous rock just above the creek that gave this god-forsaken area its name, staring at the back of Cal's house. Even when she had lived inside, it had been Cal's house. She hated everything about it—the folksy charm, the simple lines, and most definitely, the remote setting. She was sure the house was great if you were a country bumpkin.

This afternoon Marissa actually wanted to be inside, though, with Cal. Instead, the wholesome and sweet Leah Gibson had returned to what Marissa was sure she thought was her rightful place to play house with him instead. *She is pathetic,* Marissa thought. Unfortunately, Leah Gibson had finally gotten exactly what she had always wanted all the while thwarting the one thing Marissa needed.

She threw a rock into the slow-moving water. Leah was in her way, and now with the Gibson farm destined to fall into her hands, Marissa had to act quickly to win Cal over, if only temporarily, to ensure her inheritance. While everybody else in the Buffalo community was at the church for Ms. Fiona's funeral, Marissa was snooping inside the Gibson farmhouse on Leah's computer for information. She found Leah's business plan, her e-mail correspondence with Chip Moretz and lots of pictures of her friends, all women, in Virginia Beach. She needed a distraction to put a wedge between the sickeningly sweet lovebirds long enough to convince Mommy Dearest that she and Cal were working on a reconciliation.

Marissa needed a plan, something that would force Cal's attention in her direction. She sat thinking until the sun began to dip low in the western horizon between the distant peaks. Finally, an idea wormed its way into her mind and settled there, coiled and anxious to feed off of her hostility. As it grew, Marissa smiled with satisfaction. She realized her plan was devious, but she no longer cared. To get what was hers, she had to get Cal's love interest out of her way, making sure she was there to comfort him after little Leah was gone. She could play house for a little while, of course—she was, after all, an actress, but before Cal tired of her, she would lay claim to her inheritance. Then, Marissa would be long gone, living the dream in her city with this backwoods town firmly out of sight and forever out of mind.

CHAPTER 47

The weeks leading up to Leah's trip to Washington, DC were almost frenetic with spring cleaning around the farm, honing her business plans and settling Aunt Fi's estate. And Leah was thankful that she was swamped since the work kept her mind off of the impending introduction of Cal to her friends. She wasn't sure she was ready for the attention, the scrutiny, or the questions that awaited her upon their arrival.

As nervous as she was about their reception, though, Leah was eager to go and felt like the anticipation was going to kill her. She had spoken with Meg and Courtney, and they were giddy with excitement, too. Siobhan was getting through her chemotherapy by marking off the days on her calendar that would culminate with her trip to celebrate with her friends. Toni was finalizing all of the plans for her July 4th marriage to Carter and their subsequent extended honeymoon, but she relished the thought of getting away from the hospital even for this long Easter weekend to be among friends and celebrate.

Her best friends had committed to Leah's Haven in the Hollow Retreat the first week in June, and she had stayed busy outlining each day of the week with activities, both practical and social. She had developed an extensive spreadsheet of estimated costs that she hoped were validated by her actual expenditures for the inaugural week. Armed with actual costs, Leah could then determine how much to charge per participant, calculate how much she would have to earn to break even, and gauge from her friends' feedback whether the price Leah needed to charge was too much, a real bargain or just right. Her girlfriends' weeklong retreat was on her dime, and even after they protested profusely and loudly, Leah insisted. They were, after all, guinea pigs, and that meant there would be wrinkles to iron out for subsequent paying parties.

Leah smiled with satisfaction at her new-found ability to treat her friends, but she intended to entertain them with the natural and local beauty in the hollow, not splurge on frivolity or throw money around like a showoff. Leah still had poverty and destitution lurking fresh in her mind, and she intended to banish them from her life permanently and make every effort to assist others who found themselves in the same situation. She wanted to help others find a path to self-sufficiency because she knew, by a very large majority, that was what the unemployed wanted—a break, not a handout.

Even though it was only Tuesday, Leah had finished packing for Thursday's trip. She walked downstairs to the kitchen to make a cup of hot tea and sit with Pander for a while and finish crocheting a blue and white garter that she had been working on for Courtney. Looking out the window, Leah saw the beautiful early tulips peeking above the wooden container at the top of the driveway. They were pink, and the color popped against bright green shoots and the dark fertile soil from which they had sprung. Their beauty touched Leah as she recalled the winter morning she and Aunt Fi planted them together. The blooms were a bittersweet, living reminder of the circle of life, of renewal after loss.

A shadow caught her eye, and Leah looked to the tree line to determine what caused it. Home to wild turkey, white-tail deer, bobcats and the occasional black bear, the wooded mountains of the High Country were teeming with wildlife. The dawning of spring brought warmer temperatures during the day, waking the hibernating animals and stoking their desire to mate. A flash of color caught her eye and Leah quickly surmised that the lurking animal appeared to be human. An unsettling feeling crept over her, and she turned from the window to grab her coat. As she started to go out alone, she reconsidered and said, "Come on, Pander." Her trusty beagle bounded off the couch in the den and came immediately to her side.

When Leah reached for the door, Pander began to growl, and the hackles on her neck were standing up on end. Something or someone was definitely outside. Not willing to take unnecessary chances, Leah took her phone out of her purse and dialed Cal. He answered the phone immediately and asked, "Do you want me to come over and tuck you into bed?"

His question aroused her and made her smile, and she answered as calmly and coolly as she could, "I'd like nothing better than you to come over and tuck me in, but be careful, Romeo, there's something lurking in the woods."

Leah could tell from the sudden silence that she had startled him, and he asked, "Leah, did you see something?"

Seeking to downplay a shadow and a flash of color out of her window, she replied, "Just a large shadow and movement—it's probably nothing, but Pander is wary and I'd just like to be careful. I don't see any need to play Annie Oakley out there."

"I'll be right over," Cal stated emphatically. "Lock the door and stay inside until I get there."

Before she could question him further about why he was so concerned, he had disconnected the call. In the waning daylight, Leah peered again out the window and wondered if she seemed petty or silly for being afraid. She didn't say anything about the flash of bright red she saw to Cal. Maybe it was a cardinal or part of a turkey. She didn't know. Whatever it was or wasn't, Leah was just glad Cal was on his way over.

Not that she needed him to rescue her like some damsel in distress, but she also didn't need a reason to want him to come to her other than exactly what it was—pure, unadulterated desire and wanting. Cal Cunningham simply whipped her into a frenzy, and she found herself on the brink of it right now. Walking to the cabinet, she chose two wine glasses instead of tea cups, and she took a bottle of Pinot Noir from the rack that had this occasion written all over it—Tuesday night.

Leah smiled as she heard him pull into the driveway, and she went to the locked door to watch him as he got out and walked to the woods. Cal had on a navy thermal tee and a gray fleece vest with his jeans and hiking boots, and he looked so sexy and rugged. She sighed as he disappeared out of her sight behind the farmhouse then busied herself by pulling some cheese and grapes out of the refrigerator and the crackers and a jar of red pepper jelly out of the cupboard. After what felt like an eternity, Cal knocked on the door.

Leah unlocked the door quickly, but just as fast, her exuberance dissipated like a puff of smoke. Cal was worried, and it showed all over his face. She asked, "What's wrong, Cal?"

He walked inside, shut the door and relocked it then he sighed and answered, "Somebody has been walking around your house, Leah—recently."

"Pander sensed it," she said, and as calm as she sounded, Leah felt a deep-seeded fear curling in her stomach. The feeling scared her, and she visibly shivered.

The reaction was not lost on Cal, though, and he took her hand in his then asked, "What else?"

Leah sighed then detailed the little signs of something amiss over the last couple of weeks. "My computer was placed in front of the chair when we got back from the funeral. I had moved it to the corner of the table to remind myself to put it away. The closet light in the hallway was turned on. Pander was barking like a dog possessed when I got home from working at the hardware store last Friday," she detailed. "None of these little things individually meant a thing, but collectively they tell me that somebody has not only been outside, somebody may have been inside the farmhouse, too. Then earlier, I saw a flash of red, like a sweater or shirt or something."

"You didn't tell me that part," Cal said. "And somebody has clearly been walking around outside. I found fresh footprints in the dirt—small, like a kid or a woman." Cal stopped speaking abruptly, and his eyes grew dark. Leah waited silently for him to say something else. Finally, he gathered himself to utter only, "Marissa . . ."

Now it was Leah's time to get angry, and the thought of Cal's no-good, mean-spirited ex-wife in her house infuriated her. "That woman has some nerve coming into my house. She better hope I don't catch her here or I'll roll her down this mountainside like a bowling ball," she stated through clinched teeth and fists.

"She must want something or she wouldn't be playing her crazy little games," Cal said.

Leah added, "Well, she's certainly got the crazy down pat, but she's playing games on my turf now so I have home field advantage." As confident as she sounded, though, Leah acknowledged the unsettling feeling deep inside her then chose to ignore it—at least for now. In response, she stepped closer to Cal and put her arms around his waist.

"Mmm, I love when you use sports speak. Will you show me your locker room," Cal asked provocatively as he pulled her into his embrace.

"Only if you show me your equipment when we get there," Leah teased in reply.

Cal growled his approval in her ear then whispered, "I'll give you a personal demonstration on how it works too." Leah shivered with delight then turned, grabbed his hand, and ran up the stairs two at a time with Cal so close behind her that he seemed to be in chase more than in tow. Before she threw herself across the bed with him, though, Leah went to the window and pulled down the shade. Tonight, the events in this house and this room were off-limits to spectators.

Off in the woods, concealed by the encroaching shroud of darkness, Marissa let out a sigh. She was shut out of the sweet little show starring Cal and Leah. Sure, when he ran his thumb over Leah's breast, Marissa got all hot and bothered with desire. She tried to remember Cal ever being that comfortable and casual with her, but she couldn't. Cal had always been responsive, but not assertive, and his hunger for Leah pissed her off royally because Cal wanted Leah in a way he had never wanted her. Sure, Cal had lusted after her, but he desired Leah. It was all so . . . homey and quaint. Well, Ms. Goody Two Shoes could have her Norman Rockwell existence. Marissa wanted the excitement of the city and superstar living. With her impending wealth, she could have anything she wanted. Marissa's eyes were drawn back to the shadows behind the blinds. "*Almost anything,*" Leah's voice rang in her head.

Bitch, Marissa sulked as she quietly walked down the mountain to her car. Leah Gibson thought she was the luckiest woman in the world. Marissa knew she was the one who deserved fame, fortune and fun, and she was going to have them. Leah could have her luck because Marissa had a plan. The thought satisfied Marissa momentarily as she got into her car to drive away. Then, she looked back across the hollow at the farmhouse and zeroed in on the window where could still make out the shadowy movements of Leah and Cal—together. Marissa got mad all over again as she drove away. Her plan wasn't much of a consolation right now because tonight Leah Gibson was the one getting laid instead of her.

CHAPTER 48

As they pulled up to the front of the charming house that Meg and Courtney called home, Leah took a deep breath. Toni and Carter and Siobhan and Robert had already arrived, evidenced by the enormous Chevrolet Suburban parked just in front of her. Their early arrival meant the six of them were lying in wait, ready to ambush her with a barrage of questions. Leah was certain she was going to be sick.

Beside her, Cal laughed. "Are you sure these are friends of yours? You look like you're going inside for some kind of invasive medical procedure," he quipped. "Relax, Leah! I promise I won't embarrass you by picking my nose, burping loudly or unbuttoning my pants after dinner."

Leah laughed, and she did relax a little. Cal was right—these people loved her. They were her best friends, and she had talked so much about them that Cal probably felt like he had known them for years. Taking one more deep breath, she smiled and opened the door to get out. Before she could get two steps up the driveway, though, Leah was swamped by a mob of squealing and laughing women.

Cal stood back and watched them, amused by their enthusiastic welcome and thrilled by their obvious affection and love for Leah. He knew instantly he was going to like these friends of hers. Smiling broadly, he asked with mock insult, "Where's my welcoming committee?"

In unison, the band of wild women turned to him, eyeballed him head to toe before they began to catcall, whistle and laugh. Cal turned fifty shades of red before the dark, lovely brunette said, "Your real welcoming committee is more interested in the NCAA tournament, the beer and the chips than anything on this planet right now. This time of year, men prove they've evolved very little from the Neanderthals. When you go in, they'll probably greet you with a bag of chips and a cold beer. I'm Toni, by the way."

Cal walked over, shook her hand and promptly leaned down and kissed her cheek. Now Toni blushed, and Leah knew Cal already had the lot of them under his spell. Leah caught his eye and smiled, and Cal winked at her. "I'm Cal, Toni. You are even more beautiful in person than your pictures." Yep, Toni was rendered speechless.

Cal then turned his attention to the slender, sophisticated Siobhan and said, "Your Honor, it is my pleasure to see you looking so well. How are you feeling?"

Immediately riveted by his genuine concern, Siobhan walked over and hugged his neck then replied, "I'm doing well, Cal. Thank you for asking. Cancer sucks, but it has met its match in me. I knew I'd like you."

Cal smiled at her and answered, "Thank you, Siobhan." Then he turned to the petite, fiery Meg and said, "Are you ready for your big day, Meg McConnell? You look radiant! You know, though, if you get nervous, I can always be counted on to drive you to the golf course to let you work out a few jitters on some golf balls." Cal kissed Meg on the cheek. Meg beamed with happiness.

Meg said good-naturedly, "I like you, Cal, but I'd still kick your Wolfpack ass up the front nine and down the back nine even on a bad day. The Virginia Cavalier in me is still alive and well, my friend. Let me show you to the den." Looping her arm through his, Meg led Cal up the walkway to her house while the rest of his throng of new admirers followed along. As Leah fell in step with them, she breathed a huge sigh of relief. When they reached the stairs, all the attention of her friends was focused solely on Cal, and Leah laughed softly to herself with delight and simply shook her head in amazement. In the midst of this tough and discerning group of women, Cal had captured their hearts instantly and effortlessly, and Leah realized that she could finally rid herself of all those fears of scrutiny and worry she had forever. She and Cal belonged here, and her friends' approval just reinforced what she had finally figured out. Leah Gibson loved Cal Cunningham, and she always had and always would.

CHAPTER 49

The weekend together in DC flew by, and the Saturday ceremony was a beautiful and moving affair. The weather was as close to perfect in early April as anyone could remember with abundant sunshine and a mild 70-degree temperature. Both Courtney and Meg were beaming from sunrise well past sunset, and they were surrounded by family, co-workers and friends from every stage of their lives.

The vows they wrote were so poignant and heartfelt that, by the time they exchanged rings, there was not a dry eye in the house. Meg and Courtney loved each other, and that love was a powerful foundation on which they could build the rest of their lives together. As a first step, they were leaving for a long trip to England tomorrow morning, and Courtney, most especially, was ebullient with excitement.

Late into the evening, after the other guests had gone home and the eight of them were back at Meg and Courtney's house, they sat around talking comfortably and casually about the weather, the ceremony, the food, the people—everything that made the day so special. Meg opened a bottle of wine. Courtney brewed a pot of coffee.

As the night progressed, the guys moved to the den to watch NCAA basketball tournament games while the girls stayed in the dining room talking about their Haven in the Hollow Retreat in the North Carolina High Country in early June. Courtney said, "I probably won't be able to take off any more time, but Meg needs to be there. I'd love to come another time, though."

Leah answered, "You and Meg can come up together in the fall when the leaves are at peak color. The beauty is breathtaking."

Toni chimed in and said, "I can't wait to come! Siobhan, you can ride up with me."

Siobhan smiled and replied, "I'll take you up on that offer, my chauffeur—I mean Cherie." They giggled at her play on words and began planning the week as they sipped on wine and coffee.

Meanwhile, the guys in the den were taking a break from whooping and hollering temporarily and Leah knew that simply meant that one game had ended and another had yet to begin. She wondered what in the world they would discuss out of earshot of their female companions.

Carter was thrilled that Vanderbilt, his alma mater, had won the game and was now headed into the Sweet 16 next weekend. Cal had survived a nail-biter, with NC State eking out a close win over Arizona. Robert saw his Georgetown Hoyas get manhandled by their arch-enemy Syracuse Orangemen. He was already ready for next season.

With the hiatus in basketball action, the talk turned to Cal, and Robert realized that he was truly fond of him. He obviously cared deeply for Leah and by the depths of his feelings he had for many, many years. Robert hoped Cal and Leah had many happy years together, and he told Cal so.

"You are the only guy I believe I can honestly say deserves Leah," Robert said. "She is a remarkable woman, and I, like the rest of her friends, have watched her struggle, fight and survive a series of trials and tribulations that would have ploughed any one of the rest of us six feet under. Leah is the glue that holds the rest of us together as odd as that may sound. All the times when she needed nurturing and to be cared for, Leah Gibson was too busy caring for and nurturing us."

Cal paused in reverence and awe of how much a man's man like Robert Haas admired and loved the love of his life, and he pondered how he could even respond to such deep devotion. Carter, who had sat quietly listening to their conversation, nodded his head in agreement with Robert's assessment of Leah. Finally, Cal looked Robert straight in the eye and answered, "I intend to take care of her and nurture her, Robert. As a matter of fact, I plan to spend the rest of my life trying to deserve Leah."

Robert replied, "She deserves nothing less, Cal. I will tell you something else too—I have never seen her happier."

Carter chimed in then and added, "Leah is not just happy, though, she's also satisfied and settled. She has this air of knowing she is exactly where and with whom she belongs. I've never seen her look more beautiful. Leah's quite a catch, Cal."

Cal smiled but his eyes wandered across the room to Leah sitting beside Toni and across from Siobhan and Meg. Courtney sat at the head of the dining room table with her legs stretched over to Meg's chair. They were laughing, drinking wine and telling stories that involved animated hand gestures. Leah looked over and caught Cal's eye. When she smiled, her beauty almost took his breath away, and he suddenly wanted to whisk her off to bed, tear off that dress, and make passionate love to her until they both collapsed from exhaustion. Cal sighed, and as he turned his attention back to Robert and Carter, they were grinning at his obvious distraction.

Recovering his focus on the present, Cal noticed how amused they were by his love-struck ADD, and he smiled broadly back at them. Finally he validated Carter's assessment of Leah simply and succinctly and replied, "She certainly is, Carter. Leah Gibson's the catch of my life."

CHAPTER 50

The spring flew by due, in part, by the fact that there was always something to do around the house or the farm this time of the year. Today was no exception. Leah had been up since 5:00 a.m., and she had hardly made a dent in her "to-do" list. She had already weeded and watered the garden, mixed and baked a quiche for lunch, planted some annuals in her potting shed window boxes, and trimmed and edged the yard and walkway. Leah looked at her watch. It was just after 8:00 a.m.

She was heading to the hardware store to work at 10:00, and she had another meeting at 3:00 with Chip Moretz. Tonight, she wanted to finish the crisp white linen curtains she was making for the kitchen and the upstairs guest bedrooms. Last week, she washed all of the bedspreads and bed linens and painted the rooms—appropriately, butter yellow, light lavender and sea foam green for her girlfriends and their favorite colors. She had also cleaned the gorgeous hardwood floors until they gleamed. The result was simple but stunning beauty that would welcome and make even the most dour visitor smile. The farmhouse felt like a home.

Leah had also repainted the walls of her bedroom a light powder blue and bought new bed linens. She had yet to redo the bedroom downstairs that once was her Gran-Belle's and Aunt Fi's bedroom at the other end of the upstairs hall. Leah still had just over two weeks before her best friends and first guests arrived.

Meg and Courtney had returned from their wonderful trip abroad, still very much in honeymoon-mode, but both were settled back into their work in the Capitol. Siobhan had finished up her chemotherapy last Thursday, and while she was still a little sick and nauseated, she had resumed her role on the bench. She loved it. Toni was in the throes of planning her own nuptials as well as arranging to be out of work for an extended period of time beginning in two weeks with her trip to visit Leah along with Siobhan and Meg.

With over an hour before she needed to get ready to work at the store, Leah decided to make herself a cup of hot tea and work on the curtains. She pulled a mug out of the cabinet, filled it with tap water and put it in the microwave. As she reached for the tea bag, Leah's mind flashed back to the night she got the call telling her she had lost her job at the bank. In that one single moment, her life had changed forever. Her career, her home, and her daily routine were dashed to pieces. That life seemed so far in the past Leah sometimes wondered if it existed at all. Only her friendships remained to evidence her life in Virginia Beach. Oddly, Leah couldn't muster any regret.

As she walked to the den with her teacup and sat on the couch next to the lamp, she took inventory of what she had accomplished and how far she had come. Leah's days on the farm were busy studying growing cycles of fruits, vegetables and herbs. She could make beautiful and useful things with her hands. She could cook and bake. More importantly, though, Leah was in love. She had been a good niece and was able to help Aunt Fi when she needed it the most.

As she sewed the tabs on the top of the curtains, she reflected on her friendships, her values, her faith and her future. Leah had determined that she was a better friend now than she had ever been, much more comfortable in the role of giving support to her friends rather than needing it from them. She, like Aunt Fi, valued independence, but she never knew how self-reliant she was. As Leah recalled her darkest hours through the last two and a half years—the foreclosure of her house, the end of her unemployment, the loss of Aunt Fi—she realized that she alone had mustered the will and the determination to rally herself to action.

Leah wanted to marry Cal, have his children, and live the rest of her life here on this land she loved with him. She wiped away a tear of happiness, and thanked God that she had made choices that brought her home again. She looked at her watch, anxious now to see him. She put away the curtains, finished her tea and climbed the stairs to get ready to go to the hardware store, the smile never leaving her face.

For Leah, the joy of daily living went back to the faith instilled in her as a child but rediscovered through the despair of losing everything except what mattered most—her friends and her family.

Her life here reconnected her with the peace only faith provided, and she treasured the love and kindness of the people both dead and living who lived by that example. Material things were fleeting. People were not. Even after they died, the people who touched you never went away. A chill ran up Leah's arm, and she smiled knowingly. The spirits of Aunt Fi, Gran Belle and her mother lived on in her and spoke to her in these quiet moments, and anytime she needed reassurance, they were never more than a memory away.

CHAPTER 51

Leah and Cal had really gotten into a groove working together at the hardware store. Cal found that he had much more time for ordering inventory and stocking shelves when Leah was around because she did the work of two employees, and she did all of the accounting that he hated with a passion. Not that he wanted her tucked away in his office, though. Leah was also his best salesperson. She was a voracious reader and when a customer had a question, Leah would research it, learn all about the subject then answer the customer with details and supporting information. She had also reorganized his office and the cashier station as well as planted spring annuals outside to attract women in addition to his usual male clientele.

Sales this year were up almost 15 percent over last year, and Cal knew why. Leah Gibson was good for business. On Saturday mornings, she came in early to brew coffee and bring freshly baked coffee cake, muffins or Danishes for the customers. Cal was certain he would have put on ten pounds since Christmas if he hadn't kept up his exercise routine. He and Leah were now running four miles four days a week. She was in incredible shape, and he still had trouble keeping up with her, outside and inside. Leah Gibson was a dynamo.

Cal stood watching her talk to a group of high school boys in the Future Farmers of America. Leah was talking to them about organic gardening, and they clung to her every word. She could have been reading a list of ingredients—they didn't care. The young men simply wanted to look at her. Cal shook his head. Leah was a shameless flirt without even trying to be.

Seemingly still under Leah's spell, Cal didn't hear or see Marissa enter his store. When she walked up behind him, she purred, "Now that's more little Leah's speed. She can't handle a real man like you, honey."

Marissa was a black cloud on a perfect day. He wheeled around, arms crossed, and asked, "What do you want now, Marissa?"

She laughed coyly and asked, "Oh, Cal, is that any way to greet your wife?"

"Ex-wife," he replied. "Again, what do you want?"

Marissa sighed heavily and dramatically then said, "I need to talk to you, Cal. Is there somewhere we can talk privately?"

Cal stood scowling at her wondering what her angle was this time. He trusted Marissa about as far as he could throw her. He looked at his watch. It was 2:00, and Leah would be leaving to go meet Chip Moretz in a few minutes. He didn't have anybody else to work the cashier this afternoon. He finally answered, "Not today, Marissa."

"Well, how about if I come by your place tonight to talk," she offered. "I don't bite too hard," she added.

"No, it's your bark I don't like," Cal replied. "Let me talk to Leah."

"I didn't know you needed her permission," Marissa said.

"What you don't know would fill this entire store," he retorted. "Stay put."

With a noticeable scowl on his face, he walked away from her toward Leah. The closer he got the more he relaxed. When she saw the look on his face, she smiled and put her hand on his cheek. Leah said, "Your face is going to get stuck like that."

"God, I hope not! Marissa's here . . . again. She needs to talk to me," Cal said. "What are your plans for the afternoon?"

Leah looked at her watch, the wheels in her minds turning. After a short pause, she said, "I am meeting Chip at 3:00 at the farmhouse. I want him to see what I've done and what I've got planned. I should be tied up for at least three hours or so. What did you have in mind?"

Cal ran his hand over the short hair on the top of his head, "I don't know what she wants. Marissa needs to talk to me about something. Will you call me when you're done entertaining Chip?" he asked, a little perturbed.

"Of course I'll call you. Are you jealous?" she teased.

"You're damn right I'm jealous," he said softly. Cal reached down and took her hand. He suddenly didn't want to let her go or go back to Marissa. Instead, he wanted to be alone with Leah and lose their minds in the throes of passion. As his imagination ran away from him, he slid the grommet he was holding on then off her ring finger without thinking.

Leah looked up at him and smiled. Then, she answered, "Yes, if you're asking."

Cal laughed at his mindless action and said, "I would hope I could do a little better than this. You need to go. It's after 2:00. Call me when you get through. Hopefully, Marissa will say what she needs to say, ask for what she needs to get and get the hell out of my life!"

"I hope the same thing," Leah said. Before she left, she reached up and kissed his cheek. "I'll see you later tonight so you better conserve your energy," she whispered in his ear then she turned, grabbed her purse and walked out the door.

Cal closed his eyes as Leah left his field of vision, but not his mind. He was aroused and hard as a rock. God, he wanted her right now. He sighed and readied himself to deal with Marissa. Just the thought of her cooled his desire, and he walked right past her instead of to her and said over his shoulder dismissively, "You can come by my house at 7:30, and we'll talk. Now, get out of here so I can get some work done."

"I'll see you tonight, Cal," Marissa answered sweetly, but when she turned to flirt with him some more, he had already disappeared around the corner, leaving her indignant but with no audience or ally to hear her pout or complain.

CHAPTER 52

Even after Leah got back to the farmhouse, she was still irritated by Marissa's appearance at the hardware store and her obvious intention to insert herself back into Cal's life. Leah was certain she was up to no good. Not that she was threatened—she wasn't, but every time Marissa was around, Cal had to deal with her shenanigans, and they left him grouchy and morose.

Leah turned her mind back to the task at hand—showing Chip Moretz what she had done to the farmhouse and her tactical plans for the retreat week for her friends, and later, paying guests. She had placed a large canopy tent beside the potting shed for a discussion and hands-on demonstration of container gardening; bought new pots and pans for preparing gourmet dinners from organic and locally grown produce and herbs; and converted the large, downstairs bedroom into a quilting room complete with several frames and an array of fabrics, battings and threads. As the summer progressed and fresh vegetables from the garden ripened and grew, she would add a session on canning as well.

The evolution of the retreat from idea into action exhilarated Leah and she tried to look objectively at each activity and area like her guests would. She already knew the evening activities designed to pamper would be a hit with women, and she had made arrangements with Kimber Walker from the local campus of the community college's cosmetology department to provide facials, chair massages, and manicures and pedicures three nights each week for eight weeks. The sessions gave the students hands-on experience and some spending money to boot and gave Leah's guests personalized attention and pampering. Leah's plan was a win for the guests, the students, the farm and her own bank account. She would be profitable after her third week of six guests. The prospects of such success excited Leah, and she couldn't remember being as motivated or stimulated in all her years in banking.

Chip's rap on her door snapped Leah out of her daydream, and she walked quickly to let him inside. Always jovial, Chip's positive attitude was infectious and Leah laughed as he greeted her, "Hi ho the merry-o, my farmer in the dell!" Pander barked a welcome as she came running from the den, her tail wagging furiously. Chip reached down and stroked the beagle's ears. Pander nuzzled Chip playfully then trotted away from the door back to her bone in the den.

"Come in, Foolish One," she said good-naturedly. Over the last several months, Leah and Chip had become fast friends. He was connected to the state-wide network of agricultural agencies and shared best practice with Leah while she was plugged in to the latest technology and social media that provided Chip's local farmers, producers and merchants with new channels and outlets for their goods and services. Plus, both were optimistic and hard-working, and they loved the high country.

Chip's family owned a Christmas tree farm near Lansing, and he had been engaged for over five years to Sheri Hampton, the love of his life. Leah was incredulous when he told her how long he had been engaged, but he shrugged it off. He had heard it all before. Chip told her, "We'll get married when she is finished with school, however long it takes." Sheri had a Master of Science degree and was now completing her Ph. D. at Wake Forest University in biology. She had a long list of prospective employers, but was most at home among her small herd of Black Angus cattle alongside Chip's tree farm. Chip thought Sheri would probably end up teaching over at Appalachian State University in Boone.

Chip and Cal had been in school together, and they were both alumni of NC State University. They were not close friends, but they had stayed in touch with each other through their years in Raleigh and since they both returned to work and live in Ashe County. They had always been an almost friendly competition between them, but they got along well.

Leah was somewhat intimidated by Sheri before they first met. Her background and credentials made Leah feel like a cardboard farmer. Within minutes, though, the two were discussing the best methods of composting, where to find the best goat cheese and the proliferation of wineries in the region. Sheri was kind, funny and no-nonsense. Leah liked her immediately, and she realized that Sheri was the first female friend she had made in her new home, and the thought made Leah smile.

Chip was a huge coffee fan like Leah, and she had brewed a pot of freshly-ground coffee before his arrival. After she gave him the tour of the changes she had made to the farm and farmhouse, they sat down at the kitchen table over a cup of Joe to look at her newly designed website, her Facebook page with the weekly events broadcast to all of her more than 2,500 friends, and a four-color ad she planned to run in *Our State* and *Southern Living* magazines in June and July. Chip was blown away, and they continued discussing Leah's projections and the possibility of teaming up for a holiday retreat later in the year where they could visit his tree farm that he transformed each year into a Christmas village, lit with thousands of lights and decorated with holiday vignettes, including a living nativity. Leah added the idea to her list of future retreats.

As they continued planning, Leah got up and refreshed their cups of coffee. When she did, she looked down the hollow and saw Marissa walking up the Hollow Road. No doubt, she was on her way to Cal's house, but he wouldn't be home for hours. His absence would give Marissa plenty of time to make herself at home or snoop through his belongings. An uneasy feeling filled her, and Leah sighed.

Her change in mood was not lost on Chip, though, and he asked her what was wrong. Leah returned to the table and said simply, "Marissa Doherty or Montgomery or whatever she calls herself these days."

Chip shook his head and assured Leah, "That woman is a stranger here and always was. She even fancied herself too good for Boone when she let for Nashville. Besides, Cal's knows he got it right this time with you, Leah. Give the man some credit, gal. Cal's a smart man, and he's old enough now to know that booty and beauty are spelled with different letters."

Leah laughed at his cleverness and squeezed his arm, "I know, Chip, but that woman is a bad seed, and I just want to make sure she understands any roots she thinks she left in the ground before are dead and gone."

"Roots that shallow don't grow, they just create headaches trying to get them out of the way," he added softly.

"That's exactly what I'm worried about Chip. They don't make an aspirin for headaches like her either," Leah finished, and as Chip turned his attention back to her list of supplies, the foreboding of danger continued to percolate inside her, and a chill ran down her arms. Leah also could have sworn she heard Pander growl darkly.

Splitting the air like a knife, the sharp knock on the door caused Leah and Chip to jump in unison, and they laughed at their jitters as Leah got up to answer the door. "Maybe we should switch to decaf, huh?" Leah commented as she opened the door.

As she turned casually to greet her visitor, she suddenly felt like all of the air had been vacuumed from her lungs. Pander stormed angrily from the den, barking sharply as a warning that came too late. Marissa stood at the door. The hair on the back of Leah's neck stood full on end. "Marissa," she said flatly, "What are you doing here?"

"May I come in?" Marissa asked sweetly.

For an instant, Leah paused then stepped back to let her inside. Pander's growl rumbled low and long. As Marissa entered, Chip rose from the table feigning manners, but preparing for trouble. As soon as the door closed, he realized he was too late.

When he saw the shiny revolver in Marissa's hand, Chip stepped closer to Leah. The movement was not lost on Marissa, and she said, "Well, aren't you sweet trying to protect Ashe County's little flower?"

Never intending to wait for an answer, Marissa stepped closer to Leah, clearly trying to intimidate her. Pander barked sharply and bared her teeth at Marissa. Leah, though, decided to stay calm and play nice. "Marissa, just tell me what you want and I'll see if I can help you," she said softly.

Marissa laughed without humor then spat, "What I want is for you to be gone—forever—and I sure as hell don't want your help, you conniving little bitch. Now, first get that damn dog to shut up or I'll silence it forever."

Leah picked up her beagle and turned and walked the few steps toward the parlor bathroom off the den, put Pander inside and closed the door. Her companion's muffled barks never stopped. As Leah turned back to the kitchen, she quickly decided to abandon civility. She looked into Marissa's eyes and stepped toward her then said, "My dog is out of your way, but I'm not going anywhere."

Chip gingerly put his hand on Leah's elbow, trying to steer her out of harm's way, but Marissa raised her handgun even with Leah's chin, cocked the gun, then replied, "Yeah, you are—we are all going to go for a ride, but first, Leah, you are going to leave darling Cal a little note." Marissa pushed her note pad across the table and added, "Write 'Cal, I'm sorry, but Chip and I have gone away together. Leah.'"

"I won't!" Leah exclaimed.

"You will!" Marissa mocked with the same amount of emphasis. To reiterate her point, she put the gun to Leah's temple then repeated, "Write."

Leah jerked away from her grasp and leaned over and quickly scribbled the letter then pushed it to the middle of the table. Then Marissa said, "Now hand over your smart phones—and your laptop." Chip and Leah put them on the table. Marissa reached for the phones and put them in her pocket then put the computer under her arm. "Now, grab your purse and let's go," she ordered and motioned for them to go out the door with the gun.

As they walked out onto the porch, Leah looked down the hill to see if Cal was home yet. He wasn't, and she felt panic beginning to rise in her throat. She took three deep, silent breaths to keep her wits about her. She knew now was not the time to lose her head. Leah looked over at Chip. Worry was etched on his forehead, and she could almost see his mind at work trying to figure a way out of the situation. He caught her eye, and tried to reassure her with his expression.

Leah knew he would try to protect her and himself, but she also knew that Marissa, always crazy mean but now completely mad, would be a formidable foe. All they could do was play along with Marissa, and hope they could follow the invisible storyline in her head.

As they approached their vehicles, Marissa stopped behind them and said, "Get into your truck, Chip—slowly!" Chip walked toward the driver's side door, his eyes never leaving Marissa's. Leah looked back at Marissa, awaiting her own command. Marissa, further irritated by the look of contempt on Leah's face, took one step toward her, raised the pistol and put it against Leah's forehead. "Wipe that look off of your face before I blow it off! Now get in the passenger side," she growled. Leah complied, equally afraid that even if Marissa didn't simply pull the trigger intentionally she might still unload the gun by her careless and wild gestures. Marissa got in after Leah and returned the gun to her right temple. "Drive, Chip—north onto 194 toward Todd," she insisted.

The silence in the cab of the pickup was deafening, and Leah's ears rang as terror crept back into her throat. She again resorted to deep breathing, forcing herself to pay attention to which way they were going. As they past first Cal's house then Mr. C's, Leah felt almost forlorn. Marissa saw her stares to her last refuges in the hollow, and she laughed, sinister and dark then said, "Aw, poor Leah, there's no going-away party!"

Leah simply turned her gaze back to the road, trying to figure out how they were going to get out of this situation, and even what the situation was. They turned north on the highway and drove for several miles, all the while climbing higher and higher as the ridge of the mountain came into view as they wound up its side. By Leah's guess they had driven about seven miles. As they crested the mountain, a roadside turn-out on the left side of the narrow highway appeared.

Breaking the silence, Marissa shouted, "Pull onto the gravel, Chip." For effect, she cocked the gun. Chip slowed the truck, crossed the southbound lane and pulled onto the gravel. Leah noticed that the sun had disappeared behind the mountains to their west, and dusk was setting in quickly.

Chip put the truck into "park" and turned to Marissa. "What now? You need to let us get back. It's not too late to stop this madness," he reasoned.

Reason was lost on Marissa, though, and she fired back, "You haven't even begun to see madness, you hillbilly bastard! Now Leah, you get out of the truck and come with me. Chip, if I lose sight of either one of your hands, I am going to blow Blondie's precious brains out. Got it? Now put both of your hands out of the driver's window."

Chip rolled down the window as they exited his truck and he tried to watch where Marissa was going and what she was doing through the small rearview mirror. He saw her throw Leah's laptop and then their mobile phones down the mountain in front of her then momentarily go into the woods across the street with Leah. Chip tried to swallow the enormous lump in his throat. He was certain that Marissa was going to shoot Leah. Tempted to squeeze his eyes shut but afraid to let them leave the mirror, Chip knew he had never in his life been seized with fear like he was now. He could taste its rustiness in his mouth, feel its arrhythmic beat in his chest, and smell it oozing out of his pores. He knew he had to stay calm. Resorting to his Boy Scout training, Chip breathed deeply and slowly, but he never stopped looking in the mirror.

After what felt like hours, Chip saw Leah pull up behind his truck in Marissa's car, the gun still at her temple. He prayed silently that they would survive this nightmare, but he realized they might not, and he asked for mercy on their souls and for grace and peace for their obviously deranged captor. Collected if not calm, Chip watched Marissa silently giving Leah orders before the driver's door opened and they both emerged.

Marissa had hold of Leah's shirt and the gun was now in the small of Leah's back. They walked to Chip's window. Marissa stopped Leah and told her, "Get in the passenger side of the truck. Anything funny and I'll blow Farm Boy's head off—go!" and she pushed Leah toward the front of the truck to go around as she repositioned the gun to the side of Chip's head.

As Leah passed in front of the truck, she looked down the mountain. It was covered with trees, and craggy outcroppings of rocks jutted out in four or five places on the steep, almost vertical slope. The dizzying drop caused Leah to swallow hard to quell the vertigo that washed over her.

When she got to the passenger door, Leah hesitated. Marissa yelled, "Get in! Then you can get as cozy with Chip as you were with

Cal at your old aunt's funeral. How sweet," she said sarcastically. Leah opened the truck door and got in. She caught Chip's eye, and he nodded as if to reassure her that they were going to be alright. Leah slid into the passenger side of the bench seat. "Close the door. Then put your hands on the truck ceiling—you, too, plowjock," Marissa said, pointing the gun barrel up twice to reiterate her expectations.

Leah complied, and she felt her hands shaking, her palms sweating as she reached up to touch the ceiling of the cab. She had no idea what was going through Marissa's twisted brain, but she could not deny the sick feeling that had seized her stomach. Leah was terrified, and the more she focused her gaze on the darkening sky in front of her as they sat perched atop the perilous drop, the more she realized that she and Chip were in grave danger. She tried once again to reason with Marissa.

"Marissa, please, please stop this crazy shit, and let us go home," Leah implored.

A low sound rose from Marissa's chest, somewhere between laugh and growl, and as Leah's eyes met Marissa's, a feral, angry maniac stared back at her. Then she suddenly broke into song,

> *"Going home, I'm going home,*
> *There's nothing to hold me here;*
> *Well, I've caught a glimpse of that heavenly land,*
> *Praise God, I'm going home."*

When she finished the haunting refrain of the gospel hymn, Marissa leaned her head back and laughed. Then she added, "Oh, yeah, you're going home, sweet thing. Chip, put that truck into 'drive.'"

"You're crazy, woman!" Chip exclaimed. "You might as well just shoot us."

Marissa sighed impatiently then said, "As tempting as that sounds, that's not how this whole drama is going to go down."

"I'm not putting the truck into 'drive,'" Chip insisted.

Marissa glared at Chip, completely put out by his refusal to comply. She paced nervously, huffing angrily, but never lowered the gun. Finally, she snarled, "Now I'm going to get into my car, but if there is any funny stuff, I am just going to aim for your head through that back window."

Leah surmised quickly that Marissa wasn't crazy—she was completely unhinged. Her cavalier attitude with the handgun and her maniacal laugh were both windows into her instability, but Leah couldn't figure out what she was doing and Chip's refusal confused Marissa to the point that perhaps she didn't know what she was doing either. She quickly glanced at Chip. He, too, seemed perplexed, but as his eyes met hers, Leah realized he was also nervous. He quietly instructed her, "As soon as you hear that car door close behind us, you put that seatbelt on, okay?"

Leah had trouble finding her voice, but she managed, "Okay." Her breathing was ragged and shallow, and she felt like she might pass out. Leah breathed deeply from her diaphragm, trying to stay calm.

A split second after she exhaled, though, she heard Marissa's door close and she quickly reached for her seatbelt. The instant she heard the latch click into the buckle, Marissa yelled, "Bye-bye, little Leah!" and the impact from behind was so hard and so sudden that Chip's foot slipped off the brake pedal. The truck lurched forward, and even though the truck was in "park" and Chip recovered quickly to depress the brake again, it was too late. The loose gravel wouldn't stop the truck, and the front wheels left the ground as Marissa continued to push them from behind toward the edge of the mountain. Leah screamed, and she felt the truck tip weightlessly in mid-air before it made contact with the ground again then careened down the mountain into the black woods. Amidst the sounds of gnashing metal and splitting timber, Leah threw her arms over her face and felt rather than heard herself cry out with each collision before one final impact jolted her painlessly from the conscious world into a silent, blank darkness.

CHAPTER 53

The sun had completely disappeared below the western horizon by the time Cal arrived home after stopping to check on and visit with his dad for a few minutes. He looked up the hollow and even through the darkness he could make out Leah's SUV at the farmhouse. From the light burning in the kitchen, he figured Chip was still there, and he sighed softly to brush away the jealous irritation that percolated in his gut. Chip was a great guy, and he had gotten to know Leah very well over the last couple of months. They had clicked immediately and become good friends. Like Leah, Chip Moretz was never at a loss of words, and Cal knew together the two of them could talk the paint off the walls. Combined with Marissa's impending visit, he knew it was going to be a long evening.

Cal went to his bedroom and changed into his jeans and tee shirt. He sure as hell wasn't going to dress up for Marissa's arrival, and the thought of her coming over irritated him all over again. He walked to the kitchen and grabbed a beer out of the fridge. As he took his first, long swallow, Cal heard a car pull up outside. He sighed, and wished he could fast-forward to his ex-wife's departure and be done with her.

In an attempt to get this evening over as soon as possible, Cal opened the door before Marissa could knock. She, of course, mistook his gesture as being happy to see her and said in her too-sultry voice, "I couldn't wait to see you either, Cal. It has been too long."

"No, Marissa, I was thinking that eternity was not long enough. Come in and tell me what you want," he said, unable to mask his contempt.

"Why Cal, where are your manners? Aren't you going to offer me a beer?" she asked with feigned hurt.

"You know where the refrigerator is. Help yourself," he answered and casually walked to the den without her.

Marissa opened the refrigerator, cursed Cal under her breath, and grabbed a beer before she followed him. She knew he was not going to make anything easy for her, but he was being an even bigger asshole than the last time she had come to see him a month ago. Marissa chalked his attitude up to that bitch Leah. Well, no more! The thought made Marissa smile broader.

As she followed him into the den, he was sitting on the couch staring out the back window. Plastering a smile on her face that she didn't feel, Marissa said, "This room always did have a million dollar view."

"Yeah, but that wasn't enough for you because you couldn't cash it in. What do you want, Marissa?" he asked impatiently.

She took a deep breath and steadied herself then she took a drink of her beer. Finally, she said, "I want to come home, Cal."

Cal stared at her like he had been slapped. After several awkward seconds of silence, he felt an incredulous laughter bubbling up in his throat that spilled out uncontrollably. He shook his head and said darkly, "This is not your home, Marissa. It never really was and it never will be again. You need to go back to Nashville or at the very least, go home to Boone. I don't want you here."

"But Cal," she pleaded and reached over and put her hand on the top of his thigh, "You just have to let me stay here, at least for a little while. Daddy's will cut me off until I reconcile with you."

"So *that's* your angle! You came here to whore yourself for your daddy's money. I knew you wanted something. Well, let me be very clear, Marissa. Hell will freeze over before I ever reconcile with you, honey," he said emphatically as he picked up her hand and removed it from near his crotch, "but I will call your mother tomorrow and tell her you came here and tried to work it out as long as you get the hell out of my life and never come back. We're through—done—finished. Do you understand?"

Angry at his condescending tone, Marissa responded snidely, "I understand, alright. You have a substitute piece of ass to get your jollies now."

"For somebody who has never been anything but a piece of ass, I am sure you see it that way. Why don't you just go?" he said.

Marissa's angry tears stung her eyes, and she said as humbly as she could muster, "I don't have anywhere to go tonight, Cal."

Cal looked at her silently, trying to discern if she was being honest. Finally, he said, "You can stay in the guest room tonight, but after we call your mother tomorrow morning, I want you out of here—for good."

"I can't think of anything I want more myself," she all but whispered. "I'm going to get my bag, get a shower and retire for the evening. Tomorrow morning will get here more quickly that way." Cal nodded and turned his gaze back to the window where night had fallen and the stars dotted the black sky.

Marissa watched his gaze go back up the hill toward Leah's farmhouse, and she secretly reveled in the moment, forcing herself, though, to tamp down her enthusiasm over finally being rid of the nuisance known as Leah Gibson. Marissa said offhandedly, "She's not there," before she walked outside to her car, grabbed her bag and returned to the house. She had to keep herself together. As she came back inside, Cal stopped her and asked, "How do you know Leah's not home?"

Brushing off the urgency in his voice, Marissa walked to the guest bedroom at the back of the house. With her back to him, she let the burgeoning smile spread across her face. She could feel rather than see him follow her down the hall. Marissa answered, "I saw her and that Chip guy leave in his truck a couple of hours ago."

Feigning nonchalance, she turned to him. "Care to join me for a long, hot shower?"

"God, no," Cal replied immediately. "I'm going to go check on Leah. Good night, Marissa."

She slammed the door behind him, muttered, "And good riddance," under her breath then sat angrily down onto the bed. Cal was such a smug bastard, acting like he was doing her a favor by letting her stay in his country cottage on the ass side of nowhere. He could hurl insults at her and spurn her now, but soon, he would realize that she was the only option for him, and Marissa couldn't wait for him to come running back to her arms—or between her legs—once he found out that his precious Leah was gone forever.

Cal grabbed his hooded sweatshirt off the hook beside the door and pulled it over his head as he went outside and started up the path between his house and Leah's. Something didn't feel right, and he quickened his pace to a jog. As the terrain flattened back out, Cal took the steps to the front porch in one leap and knocked on the door. He listened intently for movement from upstairs, the den or the back room. All he heard were the muffled, manic barks from Pander. *Where is she?*

Peering into the kitchen from the slit in the curtains, Cal saw the coffee pot, two mugs and a piece of paper on the table. He reached for the doorknob. The door was unlocked, and he went inside. Following the sounds of her yelps, Cal went in search of Pander. She was closed inside the parlor bathroom. The unsettled feeling in his gut flared again as he opened the door and picked up the dog. She was shaking and nervous and frantically licked at his hands and his face. The sense that something was wrong intensified. Cal walked to the den and put Pander down on her bed. He gently stroked her head reassuringly.

Cal went back into the kitchen. He saw the piece of paper on the edge of the table and picked it up. As he read it, he collapsed into the nearest chair. He read it again. The note was completely unemotional, short and simple. Leah and Chip were going away together. *Going where?* Cal wondered. He looked closely at the letter. At the bottom, embedded in her four-letter, little name, he thought he saw a very light, almost indiscernible "h," "l" and "p" around the "e" in her name. Cal got up quickly to scrutinize the letters directly under the range light to be sure he wasn't imagining them.

He realized his hands were shaking. He reached over and touched the mugs on the table, still half-filled with coffee. They were cold. Cal stood and walked over to the coffee pot. It was off, but the carafe was warm. The coffee maker automatically turned off after two hours, but the two hour mark had to have passed within the last hour. Cal pulled his phone off his hip and called his dad.

Minutes later, his dad pulled into the driveway alongside Leah's SUV. Cal opened the door as his father crossed the porch. Communicating without words, Cal handed him the letter. As his dad read it, he pointed to the bottom and simply asked, "Here—do you see it?"

His dad looked at the signature then looked up and said, "It's hardly visible, but it is there. We need to call the police, son." Cal sighed loudly then nodded.

"Let me call Sheri Hampton first, though, Dad. Chip may be home," Cal added.

"You need to call Leah's mobile phone too," his father said.

Cal looked at him forlornly. His dad was right, though. That call had to be his first. He nodded again and dialed her number. As the phone rang in his ear, Cal plopped down onto the kitchen chair behind him. The long night he imagined earlier in the evening now seemed like a daydream. The call he was making seemed to unfold in slow motion, and as the phone rang in his ear, Cal held his breath, hoping that Leah answered his call on one hand, all the while praying that she didn't on the other.

CHAPTER 54

A faint, familiar melody beckoned Leah from the darkness, but the cool crisp breeze across her cheek stirred her. She tried to open her eyes, but blinking into the night only served to disorient her more. Leah wanted to go back to sleep, but her arm throbbed. The night air blew against her face again, and like a smack to her forehead, she awoke with a start. The song "My Guy" played again, and Leah realized her cell phone was ringing, and Cal was calling. *Where is my phone?*

Leah was now fully conscious, and the terrible events that landed her here—wherever *here* was—flooded her mind. She kept her eyes wide open, knowing that in a few minutes they would adjust to the darkness. She reached to her left for Chip. He didn't move. Leah cried out, "Chip! Oh, Chip, please wake up." Still he didn't move. The truck did, though.

It swayed to and fro, and Leah held her breath in fear that the terrifying fall down the mountain might resume at any time. She reached for Chip's neck, her hands trembling, and tried to find a pulse. She exhaled and sobbed out loud in one breath when she felt the soft throbbing at his throat.

Leah had to get out and go get help. She looked around, her eyes now fully adjusted to the night. Tree branches filled the space in front of them where Chip's windshield used to be. She looked out her side window into a sea of stars. Chip's window was against the ground. Leah realized they were suspended on the mountain against a tree, but she wasn't sure if they were upside down or not. She decided to unlatch her seatbelt. When she fell on top of Chip, Leah figured out the truck was lodged on its side against the ground on the driver's side. She quickly reached up to roll down her window. Her arm ached, and she wondered if it was broken or just bruised. Leah knew, though, that the severity didn't matter because she was clearly the lesser injured of the two. Chip stirred beside her and Leah rolled toward the dashboard to make sure her weight didn't exacerbate his injuries. She asked, "Chip? Can you hear me? I've got to go get help. Do you have a flashlight?"

A barely audible groan escaped from his throat and as Leah made out his face, she could see that Chip was bleeding, but she wasn't sure if it was from his nose, a laceration or something more serious. From the top of the dash, she reached up to open the glove box. Rustling with the hand of her wounded arm, she winced as she fingered the contents, each movement causing pain to shoot up her arm. As she felt a cylindrical object in her hand, though, Leah cried out with joy.

She turned on the flashlight and looked at the damage. Her right arm was swollen half way up her forearm, and Leah was certain it was broken. She shined the light toward Chip. Leah gasped out loud, and reached over again to feel his pulse. She found it, but the strength of the beats was slipping.

Leah shined the beam outside. She would have to climb out her window, onto the tree then shimmy through the limbs down to firm ground. She focused the light down the mountain. They were still a long way from the bottom. Leah whispered to Chip, "I am going to get you some help, Chip. Hang in there—Sheri is counting on you." She squeezed his hand, and she felt him try to squeeze her hand back. Leah brushed away the tears clouding her eyes with her hand. She didn't need anything to disrupt her focus.

As she positioned one foot against the steering wheel, the other against the headrest in the middle of the bench seat, Leah hoisted herself up through the window. Searing pain shot through her right arm, and she cried out in pain, but kept moving anyway, finally crawling outside the cab to where she could sit on the top of the truck to regain her strength and reassess her location. Leah was panting from the effort, but as she looked out then pointed the flashlight around her, she gasped.

The truck was wedged against one of the rocky outcroppings, held in place by one single, but enormous Virginia pine tree. Trembling in fear by the perilous drop in front of her, Leah broke into gasping sobs. *I can't do this*, she thought. She sat immobilized, afraid another move would send the truck tumbling into the black abyss, but aware that if she didn't go for help, she and Chip would die on the side of the mountain anyway.

Leah took two more deep breaths. She had to keep herself calm. Chip was depending on her. She reached over to the limb of the pine tree with her good arm and pulled herself up to standing. Then, she slowly and methodically found footing on branches and climbed down to the ground below the truck. Leah moved quickly out from underneath it and paused against a hickory tree to get her bearings. As she peered down into the valley, she could see lights in the distance shining from houses under the late spring canopy below.

Leah mentally designated the closest light and took off down the steep terrain, light on her feet, but faster than was probably prudent given that it was so dark and the rocks, tree roots and leaves below her steps were uneven and loose. She pointed the flashlight beam ahead of her with her injured arm as she ran. Concentrating on keeping her breathing deep and steady, she moved closer and closer to her destination at the bottom of the hill. She knew she had been several miles, but the light in the distance still looked miles away.

Intent on picking up the pace, Leah's foot suddenly slipped on a rock, and she cried out as she felt herself falling, trying desperately to hold onto the flashlight. She forced herself to curl into a ball and she rolled down the hill until a chestnut stump stopped her like a wall.

Gasping for air, Leah felt like screaming, but she didn't have the energy. She knew if she didn't get back up and start moving forward, she would likely go into shock. She also would be of no use to Chip. Leah pulled herself up to her knees. Tremors moved through her body, and she was unsure whether they were the result of her pain, her fear or the cold.

She felt faint, but she yelled out loud, "I will NOT die on this mountain!" In one fluid movement, Leah pulled herself to her feet using the chestnut stump as support. She moved forward again, though not quite at the same torrid pace as before. After several more miles, she didn't know how much farther she could go as waves of nausea swamped her and the shaking in her body intensified.

Ahead, Leah saw light and a small yelp escaped from her throat. Her legs felt rubbery, her arm was an inferno of pain, and the blackness of the night threatened to swallow her, but Leah mustered all of the strength she had left to scream, "Help, help me, help!" As she approached the cabin, the door opened and a woman in jeans and a flannel shirt armed with a shotgun appeared. The woman was talking but Leah couldn't hear her. Delirious and in shock, she managed one final plea, "Help me," before she collapsed in a heap on the ground.

CHAPTER 55

Chip was not home, Sheri had not heard from him in hours, and Leah wasn't answering her cell phone. Cal was certain he would go stark raving mad with nothing to do but wait. The Ashe County Sheriff's Department responded to Cal's call, but they appeared skeptical at best that anything sinister had happened to Chip and Leah. Cal could tell by the looks they traded that they fully believed the pair had run away together. Even after he showed them the faint letters indicating a plea for help, Cal knew they were not convinced.

After making his report to the deputies, they left the farmhouse. Cal wouldn't be able to file a missing persons report for 24 hours. He paced the floor trying to figure out what he could do. His father pointed out the answer, "Cal, you're going to wear yourself out. Sit down, son and let's try to figure out what might have happened here." He patted the seat of the chair beside him. Cal sighed, the sat down.

His dad said, "Tell me again about today—everything."

Cal ran his hands over his close-cropped hair and answered, "Let's see—Leah and I worked at the hardware store together until two. Marissa came in just before Leah left and said she needed to talk to me tonight. I talked to Leah about it, and she told me that she was meeting Chip at the farmhouse at three to show him all of the changes and improvements she had made and to go over her projections and plans for those weekly retreats she has planned for the summer. She kissed me goodbye. She was happy, Dad. I was the one who was grouchy and irritable because that sorry ex-wife of mine came skulking back around again trying to make trouble."

His dad asked, "What kind of trouble has she been making?"

Cal shook his head then told him all the sorry details of Marissa's visit. Then, he reminded his dad that she was still at his house. "That woman is like a bad penny, son."

"I know," Cal said. "Maybe after I call her mother tomorrow morning and tell her that Marissa tried to reconcile, the queen bee will relinquish her grip on Marissa's inheritance. Cash in hand, she'll be out of Ashe County so fast she'll leave canyons in her wake."

"Those would be welcome canyons," his dad answered.

"Amen," Cal added. "Dad, why don't you go home and get some sleep? I'm going to stay here tonight—just in case."

His dad stood and patted him on the shoulder as he was leaving then said, "I'll come up tomorrow morning at first light. You need to get some sleep too."

Cal turned out the kitchen light and walked out into the crisp, clear night with his dad, and after he saw him arrive safely down the hollow at home and flick the lights, he sat down in one of the rockers on the front porch alone in the darkness. The stars were out in abundance, and Cal immediately located Orion chasing the Seven Sisters and the Big Dipper constellations.

He felt utterly helpless, and again mentally reviewed everything that happened that day. It was a good day, he thought, with the exception of Marissa's reappearance. Cal stopped rocking and looked down at his house where his ex-wife was. He wondered if she was somehow involved in this situation, and he thought back to the afternoon when Leah saw someone sneaking around outside her house. When Cal found a woman's footprints that day, he knew they were Marissa's.

The churning in his gut returned, and Cal once again stared down the hill at his house. A shadow passed the window of his den, and he could see Marissa looking up toward the farmhouse. Cal was sitting in the darkness, so she couldn't see him, and he watched her sashay back and forth in the window in her robe with a glass of wine in her hand. A cloud partially obscuring the waxing gibbous moon cleared and the little bit of extra light illuminated Marissa's face, giving it an ominous, almost evil, glow. A chill ran down Cal's spine and in that moment, a revelation cold and true crystallized. His crazy ex-wife was the only one who had the answers to the questions surrounding Leah's disappearance.

CHAPTER 56

Katie McRae stood in the doorway of her cabin, alternately looking down her winding driveway for the ambulance and over at the injured young woman who had stumbled onto her property a half-hour ago. Katie administered the necessary first aid to stabilize the wounds the best she could. She cleaned and bandaged the cuts, put her obviously broken right arm into a sling, and covered her with every quilt and blanket she owned to ward off further shock. The stranger was dehydrated too, and Katie roused her several times from the exhaustion that dragged her into sleep and gave her glasses of water to drink. Each time she woke, she kept babbling incoherently about the same people—Chip, Cal, and Marissa.

Katie didn't know the woman, and she had lived in Ashe County for thirty years on a patch of land her late husband owned and used as a hunting cabin. After he was killed in a sawmill accident in Sparta, Katie visited the property for the first time and never left. She sold their house of ten years in town, added plumbing and electricity to the cabin, and took up hunting and gardening to minimize her trips to the stores over in West Jefferson.

Katie had a solitary but satisfying existence, and this woman's appearance at her door added a complication she didn't want or need. She sighed and looked over at her again. This visitor's presence here was not by choice, though. Katie saw the flashing lights of the ambulance coming down the long, unpaved driveway. She had warned the dispatcher that if they came with blaring sirens and lights, she would unload her buckshot in their direction. Her warning had obviously been heeded.

The woman stirred, and Katie walked to her side and tried to sit her up. "Come on, now. You're strong, I damn sure know. Let's get you up, my dear."

Leah opened her eyes and nodded and tried to sit up. She winced in pain, but she continued to work herself into a semi-upright position. "Chip . . . he's out in those woods . . . and he's hurt—a whole lot worse than I am. We've got to help him," she implored the woman attending her.

"Okay, by the way, I'm Katie McRae. Who are you?" she asked.

"I'm Leah Gibson, Fiona Parker's niece, from Buffalo," Leah managed.

Katie handed her another glass of water and said, "Drink. You're dehydrated. The ambulance is coming up the driveway. Alright Leah Gibson, who can I call for you?"

Leah grabbed Katie's hand and squeezed it tightly. Then, she pleaded, "Please call Cal Cunningham or Tom Cunningham and ask them to meet me at the hospital."

"Hardware man Cal Cunningham?" Katie asked. Leah nodded. "I know him a little bit." Katie stood to go look up the telephone number and make the call. Leah grabbed her hand again, though.

"Ms. McRae, those EMT people have got to get to Chip or he's going to die on the side of that mountain," Leah said, and she broke into heartbreaking sobs, the tears streaming down her face.

Katie sighed then patted her hand. "Okay," she said, "Tell me as specifically as you can where he is—and it is Katie, not Ms. McRae."

For the next two minutes, Leah retold the events of the afternoon beginning at the part where they were taken hostage by Cal's ex-wife. She told Katie that the best way to get to Chip Moretz was probably from the top of the mountain behind her cabin since the truck had lodged closer to the top than the bottom thanks to the sturdy pine and the rocky ledge. Katie immediately got up, retrieved the phone and called the sheriff's department. As she was explaining the urgent situation to them, the ambulance pulled up outside and she opened the storm door to let them inside.

When she hung up the phone, she returned to Leah's side and assured her the deputies, fire and rescue crews were on their way to Chip. She added, "Somebody had already reported that you two were missing."

"Cal," Leah answered. "Please call him, Katie."

"What's his number?" she asked, and she quickly wrote it down then moved out of the way of the EMTs so they could better tend to Leah. Katie walked into her tiny kitchen and called Cal Cunningham's cell.

On the third ring, Katie heard the familiar voice of her hardware store owner answer, "Hello?"

Katie sighed with relief and said, "Cal, this is Katie McRae. Leah is being taken to the hospital over in Jefferson from my house right now, and she would like it very much if you were there to meet her. Your ex-wife was almost successful in murdering Leah. Unfortunately, I'm not sure of the fate of Mr. Moretz yet."

Cal asked her a barrage of questions, but Katie was being summoned by the EMT. She told Cal, "I've got to go help, Cal, but Leah is going to be alright. I'll ride in the ambulance to Jefferson with her then we can talk once they get her inside, ok?" Katie's answer obviously satisfied Cal temporarily, and she hung up the receiver and went back to the den, shaking her head in disbelief that she had just offered to ride into town in an ambulance with a virtual stranger.

Katie figured she must be getting soft or senile. Whatever the reason, she knew that Leah Gibson possessed strength and resilience that was as admirable as it was uncommon. She had also taken an instant liking to the young woman with whom she not only could relate, but also recognized was so much like the young woman she had been so many years ago when she stumbled onto this place in the woods.

CHAPTER 57

Cal walked silently but rapidly down the mountain from Leah's farmhouse, past his own home to his dad's. It was well after midnight, but the lights in his cabin were on. Marissa was likely still awake. His dad had gone to bed, but when Cal phoned him after Katie McRae's call, he insisted he was not asleep. Cal brought him quickly up to speed then asked him not to turn on the lights because they might alert Marissa that her diabolical plot had been uncovered. Law enforcement was on its way.

Cal's truck was at his house so he asked his dad to drive him to the hospital in Jefferson to meet the ambulance carrying Leah. His dad would also need to drive Katie McRae home.

His dad offered to bring his old straight-shift Ford Bronco out of the barn so they could roll it down the mountain before starting it on Saddle Gap Road. They agreed that an engine starting this late at night or even a missing vehicle from the driveway might tip off Marissa to her forthcoming arrest.

Only once his dad pulled out the clutch and engaged the engine of the old jalopy did Cal breathe a sigh of relief. He felt even better when they passed a long line of cars and vans out on Buffalo Road that included the Ashe County Sheriff's Department, the NC Highway Patrol and even a SWAT team. Cal sure didn't know any of the details of Marissa's crimes, but he knew they were serious and that the authorities considered her armed and dangerous. Cal said out loud, "That woman is still in my house, too."

His dad answered, "True, but just thank God that you aren't. There's no telling what she might do when she's cornered. She's like a wild animal, son."

His father's comments weighed heavily on Cal, and they rode the rest of the way into town in silence. As they pulled up to the doors at the emergency entrance to the hospital, Cal got out while his dad went to park. Cal tried to stay calm, and he forced himself not to break full sprint to the nurse's station. Thankfully, Angela, the nurse on duty, and he went through school together.

"Angie, has the ambulance with Leah Gibson arrived yet?" Cal asked with urgency.

Angie reached over and patted his hand to reassure him, "Not yet, Cal, but they radioed to say they were only about five minutes away. Dodd is there with her, and he says she's going to be okay." Dodd was Angie's childhood sweetheart and now husband of more than fifteen years. Cal thought the world of both of them, and he exhaled out loud after Angie's update.

Cal then asked the question he had been afraid to ask since Katie McRae's call. "What about Chip? D-did he make it?" He searched Angie's face, her expression one of real concern, for the answers.

She sighed softly and replied, "I just don't know, Cal. They are airlifting him by helicopter to Boone. He's critically wounded."

Cal felt sick, and he steadied himself against the station counter. He thought about Sheri Hampton, and he wondered if she knew what was going on. He inquired, "Did y'all call Sheri?"

"We called her house, but we didn't get an answer," Angie said. "Do you have a cell number for her?"

Cal answered, "No, but she's over at Chip's. I'll call her there. Thanks, Angie." Angie nodded and squeezed his forearm.

While his father waited at the ambulance driveway for Leah, Angie pointed Cal to a small, private room where he called Sheri. He took a deep breath as the phone rang. It was almost one in the morning. Everybody knew phone calls in the middle of the night weren't for good news. Sheri answered, "H-hello?" Cal could hear the fear and anguish in her voice.

"Sheri," he said as calmly as he could, "This is Cal Cunningham. Are you at Chip's alone?"

Sheri started crying. He sucked at breaking bad news. "Sheri, Chip is badly hurt. He's been in an accident of some kind. I don't know a whole lot, but I know they are airlifting Chip to Boone. Have you got somebody that can take you there?"

Through her sobs, she answered that her dad was home just down the road, and that she would have him drive her there. She asked, "What about Leah? Is she ok?"

"She's on her way to the hospital here now," he replied, and he heard her sigh with a small amount of relief. "We'll be over to the hospital in Boone as soon as we can, Sheri. Hopefully, we can get some answers to what happened shortly from Leah. All I know is my ex-wife is somehow responsible. The authorities are on their way to apprehend her now. You need to go," he added. "We'll sort this out later when Chip is stabilized." She gave him her cell number, and Cal agreed to call her later to update Sheri on Leah and to find out how Chip was doing.

As he disconnected the call, his dad stuck his head inside and said, "The ambulance is pulling up." Cal stood quickly and rushed out of the room. As the doors opened, he saw Katie McRae first, and she jumped down and walked right over to him and smiled gently. Cal tried to remember if he had ever seen her smile before. He was sure he hadn't.

Katie put her hand on his shoulder and said, "You are one lucky man to have landed a catch like Leah, young man. She looks like she's been in a boxing match, but she's a champ. You better take care of her, Cal," she warned protectively.

Cal nodded then replied, "You bet I will, Ms. Katie. I will," he promised. She searched his face for earnestness, nodded and walked inside the hospital doors.

When they pulled the gurney down, Cal's knees almost buckled when he saw all of the bandages and tubes on and around Leah. He felt anger rising inside him toward Marissa. He would seek justice against her to the fullest extent of the law. As Dodd and the other EMT lowered the wheels to the ground and raised the gurney, Cal walked to Leah's side. Tears sprung to his eyes. He couldn't do a thing to help her. He finally found his voice and softly said, "Hey sunshine, I'm here." Leah's eyes fluttered open and she smiled.

She said, "Cal . . .," in a voice so breathy Cal thought his heart would break. Leah had scratches on her face, her left arm and her neck. Her hair was matted with leaves, dirt and blood. He took a deep breath to regain his composure then he leaned over and kissed the love of his life on the cheek. She smiled again, and Cal took her left hand into his, refusing to leave her side. He walked with her all the way to the doors of the operating room where a doctor stopped him.

"Are you Ms. Gibson's next of kin?" the physician asked him compassionately. Cal nodded. "We've got to get her in for x-rays then right into surgery to repair her right arm. She has a compound fracture, and we are going to set it and stabilize it," he said.

Cal exhaled loudly but replied, "Ok, doctor. Take good care of her." He nodded then disappeared behind the doors through which they wheeled Leah. Cal went back out to the waiting room to find Katie McRae. In the last twenty-four hours, the world had gone crazy, starting from the moment Marissa walked back into Ashe County. He had no idea what had happened, but he was incredibly grateful Leah was going to be alright.

He stopped walking for a moment, leaned up against the hallway wall and said a prayer. Cal prayed for Leah, Chip and even Marissa. He asked for clarity of thought and compassion of heart. He wanted answers to so many questions, but more than anything, what he really wanted were answers to his prayers.

CHAPTER 58

Marissa stood at the kitchen window. She felt like a squirrel in a cage—isolated, nervous and frantic. She felt the night closing in on her, and the feeling made her angry. Cal had not come home after he went to the recently-departed Leah's house, and she was in this backwoods hole-in-the-wall alone. After the way he insulted her earlier, he was probably afraid she would smother him in his sleep. The thought made Marissa smile.

The lights at Mr. Cunningham's house were off like those at the farmhouse at the top of the hill, but the woods felt alive, encroaching and feral. Marissa caught herself wringing her hands, and she forced herself to stop pacing. She went to the refrigerator, pulled out the rest of the bottle of white wine and filled her glass again. Perhaps she should just pop one of her pills and sleep off the day's events. She considered the idea for a moment then she resumed wandering through the empty cabin.

She walked back to the bedroom at the back where she had been banished to set up house for the night. She stomped over to the closet to hang her clothes. When she opened the door, she flew into a rage. Leah Gibson's clothes hung on the rack. Marissa pulled out the pink dress hanging alone in the middle of the rack. The dress brought back memories of the little bitch on Marissa's wedding day, and Marissa got even angrier.

Completely out of control now and just a little drunk, she threw the dress down onto the bed, opened her purse, took out her cigarettes and lit one. Then, just as calmly, Marissa lit the bottom of the pink dress, watching the flames devour the material inch by inch. Almost in slow motion, Marissa observed the flames as they spread to the bedspread then raced up the bed.

Smoke began filling the room, and Marissa snapped to her senses and ran to open the window. Instead of disbursing the smoke, the air fueled the fire and it raced up the wall to the curtains and across the ceiling. Now close to panic, Marissa backed slowly toward the door out of room, realizing that the house was going up in flames.

Outside, Marissa heard the sound of footsteps, men's voices and she screamed out in frustration. She decided to walk to the side door and blow out of this god-forsaken town tonight. As she grabbed her bag and purse to go, though, she heard a pounding on the door and a man's voice boom, "Marissa Montgomery, we have the house surrounded. Come out with your hands on your head!"

She moved back into the bedroom, and screamed, "This room was my room tonight!" The officers could hear by the tone of her voice that their suspect was almost maniacal in her rage, and they realized that she wouldn't surrender easily. Meanwhile, the flames had engulfed the back of the house and were spreading rapidly through the wooden eaves, threatening to devour the entire structure.

The voice on the megaphone tried to calm her down. He said much less forcefully, "Ms. Montgomery, come out of the house so we can talk. The flames are spreading and you are in danger."

Marissa laughed loudly then reached inside her purse and pulled out her handgun. She was glassy-eyed, and she was suddenly tired. Didn't these fools know who she was? Marissa was crying now and she said angrily to the still-closed door, "Cal Cunningham is a fool. He never wanted me! It was always *her*! Why her? He had me," she wailed.

The officer tried again to reason with her and said, "Put the gun down, Ms. Montgomery, and come outside so we can talk about everything."

"No! I'm done talking," she said, wildly flailing the gun from side to side. The smoke was growing thicker, and she coughed when she inhaled it. Marissa was hysterical, and the officers knew she was a danger to herself and everybody there.

Finally, without further warning, she fired the pistol at the closed door again and ran back down the hall. Halfway back to the bedroom, Marissa ran into a wall of flames, but as she turned to go back to the den, she realized she was trapped. She screamed with desperation as the wooden beam above her creaked a futile warning before it spilt and tumbled down on top of her. The SWAT team turned the corner seconds later, but they were too late. Marissa Montgomery lay dead on the floor.

CHAPTER 59

While they waited in the hospital waiting room, Katie recounted Leah's harrowing tale to Cal and Tom as precisely but gently as she could. Cal was visibly shaken, and he got up and began pacing back and forth in the hallway to sort through the events of the day and consider the toll his ex-wife's reckless actions had taken on Leah and Chip. Tom and Katie talked quietly as they watched Cal try to corral his frustration with Marissa and his worry over Leah with a solitary and constant march up and down the corridor.

Leah finally emerged from surgery two hours and four pins in her arm later. As she lay in recovery, the doctor came into the waiting room and spoke with them about Leah's condition, assuring them that she was going to be as good as new once her arm healed. "She's in remarkably good shape," the doctor finished.

"Well, she's a remarkable woman," Katie added. Cal and Tom nodded.

"When can I see her?" Cal asked.

"She'll be in recovery for a little while longer then we'll move her to a room for the night. You can visit her when she gets into the room, but she needs to rest," the doctor added.

"Quite frankly, so do you, son," Tom said to Cal. Then he added, "And so do Katie and I. Once Leah is in her room and resting, we'll go in and visit for a minute then I will drive Katie home and go to the house and get some shut-eye. I'd like to check on Chip first, though."

"Ok, Dad, let me call Sheri for an update because you know the first question Leah is going to ask is 'How is Chip?' I would like to know what to tell her, too," Cal said.

Cal went to the waiting room and called Sheri's cell number, both anticipating and dreading talking to her. When she answered, he sat abruptly down on the chair behind him, afraid his legs might not hold him upright. "Sheri, it's Cal. How is Chip?" he blurted out without preamble.

Sheri sighed into the phone then answered in a soft, fragile voice, "Well, his condition is still touch-and-go, but he is out of surgery finally. Chip had a collapsed left lung and has several broken ribs. His face is also a mess. He broke his nose and his left cheekbone and ruptured his left eardrum. The paramedic who rode with Chip to Boone said that the entire left side of the truck was crushed, likely from the impact with a tree. He was amazed that either Chip or Leah survived the plunge off the mountain. The doctor here says the next 24 hours are critical. They . . . they don't know if he has any br-brain damage." Sheri stopped to collect herself momentarily then asked, "How is Leah, Cal?"

Trying to take in everything Sheri said, Cal responded, "God, Sheri, can I do anything tonight to help you? What do you need me to do? Leah is being moved to a room. She is out of surgery. She has a severely broken arm. The doctor set it and inserted a bunch of pins. She looks like a boxer that lost a 15-round match too. She's cut and bruised. Dad and I are getting ready to go see her, but the doctor wants us to let her rest tonight. She is going to be alright, though."

Sheri's weeping was only discernible by her occasional sniffle, but after a few seconds she managed to say, "Well, Leah's survival is a prayer answered, Cal. For me, for Chip, just pray—just pray. I-I don't know what I would do without him, Cal," she sobbed.

Cal replied immediately, "I have prayed for all of us, even that sorry ex-wife of mine. I know Leah is going to want to head over to Boone as soon as they release her here. Do you need me to do anything at the farm or the house? Anything, just name it."

"No, my dad just left to head home. He's going to feed the cattle tomorrow morning and keep an eye on Chip's . . . our farmhouse," Sheri said. "Will you call Mike Fisher over at the Watauga County Agriculture Extension and let him know what has happened. Hopefully, he can send somebody from Boone to hold down the Ashe County fort until . . .," she broke off.

Cal answered her unfinished request immediately, "You bet, Sheri. I'll call Mike first thing." The door opened unexpectedly beside him and his father stuck his head through. Cal held up his hand to his dad to signal "hold on" then told Sheri, "I'm going to let you get back to

Chip. I'll call Mike, pray for Chip and you, and I'll call you tomorrow morning, okay?"

Sheri answered, "Okay, Cal. Thanks for calling and for the prayers. You and Leah are good friends. I'll talk to you tomorrow morning."

As soon as Cal hung up, he stood expectantly to go see Leah, but Tom put his hand on Cal's shoulder, intending the gesture to both comfort and stop him. The meaning was not lost on Cal, and he knew something else had happened. He suddenly felt like he was going to be sick. He plopped back down on the chair behind him then looked up into his father's face. "What is it, Dad?"

"Marissa, son—she's dead," he replied simply. Cal put his head down into his hands and ran them over his head. Tom cleared his throat and continued, "There's more." Cal's look begged his dad for this nightmare to end, but he continued, "Your house was burned down tonight too."

"What . . .," Cal said, trying to formulate words but ultimately just trailing off silently.

"Apparently, Marissa set the blaze as the police closed in around her. She perished in the fire. I'm sorry, son. The house is a complete loss," Tom finished.

"Dad, the world's gone crazy," Cal stated.

"No, Cal, Marissa did. Her anger and conniving got the best of her this time, and it almost got the best of a lot of good people too. By the way, Leah's in her room if you want to go see her," Tom said.

"Wild horses couldn't keep me away," Cal interjected and got up to go. As he stood, he put his hand on his dad's shoulder and squeezed it lightly. "Are you going to take Katie home?"

"I sure am," he answered. "She's a right interesting woman."

Cal smiled slightly and replied, "You don't say?"

"Mmm-hmm," Tom muttered then recovered by asking, "How's Chip?"

"He's critical, Dad. The next couple of days are going to be tough. I am going to call Mike Fisher over in Boone to cover Chip's agency office for a while," Cal said.

"I'll handle the hardware store tomorrow, Cal. I might even see if Katie will help me out some while you sort this whole fiasco out and Leah recovers," Tom stated.

"That's good," Cal said, "Walk with me, Dad. I can't wait anymore."

They walked down the hallway together without any further conversation until they got to the door of Leah's room. Katie was sitting on the hospital bed beside her, stroking her hair gently. Tom looked from inside the room to his son. Cal's eyes held tears of relief, and Tom urged him forward with a fatherly nudge. "You don't need to wait anymore, son. You two have waited the better part of your lifetimes to get to this point. Go," he whispered.

CHAPTER 60

The next five weeks passed quickly. Mr. C managed the hardware store in Cal's absence as he worked with the insurance company on the claim on his home and stayed around the farmhouse helping Leah with chores and final touches for her first retreat while her arm healed. Finally, the first Thursday in June, Leah got her cast off and while her arm was had lost some strength and looked a little puny, she was relieved that she could at least return to small everyday tasks like typing, cooking and cleaning with two hands.

Chip was released from the hospital after ten long days, and he was slowly recovering from the wounds that very nearly ended his life. He and Sheri had become best friends with Cal and Leah, and they spent a tremendous amount of time together. Chip still had several months of physical therapy and rehabilitation ahead of him, but he was poised to make a full recovery.

Cal's house was not as lucky. The structure was beyond repair and after conferring with his dad, Cal had scheduled the demolition crew to come out on Monday to clear the rest of the burned out structure away. He and Leah had salvaged everything they could. During her recovery, Cal spent his time at Leah's. He loved being at the farmhouse, and he pouted like a five-year-old when he was away from it for long.

Starting on Saturday, Cal would be spending the week at his dad's house, and he was already grouchy because of it. Thank goodness he had so much to do at work. Siobhan, Meg and Toni were due to arrive Saturday afternoon for a one-week retreat, and Leah couldn't wait. The nine weeks since Meg's and Courtney's wedding felt like an eternity because so many things had changed in that short span of time.

Cal and Sheri had helped her with the farm while she was out of commission in between everything they had to do themselves. Fortunately, she and Cal had planted her garden the weekend before they went to Washington DC. Leah decided on a big vegetable garden that included squash, cucumbers, cabbage, lettuce, okra and numerous varieties of tomatoes and peppers; a small herb garden; and a separate plot for Irish potatoes, sweet potatoes, and peanuts as well as her pumpkins and watermelons.

While she worked on the telephone and computer on her business plan and helped Chip return e-mails and phone calls, Sheri took the gas blower and cleaned the ditches beside the driveway, and Cal bush-hogged the brush and grass in the meadow below the farmhouse. They ended the afternoon with steaks on the grill cooked to perfection by Cal, music on the stereo and cold beers and hot coffee on the front porch.

On Saturday morning before her friends arrived, Leah got out of bed early and went to the kitchen to brew a pot of coffee. She had made fresh dough yesterday for fruit pies, and wanted to make Cal's favorite this morning—cherry. Leah had plenty left for her guests as well as a variety of fillings from which they could choose.

Leah sat down at the kitchen table. She was tired, and she wasn't feeling particularly well either. She was tempted to go get in the bed beside Cal, but she had a lot of loose ends to tie up before her friends arrived just after lunch. As the coffee brewed and she popped the turnovers into the oven, Leah was overcome by the hazelnut aroma of the coffee, and she felt nauseous. *Please don't let me be sick today*, she thought.

To fend off getting sick, Leah opened the kitchen door and was greeted by the cool mountain air that was present here year-round. She felt better. Grabbing a glass from the cabinet, she filled it with tap water and took a few swallows. Perhaps, she was just nervous about her friends coming to her home, and Leah hoped they were not disappointed.

Her fledgling new business was important, and Leah knew that honest feedback from her friends was crucial to making the retreat a memorable enough experience that her guests would want to return again and again. Leah would get to see what they learned, what bored them or was too difficult or time-consuming and what they wanted to do the next time they came.

Leah pulled the cherry turnovers out of the oven and inhaled. Man, they smelled good! As she let them cool slightly, she whipped up a simple icing, drizzled it on top of the turnovers and poured two cups of coffee. Then, Leah loaded up a wooden tray with the food and drink and two plates, napkins and flatware and carried it up to Cal.

Cal had been working incredibly long days since their ordeal with Marissa. In addition to tending to Leah and Chip, managing the hardware store, following up on the insurance claim on his house and dealing with his ex-wife's death and funeral, he had also been tending to her garden and keeping Leah's friends in the loop. The frenetic pace had taken its toll. Cal was tired. Sleep was recuperative for him so Leah let him stay in bed while she made breakfast. Now, it was almost 7 a.m., and Leah had plenty to do, including cleaning her bedroom, changing the bed linens and dusting before she added a vase of fresh flowers.

Leah cracked the door and looked in at him. He was still sleeping like a baby, and he looked so handsome and peaceful. Desire flickered inside her, and she walked to the nightstand and put down the tray before she leaned over and kissed him beside his mouth. Cal reached up and pulled her down beside him. Leah crawled under the covers and snuggled up close to him. He was hard as a rock, and she realized if she continued on this path, she would never get her long "to-do" list even started, let alone done. With a final kiss on Cal's chest, Leah sighed and pushed herself up off of the bed.

"Wake up, sleepyhead," she said softly.

"I *am* awake or didn't you notice," he answered playfully. "Come back over here and I will show you."

"Oh, no—I'm staying my distance. If I come back over there, the doctors will want to admit *you* to the hospital when I'm through," she teased.

"Promises, promises," Cal said.

"I made your favorite turnovers and hot coffee," Leah stated, "Sit up and eat because I need for you to maintain your strength so I can have my way with you, my dear."

"Again, promises, promises," he laughed. "Come over and eat with me." Cal patted the bed and she brought the tray, put it between them then sat down across from him. For the next twenty minutes, they ate and talked casually about the week ahead—Leah excited about the arrival of her friends, Cal trying not to be sentimental about the loss of his home. He turned his attention back to her and asked, "How is your arm feeling?" When Leah turned to pick up her mug of coffee, she again felt her stomach lurch, and fearful she was going to throw up, she quickly got up and ran to the bathroom.

Cal, obviously concerned by her sudden departure, followed her to the bathroom and asked, "Leah, are you alright?"

She was leaned over the toilet, but she stood up and shook her head, "I don't know what is wrong with me. The smell of coffee seems to be making me sick this morning. The same thing happened downstairs. I just feel queasy."

Cal walked over to her and put his hand on her back. He leaned down and kissed her blonde curls and teased, "You're not pregnant are you?"

As if she had been slapped, Leah turned and collapsed on the toilet seat. In the next few seconds, she tried to remember her last menstrual cycle. Her mouth had gone dry, and she was rendered speechless. Cal knelt down beside her. "Leah?"

"I . . . I don't know, Cal," she stammered. "What if I am?"

Cal reached over and pulled her into his arms and said enthusiastically, "Well, if you are, we have a wedding to plan sooner than later! We're going to be parents, Leah. Woohoo!"

Leah's head was spinning, and she, too, was happy, but a little more cautious. With everything she had been through in the last five weeks, maybe stress had just taken a toll on her usually consistent period. After collecting her wits again, she said, "Easy Cal, let's find out definitively before you start beating on your chest and swinging from tree to tree to announce the news all over Ashe County." Undeterred by her common sense approach, Cal simply stood up, beat on his chest and let loose the worst Tarzan call in the High Country as Leah swung between laughing at his antics and wondering if she was going to be able to keep her breakfast down.

CHAPTER 61

Siobhan and Toni talked the entire trip west from Virginia Beach to West Jefferson, and both were surprised at just how quickly the time passed. Siobhan realized that Leah's trip a little over six months ago was much longer simply because she didn't have anybody to talk to except her dog, Pander, and the thought made her appreciate Leah's resolve, independence and resilience even more.

Siobhan and Toni talked candidly about the stranger-than-fiction ordeal that Leah survived, especially after everything their best friend had endured in the two years prior to her move to the mountains of North Carolina. She was an incredibly brave woman, and Siobhan had evoked Leah's strength during her own struggle with cancer in the last three months to comfort her, inspire her, and propel her forward. Her family had been a strong source of support for her, too, but at the end of the day, the lion share of family responsibilities still fell on her shoulders. Organizing and planning for a week away was no small feat, but wow, did she need a girlfriend break.

Toni was thrilled to be free from the bonds of the hospital for the next three months, and she couldn't think of a better and more liberating way to begin her sabbatical than a trip to see her best friend in the beautiful Appalachian Mountains. Her wedding ceremony was one month away. Of course, Toni was excited about marrying Carter too . . . and the honeymoon in Europe. She had so many blessings in her life. These crazy girlfriends were among them.

As she drove down Main Street through the beautiful town of West Jefferson, Toni and Siobhan agreed that they could see why Leah loved being here and how she could call it "home." The town conveyed a feeling of warmth and community that was often lost in suburbia and more urban environments. Ahead, they saw Cal's hardware store, and Toni squealed with excitement as she pointed to Leah's SUV parked nearby. Siobhan squeezed her arm in response.

Meg was about thirty minutes behind them and had called them a little over an hour ago near Wytheville, Virginia, cruising along at light speed on Interstate 81. She left in the wee hours of the morning from home in Maryland, taking her time as she traveled south and southwest, hugging the Appalachian Mountains. The drive was peaceful, but long, and when Meg turned off onto the Grayson Parkway, she sighed with relief that she was almost there. This drive brought one stunning vista after another, and she couldn't wait to bring Courtney along next time. If Meg could be moved by such beauty, Courtney would be inspired by it. Meg smiled at the thought of Courtney's happiness.

After their honeymoon in England, Meg had returned to work invigorated and motivated to stimulate a large and almost unwieldy bunch of pharmaceutical sales representatives. The excitement and energy lasted all of about a month. Then, Spring fever had set in, and Meg had not seen a perceptible sales increase among any of the teams. Perhaps the group needed to get away to an inspiring locale like these mountains. Meg turned the idea over in her head and decided to pursue it further when she got back to the Capitol.

Meanwhile, Leah was pacing back and forth from the office to the front desk at the hardware store, giddy about being with her friends, over-anxious about making this week a phenomenal experience for them, and scared to death about the results on the little white stick she bought at Wal-Mart about an hour ago. Life had thrown her another curve ball, but Leah was learning that she had seen that pitch before, and she could hit it.

Shortly before 1 p.m., she heard the bell over the door ring, and when she looked up, Siobhan and Toni were almost on top of her, and they giggled and whooped with excitement and happiness as they exchanged hugs and kisses. Mr. C, who was at the register, simply smiled and shook his head at their silly antics. Leah introduced her friends to him, and then gave them the tour of the store, taking her time to show them through her favorite place, the garden center.

Leah poured each of them a glass of iced tea, and they gathered at the front desk with Mr. C to wait on Meg. About thirty minutes later, their fiery Irish friend came tearing through the door asking if they knew where she could buy a hammer to beat the brains out of the guy who drove 25 miles per hour the entire way into town on the two-lane road. Meg already had them rolling with laughter.

After more hugs and kisses and another introduction to Mr. C, they piled into their vehicles and made the short trek to the hollow. Leah led the way, and Siobhan rode with her the rest of the way home. As they turned off onto the highway, Siobhan asked her, "What's up with you, sunshine? You look positively radiant. After all you have endured, I was somewhat afraid that it would have worn you down."

Leah turned to her and smiled. Then, she answered, "I am so glad you're here. Just seeing you in the flesh makes me feel better. I've been worried about you, Siobhan, but I also have been nervous about you coming here. I hope you love my little piece of the world."

"We already do love it, silly. It is beautiful and peaceful—just like you, Le," Siobhan said.

"God, don't make me cry already! Here we go!" Leah said as she turned off onto Buffalo Road. She checked her mirror to make sure Toni and Meg followed suit. The mountains surrounded them as they wound left then right on the curvy road, and Buffalo Creek took turns on the left then the right side of the road.

By the time they turned onto the road that led into Leah's hollow, Siobhan was awed to silence by the overwhelming beauty of her surroundings. Leah simply turned to her, smiled and reached over for her best friend's hand before finally making the turn into the long, steep driveway. They passed Mr. C's modest cabin and the concrete pad where Cal's Craftsman-style house once stood. As she turned right into the farmhouse, Siobhan gasped, "Oh, Leah! It's stunning . . ."

Leah looked through her front windshield, trying to take in the farm with fresh eyes. Flowers popped from the window boxes, the herb and vegetable garden were lush and green, and the yard and meadow were freshly mowed and manicured. She sighed sentimentally and said, "It is home. Come on!"

Toni and Meg pulled up beside her vehicle in a parking area Leah had covered with slate gravel, and they walked together toward the farmhouse. "This place is like Shangri-la," Toni said wistfully.

"I may never leave," Meg answered, "I could call Courtney tomorrow. She would love it here too."

Leah relaxed completely and showed them to the porch swing and rockers, and they all sat down to take in the view. Leah pointed out Mount Jefferson, Three Top Mountain and Bluff Mountain for their orientation. Then she just spilled out, "I would love to have any of you closer to me so I could call on you for baby-sitting services."

The porch went silent, and her stomach lurched with fear that her friends might judge her harshly. Siobhan who was sitting next to her in the swing pulled her close into a hug, screamed with delight, and said, "Oh my gosh! I told you earlier you looked radiant—oh my gosh!"

Toni chimed in, "You and Cal are going to make great parents, Le! I am so happy for you."

Finally, Meg said as she squeezed in between Siobhan and Leah and wrapped them both up under her arms, "Does Cal know? Is he going to make an honorable woman out of you or what?" Then, she snorted with laughter and added, "Really, who gives a shit? He is completely hoo-hoo whipped anyway!"

Leah broke into a sheer horse laugh at Meg's commentary while Toni almost fell out of her chair and Siobhan doubled over with gulping giggles. This hilarious start set the tone for what was certain to be a week they would remember for the rest of their lives.

CHAPTER 62

By Friday, Leah and her guests had been pampered, eaten themselves into a stupor several times, and laughed at and with each other so many times they were certain they had cracked a few ribs. Cal had dropped by for dinner, and he entertained Leah's friends while she finished up roasting the chicken and vegetables for dinner.

When she brought everything out to the outdoor dining room so they could eat Al Fresco, her girlfriends were leaned toward Cal, clinging to his every word. Leah was so thankful that she had such a rich and full life. When she sat down, she asked Cal to bless the food. Cal stood and walked over to Leah's side. Leah was confused momentarily until he knelt beside her, then she began to cry.

"Hey! You can't cry yet! I have to ask you a question," he said playfully, reaching up to wipe away her tears with his thumb. Leah just nodded, her voice long gone. He took her hand and asked, "Leah Gibson, will you marry me and have my children?" After he asked the question, he pulled a small velvet box out of his pocket and opened the lid.

Toni, Siobhan and Meg gasped, and Leah was so struck by the sound, she started laughing. Her laughter made everybody else laugh too. She pulled Cal to her, kissed him full on the lips then answered, "Oh, yes Cal, yes. I've only waited for 20 years!" She hugged his neck and he rocked her in his arms. The girls broke out in whoops and hollers of excitement.

Cal said grace, and they ate in festive fellowship, enjoying the vegetables and herbs from the garden, and the freshly-brewed tea and the homemade bread. Leah brought out a blackberry custard pie with her soon-to-be famous vanilla ice cream. Everybody was fat and happy.

After they finished Cal said, "I have something else for you too, Leah, if you will indulge me."

Leah nodded and whispered, "Of course."

Cal stood and walked to his truck where he retrieved a large, wrapped box and brought it to the table. He put it in front of Leah and said, "Open it!"

When Leah tore off the paper and opened the lid, she completely crumbled at the sight and tears streamed down her cheeks like a river. Finally, she managed, "Oh, Cal, you replaced my dress."

"No, not exactly," he said.

Leah said, "I don't understand."

Cal continued, "This dress is longer, like a wedding dress. I want to marry you tomorrow with all of your friends here. If you'd like, I've got Dad and Katie on board, and I've already cleared Pastor Canton's schedule and put Chip and Sheri on standby. I know this ceremony might not be your dream wedding, but I don't think I can wait any longer."

"But Cal," Leah said through her tears, "this is my dream wedding. Yes, yes, yes to everything," and she got up and threw herself into his arms while her girlfriends cheered again, this time through sniffles and tears of joy.

Leah squeezed Cal's neck then kissed him deeply. She whispered, "I love you, Cal Cunningham."

"I love you too, Leah Gibson. Now, you've got a wedding to prepare. Tomorrow at the church at 12:00 noon sharp," he said.

"My posse and I will be there," Leah said. "I think I hear your daddy calling you," she teased, and Cal rolled his eyes but rose to go. Before he did, he kissed Leah dramatically one more time then waltzed around the table with each of her girlfriends to peals of laughter and perma-grins. Several minutes later, after he got out of his truck down the hill at his dad's house, he could still hear the happy sounds of celebration until he closed the door and went to get in bed for the last time without Leah Gibson as his wife.

CHAPTER 63

Saturday was a one of those chamber-of-commerce days that you hearken back on in the cold of winter. Leah woke early, not feeling too groovy, and made chocolate chip pancakes, washed some fresh blueberries and strawberries and whipped some cream to top them with her good arm. She poured herself a glass of iced tea to settle her stomach. As badly as she felt, she had never been happier.

Over the next couple hours, they ate, showered and collected their clothes and Leah's dress and headed to the church. When they walked inside, they reverted to a whisper. The full sun pouring through the stained glass gave the sanctuary an even holier aura than usual, and Leah shivered with anticipation.

The girls retired to the bridal dressing room to get ready. Toni, Siobhan and Meg, not having brought any dress clothes with them, donned their slacks and shirts then turned their attention to Leah to help her get ready. Siobhan fixed Leah's hair while Toni applied her make-up. Meg was busy wrapping a dozen pink roses filled with baby's breath with silk ribbon for Leah to carry down the aisle. Last night, Leah took the three of them into Aunt Fi's room to go through the hope chest. Inside, Leah found a handmade garter and pillbox hat with a veil attached. They fit Leah like a glove.

The simple ceremony was reverent and poignant, and by the time Pastor Canton pronounced Cal and Leah husband and wife, there was not a dry eye in the church. In addition to Siobhan, Toni and Meg, Mr. C, now presumably Dad, Katie, Chip and Sheri were in attendance. Leah could not have scripted a more perfect wedding.

Sheri had made a "wedding cake" for the happy couple, and they gathered joyfully back at the farmhouse to celebrate the nuptials. Chip played an I-pod mix of dance music, bluegrass and folk music that had them dancing, singing and laughing until late in the afternoon.

Siobhan, Toni and Meg had packed their bags for departure last night, hoping to milk as much fellowship and fun out of their last day as possible, and they did. By the time 4:00 rolled around, they

259

knew they needed to get on the road so they could get back to their respective homes before the dead of night.

Sheri and Chip said their goodbyes and their congratulations and left for home just up the road. Mr. C gave hugs all around to Leah's friends then kissed his new daughter-in-law on the cheek before he and Katie strolled arm-in-arm to his house down the driveway. Toni, Meg and Siobhan took turns packing their bags into the vehicles before they walked back to the porch to say goodbye.

They would all be together in Virginia Beach over July 4th for Toni and Carter's wedding on the beach, but it was still difficult to part. They promised to come back to visit Leah and Cal again soon. Before they got choked up again, Meg, Toni and Siobhan said goodbye. Leah thanked them for an idyllic week and for making her wedding so special. The exchanged hugs and kisses and climbed into their vehicles to go.

As they drove slowly down the driveway, Siobhan turned to look back at her best friend in the world. Cal leaned down and kissed Leah passionately while Pander jumped playfully at her side, and Siobhan smiled at the sight. All of her worries and fears about how Leah would manage alone in a new place had disappeared. Leah Gibson was going to be just fine.